DOVER

The Collected
Short Stories

DOVER

The Collected Short Stories

Joyce Porter

with a foreword
by Robert Barnard
and an afterword by
The Reverend Canon J.R. Porter

A Foul Play
Press Book

The Countryman Press, Inc.
Woodstock, Vermont

Library of Congress Cataloging-in-Publication Data
Porter, Joyce.
    Dover : the collected short stories / Joyce Porter ; with a
foreword by Robert Barnard and an afterword by J.R. Porter.
      p.   cm.
    "All of these stories originally appeared in Ellery Queen's
mystery magazine"—T.p. verso.
    "A Foul Play Press book."
    ISBN 0-88150-342-8
    1. Dover, Wilfred (Fictitious character)—Fiction.
    2. Detective and mystery stories, English. 3. Police—
England—Fiction. I. Title.
PR6066.072A6 1995
823'.914—dc20   95-30642
                                     CIP

This edition first published in 1995
by Foul Play Press, an imprint of
The Countryman Press, Inc.,
PO Box 175, Woodstock, Vermont 05091.

Text design by Sally Sherman
Printed in Canada

10 9 8 7 6 5 4 3 2 1

Contents

WITHDRAWN

Foreword

Nineteen sixty-four, the year that saw Inspector Dover trample over the threshold of an unsuspecting world, also saw the conception of another figure who was to dent the British public's childlike faith in the probity of its police force; for it was in that year that Joe Orton was writing *Loot,* with the corrupt and brutal Inspector Truscott at the centre of the farcical action.

As a homosexual, Orton had had plenty of experience with police chicanery and brutality himself, but as the figure of Truscott emerged in successive drafts of his play he became more and more like the real-life figure of Inspector Challenor, whose methods came to public attention after the visit to Britain of Greece's king and queen: Challenor's idea of protecting them from public demonstrations was to plant offensive weapons on demonstrators, beat confessions out of them, and arrest anyone who took his fancy with the immortal words, "You're fucking nicked, my old beauty."

I have no idea whether the newspaper fuss in 1963 over the antics of Challenor contributed to Inspector Dover. In some ways they are very different: Challenor was a figure of manic malevolent energy, whereas Wilf Dover is one of endemic malevolent sloth. Nevertheless, their conceptions of policing do have many things in common:

> The only thing left in life that gave Dover real pleasure was bullying the weak and helpless. Naturally he preferred pushing widows and orphans around but, failing them, Professor Ross would do. ("Dover Goes to School")

And both Dover and Truscott represent the moment when the sceptical 'sixties started examining the traditional, warm-hearted image of the British bobby, epitomised by the "Dixon of Dock Green" television series, and realized things were not like that any more. There was in the British police a soft underbelly (the image comes naturally to mind when Inspector Dover is in question) that was interested not in innocence or guilt but in a high conviction rate, performance bonuses, and generally in roughing up the British public, law-breaking or law-abiding. Being a policeman was a rough job, and that was what attracted some of the men who went in for it. This was all before the cases of the Birmingham Six and the Guildford Four, but for Orton, at least, the writing was already on the wall: The police had become a law unto themselves.

One must not attribute too serious aims to Joyce Porter. Her Inspector Dover is primarily a grotesque comic creation along the lines of such early Dickens characters as Mr. Stiggins and Mr. Bumble. Whether Dover was conceived as a way of cocking snooks at detectives such as Lord Peter Wimsey and Roderick Alleyn we can't know, but he certainly provides a commentary on such figures. Gross, flatulent, lazy and dishonest, he is everything we used to believe our policemen were not. Sexist, racist, perpetually cadging food and cigarettes and pinching other people's ideas, he spends much of his time on a case in bed in his underwear or crouched over a beer he certainly hasn't bought for himself. In the stories in this collection he usually seems to find himself at some stage on the lavatory, but that is a natural consequence of his other self-indulgences, and there is some righting of a balance here: That prominent feature of everybody's lives finds little or no place in the detective exploits of a Miss Marple or a Hercule Poirot. Joyce Porter allows for the possibility of *multum in parvo,* of great thoughts in a little room.

Inspector Dover's brutality, when he has the energy for it, is partly a comment on the "little grey cells" school of detection, on the fact that ratiocination is traditionally at the heart of the Golden Age detective novel. Dover has no truck with that, because it means taking trouble and it takes a lot of time. Thumping the truth out of suspects, or if not the truth then any kind of confession, means he can get back the sooner to sleep, or to his disgusting meals. It lacks the social and cosmic dimensions of Orton's Truscott:

TRUSCOTT (*shouting, knocking Hal to the floor*).
Under any other political system I'd have you on
the floor in tears.
HAL (*crying*). You've got me on the floor in tears.

Dover cares little about any political system. Similarly, his racism, sexism and any and every other unfashionable ism about him are less personal prejudices, more part of his general need to think badly of everybody except himself. His contempt is absolute, and it is universal: It comprises all who are not Dover.

MacGregor is a splendid foil to this figure of rampageous piggishness, but that is the only splendid thing about him. He is elegant, he has all the right instincts, he is sensitive to all the social *faux pas* Dover commits, as well as to his constant failures in human sensitivity. But he is terribly feeble, and alas he is not very bright. Joyce Porter would have made it easier for herself if she had given him something above average intelligence, since she would then have avoided what remained her great problem: How was a solution to emerge? But perhaps she thought an intelligent figure would stand out too grossly, would seem too unlikely, in a world in which her own estimate of human possibilities does not seem to differ very greatly from Dover's: Everyone is either ridiculous, greedy and corrupt, or on the other hand simply feeble. Dover falls into one category, MacGregor, poor nice young chap, into the second.

The combination works best in *Dover One*, with its outrageous farcical action, its off-colour jokes, and its larger-and-more-awful-than-life characters, all of them wonderfully fresh and with delight behind their creation. Its climax at a gruesome meal, the menu for which everyone knows except the detectives, shows at its best Porter's gift for handling hilarious and close-to-the-bone action. The whole book is instinct with that favourite 'sixties phenomenon, black humour. Joe Orton performing for the cast of *Loot* with castanets that turned out to be his just-dead mother's false teeth could come from a Porter novel. His comment that "Farce is higher than comedy in that it is very close to tragedy" is relevant to that gruesome meal at the end of the first Dover, especially when we remember the experiences of the murderers that lie behind it.

The energy that makes Porter's debut novel one of the few crime novels that make the reader weak from laughter lasted her well enough for the next four or five books. *Dover and the Unkindest Cut of All*, in particular, is a competitor in many people's mind for favourite Porter novel, mainly by reason of its splendid motivation for the crimes.

In later novels the reader becomes all too conscious of what Porter called "the sheer physical labour of pushing a pen-nib over all those acres of sneering white paper." Perhaps the device of the stupid detective became too difficult to work. Perhaps the repetition involved with a series detective (and there certainly is repetition with Dover) wearied her. Perhaps the grotesque characters stopped coming, or the jokes ran out. Comedy is much more difficult than straightforward writing. Certainly Porter seems to have been unusual among crime writers in not actually having enjoyed the business of writing.

The short stories in this volume will be new to all those who are not regular readers of the *Ellery Queen's Mystery Magazine* (it is sad that the modern mystery reader is not more drawn to the short story, granted that the great progenitor of the English mystery is the Sherlock Holmes short story). The stories here are in some ways untypical of the modern crime story, in that they tend to be mystery novels in miniature: That is, they have a cast list of suspects, one of whom will turn out to be the murderer. Few stories of that type are written these days. Christie wrote many in the early stages of her career, but her great achievements as a short-story writer are tales of a very different kind—for example, "Witness for the Prosecution." The problem, for most writers, is that the short-story length prevents them from using enough characters to provide suspense or from giving the characters the depth and vividness that alone could make the story interesting. Joyce Porter solves this by making most of her stories longer than the average *EQMM* piece, giving her just time to let Dover flex his muscles (the eating and resting ones) and to let the suspects flaunt their greed or stupidity. One of them, "Dover Sees the Trees," has a neat solution of how the truth behind the mystery is to be conveyed to the reader. They are, in all, substantial chips off the master's block, and their publication in book form is greatly welcomed.

In greeting what may well prove to be the last appearance of the old villain (one uses the term advisedly, for Joyce Porter was one of the first to blur the distinction between criminal and cop), one turns for the last time to Orton, to provide the moral justification behind the practice that Porter would probably not have wanted to give. "I think it's very unhealthy for a society to love the police the way the English do," he said. Joyce Porter, in her way, did a great deal to knock the stuffing out of that love with her series detective. Even the most cautious and conservative of us, if we were reading a Dover in bed and thought we heard noises downstairs, would think twice before reaching out to dial 999.

—Robert Barnard

Dover Pulls a Rabbit

"Good morning, Mrs. Dover." Detective Sergeant MacGregor raised his hat. He was a very polite as well as a very elegant young man. "Is the Chief Inspector ready?"

Mrs. Dover shrank farther back behind her front door and smiled apologetically. "Well, not exactly ready, Sergeant. Your call was a bit unexpected, you know. He was counting on having his day off today."

"It is a murder case," MacGregor pointed out gently.

"Oh, yes,"—Mrs. Dover wrapped her flowered housecoat closer round her and wished she'd had time to take her curlers out—"I understand. The point is, he doesn't. You know what he's like." She glanced nervously over her shoulder and lowered her voice. "He's been going on something terrible ever since you phoned."

Sergeant MacGregor contented himself with a vague smile. One hardly liked to discuss one's superior officer with one's superior officer's wife. Especially when one's superior officer might appear at any moment and catch one.

"He took senna pods last night," explained Mrs. Dover in a whisper. "You know—seeing as how he was going to have his rest day today."

"Oh, dear," said MacGregor.

"He didn't expect to have to go out, you see," Mrs. Dover went on. "He's in the bathroom now."

MacGregor was beginning to feel chilly, partly with foreboding and partly with standing in the cold morning air. "Do you think he'll be long?"

Mrs. Dover shrugged. "I don't really know."

A door slammed heavily upstairs and shook the entire house. Footsteps crashed down the stairs and the unlovely figure of Detective Chief Inspector Dover hove into view.

Mrs. Dover cowered even farther back. "Is everything all right, Wilf?"

Chief Inspector Dover grabbed his bowler hat off the hall stand. "No ith isn'th!" He tore his overcoat off its hook. "Ith's all your faulth!"

"Oh, Wilf!" wailed Mrs. Dover.

"Don'th you 'oh, Wilf' me!" snapped her husband, winding a disgusting-looking brown woolly scarf round his neck and scowling ferociously. "Whose sthupid idea was ith, eh? You and your ruddy senna pods!" For the first time he deigned to acknowledge the presence of his sergeant. "How long a drive have we goth?"

"About an hour, sir," MacGregor told him, and started a diplomatic withdrawal down the steps.

" 'Strewth!" groaned Dover. He set off after MacGregor.

"But, Wilf!" Mrs. Dover poked out a restraining hand.

"Whath is ith now? Can'th you see I'm in a hurry?"

His wife's voice was hoarse with embarrassment. "It's your teeth, Wilf. You've forgotten to put in your teeth, dear."

The trip took an hour and a half. Dover and MacGregor, equally apprehensive, spent the whole time sitting on the edge of their seats in the back of the car and spotting public conveniences.

Before long they were clear of London and its civilized amenities. MacGregor found himself looking at the countryside with new eyes. Would that clump of trees do? Could the 240-pound Chief Inspector scramble up that high bank to find a refuge behind the hedge?

"Not much further now, sir," said MacGregor, doggedly looking on the bright side. "We've just picked up the motorcyclist who's going to guide us for the last bit."

There was an ominous grunt from Dover.

"We'll be there in a couple of minutes, sir," said MacGregor, consulting his map feverishly. "We don't have to go right into the village." He braced himself against the dead weight of Dover as the car took a sharp turn off the main road.

"Damned inconsiderate!" snarled Dover.

"I beg your pardon, sir?"

"Who's gone and got himself croaked, anyhow?"

"A Miss Clarice Ebbitt, sir."

"A woman!" sniffed Dover. "I might have guessed it. Selfish bitch."

The police car, following the motorcyclist, roared at top speed up a narrow country lane. Gravel flew as they screamed to a halt outside a decrepit-looking, isolated cottage.

Dover clutched his middle. For once in his life he didn't wait for somebody else to open the car door for him. Overcoat flapping, he thundered up the garden path and stumbled clumsily over a pile of sacking which was cluttering up the open doorway.

Inside the cottage a uniformed Inspector and several plainclothesmen looked up from their various tasks.

"Where is it?" bellowed Dover, his usually pasty face now an alarming dark red.

The Inspector paused irresolutely in mid-salute. "Er—

well, I'm afraid you're—well—sort of standing on it, sir," he said unhappily, and let his hand drop.

Dover spared half a glance for the obstruction under his feet. "Not the corpse, you moron!" he yelled in distress. "The lavatory! Where is it?"

The Inspector paled. "The lavatory, sir?"

"Oh, get out of my way!" howled Dover, and barged through to the back of the house. He found a flight of stairs, and panting heavily, made a hasty ascent.

Meanwhile, back in the sitting room, MacGregor and the Inspector regarded each other in bleak silence.

MacGregor cleared his throat and introduced himself.

The Inspector acknowledged this with a thoughtful nod. "And I'm Inspector Slegge from the local police. My Chief Constable instructed me to give you every assistance."

"That's kind of you, sir."

A series of sounds came from the floor above.

"I think," MacGregor suggested tactfully, "it might be a good idea if your chaps waited outside for a bit."

Inspector Slegge agreed at once. No need to let the lower ranks see Homer nodding. He sent the plainclothesmen out. "And that's your Superintendent from the Murder Squad, is it?" he asked with a glance at the ceiling.

"Well, Chief Inspector, actually, sir."

"Really?" Inspector Slegge's eyebrows rose. "I thought they were all Superintendents that they sent out from the Yard."

"Well, Chief Inspector Dover is a bit of an exception, really, sir."

"Is that so?" said Inspector Slegge with truly admirable restraint.

For the second time that morning MacGregor's pink ears caught the slam of a bathroom door and the heavy trample of his lord and master's feet along the landing and down the stairs.

Dover crowded his unwieldy bulk into the tiny sitting room. " 'Strewth, it's a bit parky in here, isn't it? Let's have that door closed."

"We didn't want to move the corpse until you arrived, sir," explained Inspector Slegge stiffly.

"Well, I have arrived—haven't I?—so get it shifted! No, shove it *outside,* you fool! I don't want to sit with a blooming dead body round my feet, even if you do. And, Mac-Gregor,"—from long practice Dover selected the most comfortable chair in the room and pushed it nearer the hearth—"scout around for some firewood and get this fire going. They're bound to have some at the back somewhere. Oh, and if you come across the kitchen in your travels, get the kettle on. I could do with a cup of tea. It'll help settle my stomach. And," he called to his sergeant's retreating back, "a few biscuits or a piece of cake wouldn't come amiss, either."

With that settled, Dover removed his bowler and was on the point of depositing it on a small table. "Here,"—he peered accusingly at the polished top—"this is blooming dusty, isn't it?"

"It's the fingerprint powder, sir," explained Inspector Slegge.

"Got a handkerchief, laddie?"

"Er—yes, of course, sir."

"Well, what are you waiting for, then?"

In a remarkably short time Dover got himself comfortably established in the sitting room of Delphinium Cottage. He sat, fair and square, before a nicely glowing fire with a steaming hot cup of tea clutched in one pudgy fist and three cream biscuits in the other. He beamed contentedly at his two associates.

"Right," he said. "Now, let's get on with it! I haven't got all day to waste on one crummy murder."

With a tactfully suppressed sigh Inspector Slegge got

out his notebook. It provided a convenient excuse for not looking at Dover making a complete pig of himself.

"The victim, sir," he began, "is a Miss Clarice Ebbitt—"

"I know that!" snapped Dover. "How was she killed?"

"Head bashed in, sir, with that brass candlestick over there." Slegge indicated the object lying on a sheet of newspaper on the windowsill. "It's all covered with blood and hair."

"Fingerprints?" asked Dover, dribbling soggy tea-soaked biscuits down the front of his overcoat.

"We're checking now, sir. My chap found a few and photographed them, of course, but they didn't look very hopeful—too old and smudgy and not in the right place if you were using it as a weapon."

"How old was she, this Miss Rabbit?" Dover passed his cup to MacGregor for a refill.

"Ebbitt, sir," Inspector Slegge corrected him unwisely.

"That's what I said!" glowered Dover.

"Well, I suppose she was about fifty, sir."

"Live alone?"

"No, sir, she resided here with another lady, a Miss Jennifer Willoughby."

"Where's she?"

"She's at the cottage next door, sir, recovering from the shock."

"She found the body, did she?"

"Well, not exactly, sir. I'm not absolutely sure from my preliminary inquiries which one of 'em was actually first on the scene. Not that I think it's all that—"

"Right," Dover cut in; he was beginning to find Inspector Slegge a bit of a bore. "Let's have her in and see what she's got to say for herself. Any more tea in that pot, MacGregor?"

Miss Jennifer Willoughby was a prettyish woman of about thirty-five. She was white-faced and still shivering with cold and shock as she sank gratefully into the chair MacGregor pulled up for her. Although it was now after eleven in the morning she was still wearing a dressing gown and slippers and had a gray blanket wrapped round her shoulders.

Dover took one jaundiced look and didn't reckon he was going to have much trouble with her. He turned on his most hectoring tone. "How long have you and this Miss Rabbit been living here?"

"Ebbitt," said Miss Willoughby faintly. "About eight or nine years, I suppose."

"And what did you quarrel about?"

"Quarrel? We didn't quarrel about anything."

"Aw, come off it!" sneered Dover. "Two women living together for nine years and you didn't quarrel about anything?"

"No, really. We got on very well together. Poor Clarice was older than me, of course, but we were always the best of friends, I do assure you. My being out at work most days helped, I suppose. We weren't always on top of each other, if you see what I mean." She glanced somewhat timidly at MacGregor, who was writing all this down. "I work at the public library in Chuddington."

"Nearest town," explained Inspector Slegge. "About five miles away. Frequent bus service."

"That's right," agreed Miss Willoughby. "I usually catch the eight twenty-five at the bottom of the lane. That gets me to work in very nice time."

"Did this Miss Rabbit go out to work?" demanded Dover, undoing the buttons of his overcoat as the heat from the fire grew fiercer.

"Oh, no. She had a small annuity, you see. She stayed at home and looked after the cottage. Naturally we shared all the household expenses."

"All right," said Dover impatiently, "let's get to this blooming murder. What happened?"

"Well, I heard all these dreadful screams and I came rushing downstairs and there she was, lying all huddled up in the doorway and covered with blood and—" She broke off with a choked sob and groped in the pocket of her dressing gown for a handkerchief.

Dover regarded her with distaste. He couldn't stomach these sniveling witnesses who got their stories all jumbled up and gave him the trouble of sorting them out.

"What time was all this?"

"About seven o'clock, I think. I remember glancing at my alarm clock and seeing that it said five past seven. I always keep it a few minutes fast."

"You were still in bed?"

"Oh, yes. We never get up before half-past seven. That's why I was so confused at first, you see. I went rushing into Clarice's room because, naturally, that's where I thought she would be. I imagined she must be having a nightmare or something. Then I tried the kitchen. It was only after that I came running in here."

Dover wiped the sweat off his forehead, closed his eyes, and laboriously thought this out.

"Normally," he said after a bit, "you both stayed in bed till half-past seven?"

"Oh, yes. That gave me plenty of time to get dressed, have my breakfast, and catch my bus."

"But this Miss Rabbit was up before half-past seven this morning. Why?"

"I don't know," moaned Miss Willoughby, starting to weep again.

Dover turned to Inspector Slegge. "Any signs of breaking in?"

"No, sir, none at all. All the windows are securely locked and the back door's fastened with a lock, heavy bolts top and bottom, and a chain. This front door's equipped the same way, sir, although of course that was wide-open."

"Poor Clarice was very nervous," said Miss Willoughby, "living out here in the country and all these dreadful things you read about in the papers. And tramps, you know. I did want her to get a dog, but she didn't like dogs. They do bring a lot of dirt into a house, one must admit, but even so—"

"If," said Dover, ruthlessly stemming the flow of Miss Willoughby's whining voice, "nobody broke in, then this Miss Rabbit must have opened the front door herself, mustn't she?"

"Unless Miss Willoughby did," said MacGregor, who felt under an obligation to prevent Dover from cutting too many corners.

"Well, she didn't!" snapped Dover. "She's already said she was in bed, hasn't she? That door was locked last night as usual, wasn't it?"

"Oh, yes," Miss Willoughby nodded emphatically. "I always locked the whole house up every night—that was my little chore—and then, when she'd washed up the supper things and made the cocoa, Clarice would go round and check it again. Last night was the same as usual."

"Hm." Dover let his eyelids droop again. It was really getting very hot by the fire.

MacGregor thought it might be a suitable moment to stick his oar in. "Did somebody knock at the door?"

Miss Willoughby jumped a little at the sound of this new voice putting the question, and looked at MacGregor uncertainly. "I don't think so."

Inspector Slegge leaned forward. "But you would have heard a knock, wouldn't you? After all, your bedroom is upstairs, isn't it? Right over the front door? And Miss Ebbitt's room is downstairs, opposite the kitchen and at the back of the house?"

"Well, poor Clarice was a very light sleeper," said Miss Willoughby.

A piece of coal fell in the hearth and Dover came to with a start. "Yes," he said, for all the world as though he hadn't dozed off for a minute. "Well now, when you found this Miss Rabbit as dead as a duck in the open door, did you see or hear anybody else?"

"No. Only Mr. Lurgan from the cottage next door."

"Lurgan?" repeated Dover crossly. "Who's Lurgan?" He glared accusingly at MacGregor and Inspector Slegge. "Nobody's told me anything about anybody called Lurgan."

"He's waiting in his cottage, sir," Inspector Slegge hastened to explain, quite forgetting whose fault it was that Dover knew next to nothing about the case. "I told him you'd be wanting to see him."

"Yes," said Dover doubtfully. He was loath to leave the comfort of his chair by the fire, but the rumbles in his stomach couldn't be ignored. "Well, after lunch, eh? I reckon we've done enough for one morning."

Inspector Slegge's firm, closely shaven jaw dropped slightly. "But, sir, it's only a quarter to twelve!" Dover's bottom lip pouted out in a way which should have been a warning. "And Lurgan's missed half a day's work already, sir, and they're very busy on the farm. I promised him faithfully he could go in this afternoon. If you could just see him now, sir, I'm sure it wouldn't take more than a couple of minutes."

"God help you if it does!" growled Dover.

Miss Willoughby gazed sadly at the empty tin of her

favorite biscuits. "Have you finished with me now?" she asked.

"For the moment," said Dover, still aggrieved at being forced to work what he considered overtime.

"Well, do you think I could go back upstairs and get dressed? It's not very nice, being in my night clothes with all these policemen about the place. And it's not very warm, either."

"No," said Dover, happy to be awkward, "you can't. I haven't completed my examination of the premises yet and I don't want you mucking everything up."

Miss Willoughby, her ladylike protests falling on deaf ears, was sent back to the next-door cottage and Fred Lurgan summoned to take her place.

Fred Lurgan was a strapping, rosy-cheeked young fellow with a cheerful nature which not even Dover's sullen presence could dampen.

"I was just coming out of the front gate," he told them, "when I heard all these blood-curdling screams, see. Just gone seven, it'd be. I was on me way to work. Well, for the moment I couldn't think what it was or where the dickens it was coming from. Had me right flummoxed, it did. Didn't sound like a rabbit or a hare or anything, and then I bethought meself of this place. So, I come running as fast as I could make it."

"How long do you think it was between hearing the screams and getting to the cottage here?" asked MacGregor after a sidelong glance to see if Dover had got over his sulks yet.

"Oh, not more'n a couple of minutes at the very outside. We're not more than a hundred yards down the lane. Soon as I turned in at the gate I saw her, of course. Miss Ebbitt, that is. Lying right across the threshold of the front door with Miss Willoughby just coming into the sitting room from the back of the house. Terrible state she was in. I dunno what had got her most bothered—Miss Ebbitt getting her head bashed in or me seeing her in her nightie." He chuckled good-humoredly. "Right couple of old maids, they are. Run a mile if they see a pair of trousers, God alone knows why!"

"So you and Miss Willoughby arrived on the scene at more or less the same time, then?" mused MacGregor.

"Seems like it, mister. I had a quick look to see if there was anything I could do, but she was as dead as a doornail, poor old thing. Well, I didn't like leaving Miss Willoughby all alone, see, so I took her straight back to our place and then I got me bike out and went down to the village to get the policeman. That was right, wasn't it? I didn't touch anything. Hardly set foot in here, really."

"When you first heard the screams," said MacGregor, "could you actually see this cottage from where you were standing?"

"Oh, no. It's round the bend in the road from us, you see, and there's all those trees in between as well. I couldn't actually see this cottage till I got to the garden gate, like."

"And you didn't see anybody running away? Or hear footsteps on the road? Or the sound of a car?"

"Not a damned thing. If he'd come out into the lane, though, you'd have thought I'd have heard him at least, wouldn't you? 'Specially if he was running."

"Could he have been hiding somewhere?"

"Well, not in this front garden, that's for sure. You couldn't miss a field mouse there, it's that small. He might have slipped through to the back, I suppose."

"No," Inspector Slegge put in efficiently, "the gate through to the back is locked from the other side and that fence is six or seven feet high. He'd have had a job climbing over that before Lurgan came on the scene."

"Could he have got off the lane somehow?" MacGregor tried again. "Into one of the fields, perhaps?"

Fred Lurgan shook his head. "We've got these high banks, see, and they've just finished the hedging only this week. Filled up all the gaps, see. Of course, you could break your way through, but that'd take time and make the devil of a noise. Once I got round the bend in the lane I'd a clear view for half a mile down to the main road. I wasn't what you might call looking for anybody, of course, but I reckon any movement'd have caught me eye."

Dover showed signs of returning to life. The three men waited for the oracle to speak.

"Anybody got a cigarette?" asked Dover through an enormous yawn.

MacGregor counted silently up to ten and offered his cigarette case.

Dover blew the smoke out with a deep sigh. "You on pretty friendly terms with these two women, eh?"

When Fred Lurgan finally caught on that this question was being addressed to him, his face broke into a big grin. "Well, I'd hardly call it that, sir. They keep themselves very much to themselves, they do. Shirl—that's my missus— she's tried to be neighborly, but you could see with half an eye that they weren't a bit keen, 'specially Miss Ebbitt. Mind you, I reckon they're as poor as church mice and proud with it, if you follow me. Didn't want to accept any hospitality that they might have had a bit of a struggle to pay back, like. Well, you've only got to look round here, haven't you? They haven't even got a telly."

"Did anybody ever come visiting?" asked Dover, looking for once mildly interested in the answer.

"Nary a soul, sir, as far as I know—apart from the milkman and such-like which you'd hardly count. We've been living next door for five years now, and I don't reckon they've ever had anybody in here for so much as a cup of tea. Oh, the vicar called once, I think, but he never got across the front doorstep, I'll be bound."

"They aren't churchgoers, then?" asked Dover, finally conceding defeat and moving his chair six inches back from the fire.

"No. Well, nobody is in the village, see, except for the people who work on the estate and they don't have much choice, do they? Seeing as how old Mrs. Leatherside's the patron of the living. Very High Church, she is, and scared by a curate in her youth, they do say. So the upshot is the parson's always got to be a bachelor and the services are enough to make you turn in your grave. My old granddad says they're burning that incense stuff and ringing bells— well, people don't like it, not round here they don't. If they go anywhere, they go to the Chapel and you can't blame 'em, can you?"

But Fred Lurgan had lost Dover a long way back. The Chief Inspector's bird-brain was now fully occupied with wondering what it fancied for its supper.

"Have you seen any tramps about, Lurgan?" asked Inspector Slegge. His already low opinion of Scotland Yard was being reinforced every minute. Why, damn it, that fat lump hadn't done a blessed thing since he'd arrived except swill tea and shove biscuits down his throat!

"Tramps?" Fred Lurgan shook his head. "No, I've not seen any about lately and I've not heard of any, either. Besides, what'd a tramp do this for? Even allowing that he'd be daft enough to come round on the scrounge at seven o'clock in the morning. Nothing's been stolen, has it?"

"No escaped prisoners or lunatics in the neighbor-hood?" MacGregor looked questioningly at Inspector Slegge.

Another negative shake of the head.

" 'Course," said Fred Lurgan dubiously, "I suppose if he was pretty fast on his feet and wearing soft-soled shoes, he could have made it to Donkey Lane before I got round the bend."

"Donkey Lane?"

"A footpath off to the right," explained Inspector Slegge crisply, making a determined effort to stop staring so rudely at the somnolent Chief Inspector, "between here and the main road. You'd pass it as you came in. It runs down the hill past the church to the village. That's right, Lurgan, isn't it?"

"By foot it's the quickest way to the village," agreed Lurgan, "but it's as muddy as all hell. You'd be up to your ankles in it this time of year. Besides," he frowned, "would a fellow who's just committed a murder run towards the village? I should think he'd have headed for the open country somewhere, away from people, like."

Dover blew suddenly down his nose, and everybody jumped. "This Miss Willoughby," he said, "you say you took her back to your cottage?"

"That's right, sir."

"Did you let her go back upstairs first?"

"Oh, no. She was as near passing out as makes no difference, so I just put me arm round her and helped her straightway over to our place."

"Did you go upstairs yourself?"

Lurgan shook his head. These coppers took a long time to catch on, and no mistake. He'd already told 'em all this once. "I didn't come no further than the middle of this sitting room, and that was just to catch Miss Willoughby before she hit the floor."

MacGregor's ears pricked up. "Ah, I see what you're getting at, sir," he said eagerly. "You mean that the murderer

could have escaped into the rear of the house and concealed himself there until Lurgan and Miss Willoughby
had gone?"

"I don't mean anything of the sort!" roared Dover. "And
don't you start fathering your crackpot notions on me!
How could he have concealed himself in an undersized
chicken coop like this with Miss Willoughby coming
down the stairs and looking all round the place for her
friend? Why don't you try keeping your ears open and
your trap shut for a change?"

MacGregor lapsed into an offended silence. Dover
turned his attention to Inspector Slegge. "You—how much
mucking about did you let your lot do before I got here?"

"Well, I'd hardly call it mucking about, sir," Inspector
Slegge retorted with some indignation. "I hope that, after
all my years in the force, I know—"

"How much?" repeated Dover.

"Well," Inspector Slegge thought carefully, "the village
constable looked into every room as soon as he got here,
just to make sure that there was nobody hiding. He
assured me that he did no more than just stand in the
doorways and look. Then I arrived with the police surgeon
and the C.I.D. team. We'd only just started on the routine
examination of this room when you came, sir."

"Did any of your men go upstairs?"

"No, sir, though I myself had a quick glance round to
ascertain the layout. Naturally I didn't touch a single
thing."

"Humph!" Dover slumped moodily back in his chair.
"Well, what time is it?"

"Half-past twelve, sir," said MacGregor.

"Lunch," said Dover firmly. He glared at Fred Lurgan.
"If I want you again, I'll send for you. Meanwhile,"—the

admonition was accompanied by a fearsome scowl—"keep your lip buttoned!"

Lunch turned out to be only a qualified success. Inspector Slegge, erroneously assuming that the great detective from Scotland Yard would be too engrossed in his investigations to wish to interrupt them by a trip to a nearby hostelry, had persuaded his wife to pack a picnic hamper. Dover was furious. A lunch consisting of nothing but hot oxtail soup from a thermos bottle, pork pies, cold chicken, ham, tongue, hard-boiled eggs, homemade bread and farm butter, apple pie, cheese, and four bottles of beer each was not, as he kept on remarking, the sort of hospitality he expected from those local police forces lucky enough to acquire his services. Grumbling and complaining through every mouthful, he shoveled the lion's share of the goodies down his maw while MacGregor and Inspector Slegge looked rather wistfully on.

By half-past one Dover was flat out in his chair again. The gobbling and guzzling had mercifully ceased and he was now at peace with the world. He stuck his legs out, undid his top trouser button to relieve the pressure, and let the comfortable warmth of the fire play on his distended stomach.

"What happens now?" Inspector Slegge asked in hushed and mystified awe.

"We get an hour's peace and quiet—if we're lucky," replied MacGregor nastily, "before he wakes up in a stinking temper and remembers that he's no nearer solving the case than he was before he left home this morning."

"He's a bit of a one, isn't he?"

"He's a pig!" retorted MacGregor. "It's the same on every job we go on. He never does a damned thing! I'm the one who's got to do all the work."

"He's certainly not much of a one for sticking to the book," observed Inspector Slegge, not knowing whether to admire or condemn.

"Sticking to the book? That lazy old slob hasn't even read the book! Talk about not having a clue—he wouldn't recognize one if you shoved it up his snout. Look, while he's having his nap, I think we'd better discuss what we've got so far and plan our future actions. If we don't do something, this is just going to be one more in the long list of Chief Inspector Dover's unsolved cases. Keep your voice down, though, because we don't want the old fool waking up. Now, as I see it, we've got three possibilities: one, Miss Willoughby did it; two, Lurgan did it; three, some passing stranger did it."

"Well, my money's on Lurgan. I can't see Miss Ebbitt opening the door to a complete stranger at that time in the morning, but she'd trust Lurgan. He could spin her some cock-and-bull story and she'd open up and let him in. We've only got his word for it that he was outside his cottage when he heard the screams. And look how clever he's been about saying he didn't see anybody running away! He's been very careful not to commit himself to anything we might possibly be able to check."

"Motive?" asked MacGregor doubtfully.

"Oh, robbery, I should think. Don't forget he was the one who was so keen to impress us that there was nothing here worth stealing. How do we know? Miss Ebbitt might have had a fortune hidden away under her mattress."

"Well, possibly." MacGregor spoke without much enthusiasm.

"Or, of course," Inspector Slegge added primly, "it could be one of those sex crimes. You know what some of these country people are like."

"I think it's Miss Willoughby, myself," said MacGregor.

"I can't understand why, if Lurgan or anybody else came knocking at the door, she didn't hear it. And then there's the murder weapon—that came from inside the house. Lurgan would have brought something with him, wouldn't he? He'd never have relied on having to get inside this room to pick up that candlestick when he could have hit her with a hammer or something as soon as she opened the door. My theory is that Miss Willoughby woke Miss Ebbitt up and lured her down here. Maybe she even persuaded her to open the front door. Then, when her back was turned, she struck her down with the candlestick. If it was Miss Willoughby, you see, she'd have heard Lurgan dashing up to see what all the screaming was, and she'd have had time to get to the hall door before he actually arrived on the scene."

"But what's her motive?"

"Well, as my esteemed Chief Inspector said, two women living together could have had a quarrel about practically anything, couldn't they? Even a man, eh? Or maybe Miss Ebbitt isn't as poor as all that and she's left all her money to Miss Willoughby. We'll have to check, of course, but there's bound to be something."

"What about the passing stranger theory?" asked Inspector Slegge.

"The passing stranger?" MacGregor pursed his lips. "I don't think so. An innocent Miss Willoughby would have heard the knock on the door. An innocent Lurgan would surely have seen somebody running away. Either way it seems to rule out the passing stranger theory. By the way, we must check the distance Lurgan had to cover after he heard the screams. It might tell us something. What I'd really like to do is get hold of some of your chaps and do a reconstruction of the crime."

"My chaps'd be delighted. They've been kicking their

heels outside all morning, you know." Slegge stole a glance at Dover.

"All the same," MacGregor mused, "I still can't see Miss Ebbitt letting a total stranger into the house, especially when she was in her nightie. She'd have left the chain on, at the very least."

"Well, I can't see Miss Willoughby smashing her friend's head in with a brass candlestick, either," objected Inspector Slegge. "She just isn't the type. My guess is that Miss Ebbitt was the sort of tough, masculine one in the partnership. She was a big strapping woman with quite a pronounced mustache."

MacGregor snapped his notebook shut. "What it really boils down to is that, as of this moment and thanks to Sleeping Beauty there, we just haven't enough solid factual information to go on. What we need to do now is go over this cottage and the area surrounding it in a proper scientific manner. I wonder," he sighed disconsolately, "if I could persuade the old fool to let me do it. Talk about being past it—they ought to have put him out to pasture years ago. Or shot him."

A loud belch came from the chair by the fire. "Clues!" snorted Dover, half to himself. "Reconstruction of the crime! Scientific investigation! 'Strewth!" Dover opened his beady little eyes and glowered accusingly at his juniors. "Sitting there nattering away like a couple of old women over the back fence!"

"We were just trying to clarify our minds, sir," explained MacGregor stiffly, "and plan the next steps in the investigation."

Dover contented himself with rolling his eyes dramatically up to the ceiling as if seeking sympathy and understanding for his burdens. Then he gave one of his enormous yawns and scratched his head. Inspector Slegge watched fascinated as the dandruff flaked down onto the shoulders of the great man's overcoat.

Dover yawned again. "No need for you to go busting a gut with thinking," he observed with a marked lack of charity. "I've already solved the case."

MacGregor's heart sank. When Dover got bored with a case, he had a distressing tendency to close his eyes and, figuratively speaking, stick a pin in the list of possible suspects. MacGregor had no doubt that this was what had happened now. Dover couldn't possibly have solved a problem about which he, MacGregor, was still in the dark.

"But, sir," he wailed, "you can't have solved it! I mean, we haven't even done anything yet."

"Done enough for me," was Dover's rejoinder. One of his chief pleasures in life was baiting his snooty young sergeant. "Or for anybody else with a ha'p'orth of brains."

Inspector Slegge was open-mouthed. Had he been wrong? Was this really a Master Mind after all? "You actually know who killed Miss Ebbitt, sir?"

"Good as," said Dover.

MacGregor relaxed slightly. "Perhaps you could explain your theory, sir?"

Dover was offended. "It's no bloomin' theory," he grumbled. "It's just a question of putting a name to the one who did it."

MacGregor relaxed still more. Quite clearly Dover had as little idea as anybody else who the guilty party was. He was just trying to be clever. "Inspector Slegge and I," he began rather patronizingly, "were just discussing the idea of some stranger being responsible, sir, but we have discounted it. Miss Ebbitt, you see, sir, would never have opened—"

"Of course she wouldn't," agreed Dover unexpectedly. "No need to, was there? The murderer was already inside the house."

Inspector Slegge was disappointed. "You think it was Miss Willoughby, then, sir?"

Dover turned on him irately. "Why don't you wash your ears out?" he demanded. "I've just told you I don't *know* who it is, haven't I?"

"But Miss Willoughby was the only other person in the cottage, sir," said MacGregor. Then a horrible thought struck him. "You surely don't think it was suicide, do you, sir?"

"Suicide?" Dover's face crinkled in disgust. "How could it possibly be suicide, you blockhead? 'Strewth, if that's an example of what they call detection these days—roll on, crime!"

MacGregor took a deep breath. "You said the murderer was someone inside the house, sir. Only Miss Willoughby and the deceased were inside the house."

"That's what you think!" sneered Dover. "There was somebody else."

"Really, sir?"

"Yes, really, you young pup! And don't you take that hoity-toity, looking-down-your-nose tone with me, laddie, or you'll wake up wondering what hit you! If you'll just shut up for a couple of minutes I'll explain the whole thing to you in words of one syllable."

Dover's promised elucidation, however, was destined to die unuttered on his lips. Just as he was demanding another of MacGregor's cigarettes as his price for revealing all, there was a hesitant tap on the front door. On a nod from Dover, Inspector Slegge opened it. A tall lank clergyman in biretta and cassock stepped gingerly into the sitting room.

"Oh—ah—is Miss Willoughby here? The police constable outside suggested that I should—ah . . . I don't—ah—want to disturb you gentlemen but I would like a word—"

"Who the blazes are you?" demanded Dover.

The clergyman looked at the person who had addressed him so abruptly, blinked, and looked again. Few people could believe their eyes when they saw Dover for the first time. "I'm—ah—Father Potsford, the incumbent of St. Hilda's in the village."

"Wadderyer want to see the Willoughby woman for?"

"Well, I heard of the—ah—tragedy and I thought it my duty to come along and offer what—ah—spiritual comfort I could."

Dover frowned. "Wafor?"

"I—ah—beg your pardon?"

"This Willoughby woman doesn't attend your church, does she?"

Father Potsford was rapidly acquiring a hunted look. "No, she—ah—doesn't actually, but of course my pastoral care covers everybody living within the boundaries of my parish. Strictly speaking, it doesn't matter which church people belong to, or—ah—indeed, if they attend none at all. Besides," he added before Dover could get in with a comment, "I think I can—ah—count Miss Willoughby as a personal acquaintance. She has been most helpful to me in my—ah—researches at the public library. I am in the—ah—process of writing a little work on the Anglo-Catholic tradition at St. Hilda's and—"

"Come by bicycle?" asked Dover abruptly.

Father Potsford blinked again, then looked down at his feet. "Ah," he said with a fatuous grin, "the bicycle clips! I suppose my cassock doesn't quite cover the bottom of my trousers. Most—ah—observant."

Dover ignored the compliment and turned to MacGregor. "That's him!"

"Sir?"

"The murderer, you fool! He's the one that snuffed out your Miss Rabbit."

MacGregor had had many embarrassing experiences with Dover, but this threatened to be the worst. Frantically he sought for something to say or do which would get them out of the mess that the Chief Inspector's outrageous pronouncement had dropped them into. Father Potsford might look more than a bit of a fool, but the clergy are notoriously sensitive about being accused of murder, especially in front of witnesses. Could Dover's injudicious accusation be laughed off as some sort of gruesome joke? MacGregor's blood ran cold as he imagined what his superiors would say if they ever heard about it. Or the Sunday papers—

Meanwhile Dover, as cool as a cucumber and behaving as though he was still in his right mind, was tackling Father Potsford. "You might just as well come clean," he told him. "The Willoughby woman's given us a full confession."

"I don't believe it!" bleated Father Potsford, backing away as far as he could in the tiny room.

"Suit yourself," said Dover with massive indifference, and began exploring his left ear with his little finger.

"Sir!" MacGregor hurried to the fireside chair and whispered urgently in Dover's other ear. "Don't you think Father Potsford had better wait outside for a moment while we talk this over? We can't just make wild accusations like this without any evidence. There'll be the most frightful row."

Dover looked at his sergeant with acute distaste. "Row? Who's going to kick up a row? That baa-ing ninny's as guilty as sin. If he doesn't get a move on and confess pretty damn quick, I'll thump the living daylights out of him!" So saying, Dover clenched one beefy fist and waved it threateningly.

MacGregor played his last card. "How about a nice cup of tea, sir?"

"Afterwards," said Dover, and rose ponderously.

But Father Potsford had got over the initial shock and was rallying. "I don't know what this is all about," he proclaimed indignantly. "I demand an—ah—explanation of this terrible accusation!"

Dover scowled. He thoroughly disapproved of people who insisted on putting up a fight. "I'll give you an explanation, mate!" he bellowed. "What about you and your popsie for a start, eh?"

"My—ah—*popsie?*" gabbled Father Potsford. "How dare you make slanderous accusations—"

"Oh, shut up," snapped Dover. "Don't start coming the innocent with me! You and Miss Willoughby spent last night together upstairs in her bedroom, you don't deny that, do you? At seven o'clock this morning you pussy-footed downstairs and this Miss Rabbit caught you red-handed. Whereupon you picked up the nearest available weapon and clobbered her with it."

To MacGregor's intense amazement and everlasting chagrin Father Potsford crumpled without warning and sat down heavily on a convenient chair. "Do you think I could have a glass of water?" he asked pathetically.

MacGregor stared at him in horror. "You didn't really kill Miss Ebbitt, did you?"

Father Potsford sighed and dashed all MacGregor's dearest hopes. "I'm afraid so. In the heat of the moment I did—ah—strike the woman. She wouldn't let go of me, you see, and she was making the most dreadful—ah—accusations, threatening to expose me to my bishop. I fear I lost my head. All I could think of was getting away, you see. I grabbed the—ah—candlestick and struck her. I just wanted to make her let go of me, that's all. I never meant to kill her." He looked up. "I've been on my knees all morning, praying for the repose of her immortal soul."

"That's nice of you," scoffed Dover, returning to his chair. "Well, now you've started, you might as well spit the rest out." He didn't hold with things like cautions and informing suspects of their rights under the law.

Luckily MacGregor did, and the formalities required by the Judges' Rules were carefully observed before Father Potsford was allowed to complete his sordid little story.

He and Miss Willoughby had met and fallen in love in the public library at Chuddington. Marriage, or even the announcement of an engagement, would have meant the immediate loss of his parish. "Mrs. Leatherside, my patron, would have quite—ah—simply thrown me out, neck and crop," he explained as MacGregor's pencil raced over the pages of his notebook and Dover closed his eyes to rest them. "She just doesn't hold with married priests. Miss Willoughby was also worried about the reactions of her—ah—friend, Miss Ebbitt. We both needed a little time to set our affairs in order, so we decided to wait until I had secured another position.

"Regrettably our—ah—passion proved too strong for us. It was so difficult for us to meet anywhere. Both Miss Ebbitt and my—ah—housekeeper are women of extraordinary suspicious natures. Then Miss Willoughby had this idea. The woman—ah—tempted me and I fell." Father Potsford shook his head over the wickedness of the female sex.

"Every Thursday night Miss Ebbitt took a bath before retiring to bed. A week ago, while her friend was thus engaged in her ablutions, Miss Willoughby surreptitiously let me into the cottage and—ah—up to her room. Oh, that I should ever have been such a reckless fool! In the morning I let myself quietly out before Miss Ebbitt was awake. As soon as her alarm clock went off, at half-past seven, Miss Willoughby hurried downstairs and on the pretext of getting the milk in, concealed the—ah—fact that the front door was unlocked. On this first occasion everything went most smoothly." He gave a deep sigh.

"Last night we—ah—repeated our little deception. But this time, as I crept down the stairs, I found Miss Ebbitt waiting for me at the bottom. Somehow we must have aroused her suspicions. What happened then I have already—ah—told you." He covered his eyes with his hand. "I opened the front door—she was still clinging to me—and rushed out. My bicycle was concealed in the hedge by the garden gate. I mounted it and rode away."

"See?" Dover broke in smugly. "A bicycle! That's why Lurgan didn't see or hear anybody on the road. Silent and swift. Get it?"

MacGregor repressed a desire to wipe the smirk of triumph off Dover's face. It was aggravating enough to have the Chief Inspector actually solve a case, but it was positively unbearable not to be able for the life of him to see how he'd done it. While Inspector Slegge busied himself with getting the now maudlin Father Potsford bundled off to the police station, MacGregor wracked his brains. What could Dover have spotted? Could it all have been pure guesswork? Had he hit the bull's-eye by sheer chance?

MacGregor carried the tea tray into the sitting room once again and found Dover girding his loins to repeat his bully act with Miss Willoughby. The Chief Inspector restored his energies with a pot of tea and another of MacGregor's cigarettes. "Fifteen minutes," he instructed Inspector Slegge sternly, "and not a second sooner. Then wheel her in."

"Yes, sir!" Inspector Slegge was practically groveling. What a genius this fellow was! It just showed that you could never judge by appearances. Inspector Slegge threw Dover a cracking salute and marched off to stand guard over Miss Willoughby.

But MacGregor went straight to the point. "How on earth, sir, did you know it was Father Potsford?"

It wasn't often that Dover got the chance to put one over on Clever-Boots MacGregor. "Oh, simple deduction, laddie," he said airily. "It was all pretty obvious, really. I'm surprised," he added maliciously, "that a bright boy like you didn't work it out before I did."

"But what started you off, sir?" insisted MacGregor, still hoping against hope that the whole thing was a fluke.

Dover chuckled. It was quite funny, really, when you came to think of it.

"The seat," he said.

"The seat, sir?"

"Remember that as soon as I arrived here I had to go upstairs to the bathroom? Well, the seat there was *up.*"

No enlightenment dawned across MacGregor's handsome features.

"Oh, come on, laddie! You're not as prim and proper as all that! A house with two women in it—why should the lavatory seat be *up?*"

MacGregor was aghast. "And from *that* you deduced Miss Willoughby had a lover, sir?"

"Well, not at first," Dover admitted with spurious modesty. "I merely deduced that there'd been a man in the bathroom. Then I found out from the evidence of the witnesses that there couldn't—or at least shouldn't—have been."

"But, sir, there could have been a hundred explanations for the—er—seat being in that position."

"Could have been," agreed Dover with infuriating reasonableness, "but there weren't. Once you know there's been a man kicking around, the rest follows logically, doesn't it? Miss Willoughby—she's the younger one in the twosome—she goes out to work and she sleeps upstairs. So she must have known about the man up there. But she wasn't murdered, was she? Add it all up, and it means that Miss Willoughby has a boy friend staying the night, and the jealous Miss Rabbit catches him. Bingo!"

"Well, yes," said MacGregor unwillingly. There was something cockeyed somewhere. He only wished he could spot what it was. "But—Father Potsford?"

"Why did the boy friend kill Miss Rabbit? Because he didn't want it to get around that he was having a tumble with Miss Willoughby. That means he'd got some sort of position to protect, doesn't it? Well, when I'm handed an unmarried parson who'll get the boot if he so much as touches a woman, I don't have to sweat about it any more, do I? Especially when he returns to the scene of the crime on a bicycle. They do that, you know."

"I don't follow, sir."

"Murderers, you fool! They always return to the scene of the crime. 'Strewth, call yourself a detective and you didn't even know that?"

MacGregor let it pass. If Dover believed that, then he'd believe anything.

"I'm surprised," Dover continued, gleefully rubbing it in, "that you didn't think about the murderer getting away on a bicycle. He rode down this Donkey Lane, you see, right back to his vicarage. Lurgan said that lane led to the church."

"I seem to have been rather dense about this whole thing, sir," MacGregor admitted miserably. "Though, to be perfectly frank, I really don't see how—"

"Senna pods," said Dover with a perfectly serious face. "I owe it all to senna pods. You ought to try them yourself sometime, laddie. It might sharpen you up a bit."

—1968

Dover Tangles with High Finance

The directors of Sewell & Vallotton Company, Limited, together with the upper echelons of management, enjoyed a rare privilege in their London offices. They had their own private entrance hall and over the years a great deal of care and company money had been lavished on it. Delicate works of art and exquisite antiques were dotted about the vast expanse of the hall with a tastefulness which was always being photographed by the glossier monthly magazines. Whatever economies might be made elsewhere, nobody begrudged the extravagant luxuries here, and even the doormen had their uniforms made in Savile Row.

Not that the doorman on duty at the moment was looking particularly happy as he lurked behind an expensive sculpture by Henry Moore and waited for the next batch of policemen to arrive.

He brooded resentfully about the lot he already had upstairs, trampling round in their great boots and upsetting everything. He realized, of course, that when one of your directors gets himself murdered in his own boardroom there's bound to be a bit of a disturbance; but, the doorman reminded himself, there's moderation in all things. He'd been watching directors come and go for the last twenty-five years and he was blowed if he could see that one more or less made that much difference.

He looked at his watch. Half-past eleven! Blimey, how much longer were they going to be? You could walk it from Scotland Yard in ten minutes! He'd been hanging about here for nearly an hour already and had missed his coffee break in the bargain.

A big black car drew up in the private driveway. The doorman smoothed down his jacket and peered through the holes which Mr. Moore might have placed there for just such a purpose. Two of the occupants of the car appeared to be trying to extricate a third from the confines of the rear seat. The doorman sniffed contemptuously. Yes, well, if it hadn't been for the murder, that fat one coming out of the car like a tight cork out of a bottle wouldn't have got his foot over the threshold! What a lout! A filthy bowler hat and a disgusting old overcoat—*not* the sartorial standards you expected in the Sewell & Vallotton directors' private entrance hall!

The fat man was now laboring up the short flight of marble steps with a younger, thinner fellow chasing athletically after him. The doorman stood his ground. He'd long ago given up falling over himself to welcome anybody, never mind a couple of peasants like these.

The plate-glass doors, untouched by human hand, swung noiselessly open and the two new arrivals moved forward to receive a blast of warm scented air on the top of their heads. Another step and—

"'Strewth!" exploded Detective Chief Inspector Wilfred Dover.

There was a fastidious shiver from the glass in the chandelier but the attention of "Fattie of the Yard" was riveted on the floor. Eyes popping, he watched in astonishment as his boots sank up to the ankles in the thick pile of the carpet. For one who had spent his life wallowing in lower middle-class squalor it was an intriguing, if unnerving, experience.

The younger, thinner man—Detective Sergeant MacGregor—went a bright pink as he always did when his superior made an exhibition of himself in public. The sergeant was just as impressed with the opulence of his surroundings as Dover was, but he would have died rather than show it.

The doorman adjusted his sneer and came forward, casually skirting the five-foot-high T'ang vase and arriving just in time to stop the fat man getting his paws on a charming little Fabergé clock which was standing defenseless on one of Sheraton's finer tables.

"H'are you the—er—gentlemen from Scotland Yard?"

Poor Sergeant MacGregor was cut to the quick by the doorman's hesitation, but if you wanted to insult Dover you had to use a sledge-hammer. In any case Dover was far too busy gawping enviously round to pay much attention to the doorman. This lot must have cost somebody a pretty penny or he was a Dutchman! What about that picture? Looked as though it had been done by a two-year-old kid with its feet but they wouldn't have stuck it in a posh frame like that if it weren't valuable. And that dirty great mirror over there? Dover swung round suddenly on the doorman.

"Here—you got all this junk properly insured?"

That took the wind right out of the doorman's sails and without another word he led the two detectives over to the directors' own personal elevator, ushered them in, showed MacGregor which button to press, and thankfully watched them slowly disappear from sight.

The directors' own personal elevator was worth a king's ransom on its own account. The wrought-iron gates were

fifteenth-century Florentine work and the two carved clus-
ters of fruit on the side walls had been confidently attributed to Grinling Gibbons; but it was the icon on the rear
wall that caught Dover's eye. Not that Dover was exactly a
connoisseur of early Novgorod religious painting but he
found the gold and jewels with which this particular
example was covered well-nigh irresistible.

"Do you reckon those rubies are real?" he demanded as
the elevator wended its way gently upward.

"Oh, I should think so, sir," said MacGregor, noting
with relief that the icon seemed to be securely bolted to
the wall. "They wouldn't have any imitation stuff here."

Dover's hand was already moving toward his trouser
pocket. "I'll bet you could prize 'em out easy as pie with a
penknife," he observed as though challenging his sergeant
to say that you couldn't.

But MacGregor was quick to scotch any bright ideas in
that direction. "I don't advise you to try, sir. Sewell and
Vallotton's collection of antiques is very well-known and
you can be quite sure they've taken all the necessary precautions against theft. I imagine this place is absolutely
crawling with burglar alarms. Closed-circuit television
cameras, too, I shouldn't wonder."

"Oh." Dover continued to stare wistfully at the rubies
while MacGregor hoped fervently that Sewell & Vallotton
had indeed got everything portable well nailed down. "I
didn't know they were second-hand furniture dealers."

"Sir?"

"This dump. I thought it was some sort of an office
building we were coming to."

"It is, sir. It's the head office of Sewell and Vallotton.
You know"—MacGregor, who was more than a bit of a
snob, looked down his nose—"they make soap."

"Soap?"

"Well, detergents now, I suppose, but they started off making soap. They're one of the biggest firms in that line in the country. Blanchette, Squishy-Washy, Alabas, Sparkle-Spume, Blua—they market all that and a dozen others besides."

"Well, what's all this stuff then?" Dover jerked an inquiring thumb at the icon.

MacGregor shrugged. "It's just their gimmick, sir. Some firms sponsor golf matches or horse shows; Sewell and Vallotton buy and display works of art. They make a specialty of saving national treasures from going abroad. It brings them millions of pounds' worth of free publicity and I suppose the antiques themselves are a pretty gilt-edged investment."

"Seems a funny way of going on," sniffed Dover.

"Sewell and Vallotton can more than afford to indulge their whimsies, sir."

Eventually the elevator reached the top floor, and Dover and MacGregor emerged to find themselves in what was known as the Directors' Suite. Here, too, money had been splashed around with a most liberal hand, as witness the fine Aubusson tapestry which covered the whole of the facing wall.

As MacGregor was closing the elevator gates they heard the creaking of regulation boots and a second later a young chubby-faced policeman came tiptoeing toward them, his cap tucked underneath his arm.

"Chief Inspector Dover, sir?" he inquired in a respectful whisper.

"Who are you?"

"Police Constable Saunderson, sir. C Division. Me and my mate answered the original 999 call and we've sort of been holding the fort ever since." In his innocence P.C. Saunderson considered himself entitled to administer a mild rebuke. "We thought you was never coming, sir."

Dover's face went black but MacGregor stepped in with a ready lie. "We were held up by the traffic," he explained quickly. "Now, what's going on here?"

"Well, nothing really at the moment, Sarge," replied P.C. Saunderson who was proving to be a rather complacent sort of lad. "I think you might say that me and my mate have got the situation well under control." He started to get his notebook out of his tunic pocket. "You've missed all the excitement—see?—what with you being held up by the traffic and everything. Now"—he flicked the pages of his notebook over—"me and Stokes—he's my mate—we got the 999 call relayed to us at ten seventeen precisely.

"A sudden death in suspicious circumstances was the message and we arrived downstairs at ten twenty-one. A nippy bit of driving that but, of course, the streets are pretty quiet round here in the middle of the morning. Or, at least, that's been my experience. Right—well, by ten twenty-three approximately we was up here and I conducted a preliminary examination of the deceased. Strictly between you and me, old Stokes is a bit of a dead loss when it comes to First Aid.

"Now, at ten twenty-five I turned to Stokes and said,"—P.C. Saunderson solemnly consulted his notebook—"'I reckon this is a blooming murder, Jack, or'"—he turned over a page—"'or maybe he croaked hisself.'"

"For God's sake," snarled Dover, his feet giving him hell as usual, "do we have to stand here all day listening to this twaddle?"

P.C. Saunderson, whose romantic ideas about Scotland Yard's glamorous murder squad were about to take quite a beating, was disconcerted by the violence of the interruption. "Did you want to see the body, sir?" he stammered.

"Not likely!" came Dover's indignant retort. "If I'd wanted to spend my life looking at corpses I'd have joined a blooming mortuary, wouldn't I, blockhead? Isn't there somewhere we can go and sit down?"

"Oh, yes, sir! As a matter of fact I've already requisitioned the secretary's office for your use."

"And where's the secretary?" demanded MacGregor sharply, because somebody had to keep a check on these things.

"Having hysterics in the ladies' cloaks, I shouldn't wonder," chuckled P.C. Saunderson as he led the way down a corridor devoted exclusively to masters of the seventeenth-century Dutch school. "Funny how it takes some people, isn't it?"

"Good God, man!" shouted MacGregor. "You don't mean to say you've let her out of your—"

"Now, now, Sarge," said P.C. Saunderson soothingly, "give us credit for a bit of the old common or garden. She's in the clear. Never went in the boardroom after the bottle of sherry was opened. Everybody agrees about that. And she didn't have any contact with the suspects after the old fellow snuffed it either, so she can't be an accomplice. Ah"—he opened a door—"here we are! Think you can pig it in here?"

The secretary's room was startlingly elegant but the furnishings were merely expensive and not priceless. Dover didn't care. He homed to a comfortable-looking chair behind the desk and flopped into it with a sigh of relief. MacGregor propped himself up against a filing cabinet and got his own notebook out. P.C. Saunderson decided not to push his luck and remained standing by the door.

"Sherry?" prompted Dover, ever hopeful.

The constable twinkled roguishly at him. "The murder weapon, sir."

"The murder weapon? Do you mean the victim was hit over the head with a bottle?"

"Oh, no, sir." It was P.C. Saunderson's turn to register surprise. "He was poisoned. Didn't they tell you?"

"Nobody ever tells me anything," grumbled Dover, with considerable justification. "And that goes for you too, laddie, so you can wipe that stupid grin off your face! I don't know what you young coppers are coming to, straight I don't! Why, when I was your age I'd have had the bloomin' case solved by now."

"Give us another half hour, sir, and I'll have it all tied up for you," responded P.C. Saunderson eagerly and watched with some trepidation as Dover's usually pasty face turned dark crimson.

The trouble with Chief Inspector Wilfred Dover was that he had a rather dog-in-the-manger attitude to work. He didn't want to do it himself, but he got exceedingly nasty if anybody else tried, too obviously, to relieve him of the burden. MacGregor, who had more experience than anybody else in the delicate art of handling the old fool, stepped in once more to smooth things over.

"Just give us the facts, Constable," he said, "and leave the detective work to us."

And, sulkily hoping that everybody realized how hurt his feelings were, P.C. Saunderson did just that.

The crime had occurred just as the monthly board meeting of the Sewell & Vallotton directors was about to start. Only five directors had been present and they had eventually divided themselves up neatly into one victim and four suspects.

"And the name of the dead man?" asked MacGregor.

"Sir Holman Hobart." P.C. Saunderson dutifully waited while MacGregor wrote it down. "He was Chairman of the Board. Chap in his early sixties, I should think."

MacGregor nodded and the story continued.

The five directors had all arrived for their meeting at about ten o'clock. According to Mrs. Doris Vick, the secretary who had welcomed them and taken their hats and coats, they had behaved quite normally and gone straight into the boardroom. When everybody had arrived she had closed the door and left them to their weighty deliberations.

MacGregor looked up. "That's a bit odd, isn't it? Doesn't the secretary usually sit with the board and take down the minutes or something?"

"I believe that is the accepted procedure, Sarge, but from what I've been able to ascertain that lot in there"— P.C. Saunderson inclined his head toward the beautifully inlaid double doors in the wall directly opposite the secretary's desk—"are a bit of a law unto themselves." The constable lowered his voice. "Seems they prefer to have all their argy-bargies in private and *then* call Mrs. Vick in and dictate an expurgated version of what happened. She says they're real gentlemen and they don't like cussing and swearing in front of a lady."

"What the hell," demanded Dover, temporarily abandoning his search for some decent writing paper that wasn't defaced by Sewell & Vallotton's engraved letterhead, "are you whispering for?"

"Well," said P.C. Saunderson defensively, "we don't want them to hear us talking about them, do we, sir?"

"No skin off my nose," grunted Dover and opened another drawer.

MacGregor, however, was blessed with a more inquiring mind. He pointed his pencil at the double doors. "That's the boardroom, is it?"

"Right, Sarge."

"And the dead body?"

"Oh, that's in there too, Sarge." P.C. Saunderson drew himself up proudly. "The doc wanted to take it away with him but I said no, not until you'd had a chance to look at it."

"The police surgeon's been and gone?" asked MacGregor, shooting an anxious glance at Dover.

"Said he couldn't hang about any longer, Sarge. Still, I made him give me his preliminary report. He can't tell us anything more until he's done the postmortem."

"But I don't get this," persisted MacGregor. "You mean that all the surviving members of the board are sitting in there with the corpse?"

"It's nicely covered up with a sheet, Sarge, and they insisted. Of course, I've got my mate, Stokes, in there too, keeping an eye on them. I told you they was a queer lot, didn't I? Not one of 'em has so much as set foot outside that room since the old boy dropped down dead."

MacGregor took a deep breath to steady himself. "Yes, well, let's get back to that, shall we? You can explain these peculiar goings on when we come to them. Now, we'd got as far as the five of them having their board meeting."

But P.C. Saunderson was a stickler for accuracy. The board meeting, he ponderously pointed out, had not actually started. There was, it seems, a rather charming tradition at Sewell & Vallotton according to which the directors, before settling down to their meeting, refreshed themselves with a glass or two of choice sherry. Poured, added the constable looking meaningly at MacGregor, from an unopened bottle.

Dover, who had been quietly resting his eyes, opened them and smacked his lips.

"You're sure of that?" asked MacGregor.

"Quite sure, Sarge. I got it from that commissionaire chap downstairs. It's his job to supply two bottles of sherry for each board meeting. Anything the directors don't consume is his perks. He bought the bottles on his way to work this morning from an off-license in Pewter Street and he'll take his oath that they hadn't been tampered with when he left 'em on the table in the boardroom. Anyhow, we don't need to worry too much about what happened to the sherry at this stage. If the poison had been put in the bottle, the whole lot of 'em would have died, wouldn't they?"

MacGregor chewed the end of his pencil and admitted somewhat helplessly that this would appear to be so.

P.C. Saunderson looked pleased; then, sucking in his second wind, he continued inexorably. One of the directors, the Marquis of Arnfield, had opened the sherry and poured it out, but the tray of glasses had been handed round by another director, the Honorable Gisbert Fittsarthur. Presumably either nobleman could have surreptitiously slipped in the fatal dose, but it was a little difficult to see how they could have insured that Sir Holman took the right glass. As Chairman he had been served first out of courtesy and had had the choice of five more or less identical goblets.

"You can hold a tray so that a man will probably take a particular glass," MacGregor pointed out doubtfully. "Still, it's pretty risky. What happened next?"

Nothing, really. The directors had stood around, sipping their drinks and chatting. After about ten minutes Sir Holman had called to them to order and suggested that they might as well make a start. Everybody was just beginning to sit down when Sir Holman, standing at the head of the table, had gasped, clutched his throat, choked, retched, doubled up in obvious agony, and dropped down dead.

"And the funny thing is, Sarge," P.C. Saunderson went on with a wondering shake of the head, "that none of 'em seems to have doubted for a minute that he'd been poisoned. And not accidental, neither. They spotted straight off that they'd all be under suspicion, so they called the secretary on the intercom and told her to get the police. After that they just sat tight, watching each other. Until me and Stokes arrived nobody was allowed to enter or leave the boardroom. What do you think of that, eh?"

MacGregor shrugged.

"If you ask me, Sarge, it's a conspiracy."

"Well, nobody is asking you, laddie, so shut up!" Dover, having delivered himself of this pleasantry, crooked a finger at his sergeant. MacGregor hurried over to the desk. "Sling him out!" Dover ordered.

"Sir?"

"You heard me! Cocky young smart aleck—get rid of him!"

P.C. Saunderson might have his faults but being stone-deaf wasn't one of them. "I haven't quite finished my report yet, sir," he said and went so far as to produce a friendly man-to-man smile.

Dover's habitual scowl deepened. "You were finished ten minutes ago, laddie," he growled ominously. "Take my word for it."

MacGregor moved in smartly before the situation could degenerate any further. He caught the constable by the arm and began to lead him over to the door. "Well, come on!" he urged impatiently. "What else is there? And for God's sake keep it short!"

"It's just that me and Stokes searched all the suspects, Sarge."

"And?"

"I thought that whoever brought the poison into the room must have carried it in something—see?—and they might still have the container on their person."

MacGregor gave the arm he was grasping a warning shake. "Did you find anything?"

"Well, not exactly. I haven't had time, have I? But I confiscated everything they had in their pockets. I've got all the stuff locked up in that filing cabinet and I'd just finished making a list when you arrived." P.C. Saunderson risked a sideways glance in the direction of the desk. "I hope I did the right thing."

MacGregor opened the door with one hand and held out the other. "Give me the key. Now"—he dropped his voice and spoke more kindly—"take my advice and stay out of sight for a bit. No, better still, see if you can't rustle up some coffee for him, and a few biscuits. He's generally a bit more amenable when he's been fed."

With the door open and escape in sight, P.C. Saunderson threw the discipline of years to the winds. "What's his favorite food, Sarge?" he demanded in an aggrieved whisper. "Babies?"

Dover watched in gloomy silence as MacGregor unlocked the filing cabinet and brought out five small cardboard boxes, all neatly labeled with names. It was only when the boxes had been deposited on the desk in front of him and he caught sight of the contents that he sat up and began to take notice.

"Blimey!" he squealed. "Get an eyeful of all that!"

"Oh, sir, I don't think—"

MacGregor was too late. Chief Inspector Dover had already got at the loot and was dribbling gold watches, silver cigar cutters, platinum ballpoint pens, and plump soft leather wallets through the stickiest fingers in the Metropolitan Police. MacGregor scrabbled desperately, trying to return each avidly snatched-up goodie to its own box.

"Who are they, for God's sake?" gasped Dover, flicking away unsuccessfully at a diamond-studded lighter before abandoning it for another in opalescent strawberry enamel. "Bleeding millionaires?"

MacGregor caught the diamond-studded lighter just before it hit the desk. "As near as makes no difference, I believe, sir. Now, which box did this come from? Oh, sir, please, we shall get them all muddled up and—"

"It's downright unfair!" whined Dover, grabbing for an alligator-skin wallet. "Nobody ought to be this rich! 'Strewth, look at this!" He opened the wallet to reveal a thick wad of five-pound notes. "I'll bet he doesn't even know how much he's bleeding well got!"

"He may not, sir," said MacGregor, literally pulling the wallet out of Dover's stubby fingers, "but P.C. Saunderson certainly does. He's made a complete inventory of everything."

"He would!" Dover looked around for a consolation prize. A heavy gold cigarette case caught his eye and by the time MacGregor had returned the wallet to its box Dover was already lighting a fat white cigarette with the enameled lighter.

"Oh, *sir!*" said MacGregor.

Dover ignored the reproach and went through the routine of hacking, coughing, and spluttering which, more often than not, accompanied his first puff.

"Don't you think we'd better start questioning the people concerned, sir? They must be getting very impatient at having to wait so long."

Dover mopped his eyes and regarded his purloined cigarette with disgust. "Talk about sweaty socks!" he observed disparagingly. "What did you say? Oh, I suppose we might as well. Wheel the first one in."

In some bewilderment MacGregor examined the

names, titles, and decorations which P.C. Saunderson had painstakingly written on the little boxes. How was one with only a scanty acquaintance of the beau monde to sort out the precedence in this bunch? Of course Sir Holman Hobart Bt., K.C.V.O., C.B., D.S.O., M.C. (the deceased) could be ignored; but that still left the Marquis of Arnfield, M.V.O., M.B.E., T.D.; Dr. Benjamin Zlatt, O.B.B., Q.C., M.Sc., LL.D., F.R.I.C.; Vice-Admiral T.R. Jonkett-Brown, C.B.E., D.S.O., D.S.C., R.N. (Ret.); and the Honorable Gisbert Fittsarthur, B.A., F.R.G.S.

"Alphabetical order!" grunted Dover, cutting the Gordian knot.

As a matter of fact, almost any sequence would have served as there was a remarkable similarity in the appearance of the surviving Sewell & Vallotton directors. Dover, indeed, never really did get round to telling t'other from which. It was almost as if all four of them had been cast from the same mold and only as an afterthought had a few superficial details been added to distinguish one from the other. Each was vaguely middle-aged, aggressively well-nourished, beautifully groomed and suited by a tailor who knew, where necessary, how to conceal an incipient paunch.

The Marquis of Arnfield, as befitted a peer of the realm, played it very aloof and distant. He waited with only the merest hint of impatience as MacGregor placed a chair for him in front of the desk.

Dover was busy examining a packet of picture postcards which he had found tucked away in Admiral Jonkett-Brown's possessions, but the Marquis appeared not to notice the snickers and grins which ensued. He had condescended to make a statement to the police but that was going to be the limit of his social contact with them.

"I think I should say right at the beginning," drawled the Marquis, gazing at a delightful little Gainsborough which hung on the wall over Dover's right shoulder, "that I did not murder Sir Holman Hobart."

"Disgusting!" chuckled Dover under his breath. "They bloomin' well want running in for having muck like—oh, crikey!" And then, just to show that his mind really was on his work, he swung round suddenly on the Marquis. "You seem damned sure it's murder."

"Accident would appear to be extremely unlikely and Sir Holman was the last man in the world to commit suicide, especially in public."

"Might have been a heart attack or something," said Dover, wondering why he hadn't thought of that lovely labor-saving idea before.

The Marquis continued to feast his eyes on the Gainsborough. Most people, finding themselves face to face with Dover, would have done the same. "Your police doctor didn't think so."

Dover sighed and shuffled through his picture postcards. "Who are you putting your money on?"

The Marquis didn't bother pretending not to understand. "I'm afraid I haven't the faintest idea. They say poison is a woman's weapon, don't they? Perhaps you ought to arrest our faithful Mrs. Vick."

"The secretary? But I thought she—"

The Marquis deigned to look straight at Dover. "I was being facetious," he murmured. "But, since we are on the subject of poisoning, perhaps I ought to mention that Dr. Zlatt is a qualified chemist."

"Is he now?" said Dover, pushing the picture postcards to one side.

"And a very distinguished one. Sewell and Vallotton often employ him as a consultant and so do several other firms. He must have unrestricted access to a number of industrial research laboratories."

"Fancy." Dover looked up hopefully. "You didn't happen to see him slipping anything in Sir What's-his-name's drink?"

The Marquis squinted down his nose. "Of course not."

Dover sighed again and dragged some sheets of typing paper over in front of him. "You'd better tell us what happened in there, I suppose," he grumbled and began hunting through the boxes in front of him. Eventually he selected an old-fashioned fountain pen belonging to the Honorable Gisbert Fittsarthur and unscrewed the top. "You're the one who poured the sherry, aren't you?"

"Yes. I always do. I filled the five glasses on the tray, took my own, then old Gissie Fittsarthur handed the others round. He loves appearing generous when somebody else is footing the bill."

There was a strong rumor circulating round Scotland Yard that Chief Inspector Wilfred Dover couldn't even write his own name. Judging from the way he was futilely scratching with the borrowed fountain pen, the rumor was probably true. MacGregor watched him jabbing the nib irritably into the paper and decided that he had better carry on with the questioning until Dover had less important problems on his mind.

"Did you speak to Sir Holman, sir, after you poured out the sherry and before he died?"

The Marquis acknowledged MacGregor's presence by a languid quarter turn of his head. "Naturally. I went over to have a word with him as soon as I'd finished pouring the sherry. I suppose we stood chatting over by the window for several minutes."

By the judicious use of his teeth Dover managed to restore the fourteen-carat gold nib to something approaching its original condition. MacGregor hurried on with his next question.

"What happened after that, sir?"

The Marquis withdrew a fine linen handkerchief from his cuff and waved it negligently across his nose. The scent of lavender filled the air. "After that? Well, Sir Holman was called away by Dr. Zlatt. Zlatt had a great sheaf of papers in his hand and the pair of them stood looking at them. I joined Gissie Fittsarthur and the Admiral by the sherry table. Gissie was knocking back as much free drink as he could get his hands on, of course. Then Sir Holman started walking to the head of the table to call the meeting to order and Admiral Jonkett-Brown muttered something about wanting a quick word with him. He caught him about halfway up the table and they had a brief chat. After that Sir Holman suggested that we should all take our seats."

Dover chucked the fountain pen back in its box and scowled disagreeably at the Marquis of Arnfield. "So the whole bang shoot of you talked to Sir What's-his-name while he was guzzling his sherry?"

An expression of acute distaste passed over the Marquis' countenance. "Not exactly. Gissie Fittsarthur didn't speak to him, as far as I can remember."

Dover grunted and returned to an examination of the little boxes.

The Marquis wafted his handkerchief over his face again. "Is that all?" he asked MacGregor faintly.

"Well, just another question or two, if you don't mind, sir." MacGregor cringed visibly as Dover emerged triumphant with a carved ivory toothpick. "When Sir Holman left you to go and talk to Dr. Zlatt, can you remember how much sherry he still had left in his glass?"

"Yes."

"I beg your pardon, sir?"

The Marquis closed his eyes in a slow blink of martyr-dom. "I said, yes, I do remember how much sherry he still had in his glass. He had it all left."

"All, sir?"

The Marquis directed a bleak stare at MacGregor. "Are you having difficulty in hearing me, my good man?"

MacGregor blushed. "No, sir."

"I am glad to hear it. I rather pride myself on the clari-ty of my enunciation. Now, as I was saying, when Sir Hol-man left me to talk to Zlatt he hadn't touched his sherry. There was nothing unusual about this. Sir Holman was a whiskey man and didn't care much for sherry. However, it is the tradition at Sewell and Vallotton to serve sherry before each board meeting, so there was nothing Sir Hol-man could do about it. He just used to carry his glass around until he was ready to open the meeting. Then he went to the head of the table, tossed the whole glassful down at one go, and called us to order. Like," added the Marquis with a very aristocratic sneer, "someone drinking cough mixture."

"That's very interesting, sir," said MacGregor and shot a glance at Dover to see if this vital piece of information had penetrated the solid ivory. Was there a momentary hesita-tion in the delicate exploration, with the borrowed tooth-pick, of the Chief Inspector's left ear? It was difficult to tell. MacGregor turned back to the Marquis. "I suppose every-body in the boardroom knew that Sir Holman usually drank his sherry like that?"

"Of course." The Marquis flourished his handkerchief with studied grace. "It was no secret. He did it for years."

MacGregor tried to hide his excitement. "No doubt that's why he never noticed the poison."

"No doubt. Is there anything else?"

"Er—just one more point, sir." MacGregor turned back a page or two in his notebook. "Ah, yes. Could you tell me what you and Sir Holman were talking about, sir?"

The Marquis looked annoyed. "I fail to see what damned business it is of yours," he snapped, "but, if you must know, we were discussing my re-election to the board. I am due to retire in a couple of months under our rules and I wanted to be quite sure that our chairman knew that I was intending to stand again."

"There was no quarrel or disagreement, sir?"

"None. Sir Holman assured me of his full support." The Marquis stood up and glared icily at Dover who was now engaged in trying to get the top off the Marquis' own pocket flask. "No doubt you will be returning my personal possessions in due course. I would prefer to have them in an undamaged condition, if that is possible."

The Honorable Gisbert Fittsarthur was a watery-eyed, shriveled old chap who was clearly keen to get on pally terms with two real-life detectives.

"Always been a great one for mystery stories," he confided as he hitched his chair nearer to the desk. "Started as a nipper with those Sherlock Holmes ones and never looked back since, hm? Borrowed 'em from the library, don't you know. Can't afford to buy books with the surtax the rate it is. So—you've me to thank that there was no tampering with the evidence in there, hm? Knew there was something pretty fishy about the way old Holman keeled over. Fit as a fiddle, he was. 'Don't touch anything!' I told 'em. 'And nobody's to leave the room, either!' I knew exactly what to do, hm?"

Dover scowled resentfully and pulled the Honorable Gisbert's box in front of him. The old-fashioned fountain pen, a rather shabby wallet, four pieces of string, three bus tickets, a large sheet of hastily folded blotting paper—the Honorable Gisbert's personal possessions were not up to the high standards Dover had come to expect. He opened up the sheet of blotting paper and glowered at its virgin whiteness.

The Honorable Gisbert grinned sheepishly. "Always stock up on a bit of stationery, hm? Well, Sewell and Vallotton won't miss it, will they?"

Dover pushed the box away and got down to business. "You were the one who handed the sherry round?"

"Ah! Yes, well, I can explain that. Innocent as a newborn babe, hm? Sherry glasses all laid out on a heavy silver tray. Lord Arnfield pours the sherry out. I pick up the tray. Both hands, see? Takes both my hands to lift the damned thing. Couldn't possibly have held it in one hand while I popped the poison in. Besides, how did I know which glass poor Holman was going to take?"

"You served him first," Dover pointed out through an enormous yawn.

"Who told you that? Oh, Arnfield, of course! Well, if it's a suspect you're after, have a good look at our noble Marquis, hm? *Cui bono*, that's what I always say."

MacGregor knew it was no use waiting for Dover to respond to a Latin phrase, however well-known. "Are you suggesting that the Marquis of Arnfield benefits from Sir Holman's death?" he asked.

The Honorable Gisbert bared his yellow teeth in what could have been a smile. "Five thousand a year. What I'd call a substantial motive, hm?"

"He stands to inherit that, sir?"

"No, not inherit! Keep. That's what he gets for serving on the board, don't you know. Arnfield's term of office coming to an end. No re-election for him without poor Holman's backing. Ergo, five thousand a year gone up the spout and Arnfield's got some very expensive hobbies to keep up."

"And Sir Holman was not going to support him, sir?"

The Honorable Gisbert winked, tapped the side of his nose, and leered knowingly. "Little bird!" he sniggered. "Little bird, hm? Holman wanted the seat for his nephew. Everybody knows that."

"You accusing this Marquis of Who's-your-father of murder?" demanded Dover who could occasionally get to the point with amazing speed.

The Honorable Gisbert squirmed uncomfortably. "Hey, steady on!" he whinnied. "Arnfield and I belong to the same club. Not that I'll be able to keep my dues up much longer with the way—"

"Well, who do you fancy then?" demanded Dover.

"I'd give you six to four on Zlatt," responded the Honorable Gisbert maliciously. "Well, you can't call poisoning an Englishman's crime, can you?"

Dover had found himself an ebony comb in a chased silver case. "That's all you've got to go on? That Zlatt's not an Englishman?"

"No. He's got a motive, too."

"So has this Marquis fellow."

"Zlatt's is bigger," said the Honorable Gisbert. "*Cui bono*—told you that before." He paused in wonder as Dover slowly drew the comb through his meager tufts of hair. "I say, that's a bit unhygienic, isn't it?"

"Why?" asked Dover, continuing his combing unperturbed. "Zlatt's not got dandruff, has he?"

"That's Zlatt's comb?"

"In his box," said Dover, idly running his thumbnail along the teeth.

The Honorable Gisbert whickered like a senile horse. "Bald as a coot!" he tittered. "What's he want a comb for?"

"Maybe it's a reminder of happier days," chuckled Dover and warmed to the Honorable Gisbert as this shaft of wit was greeted by flattering guffaws.

MacGregor, who had lost his sense of humor the day after he was appointed Dover's assistant, cleared his throat. "You were telling us about Dr. Zlatt's motive, sir."

"Ah!" The Honorable Gisbert pulled himself together. "Next chairman of Sewell and Vallotton. No doubt about it. Ten thousand a year plus perks." The yellow teeth were revealed once more. "Might be tempted to commit murder myself for that, hm? And he had the opportunity. While he was showing poor Holman those papers. Quickness of the hand, hm? Juggling about like that he could easily have dropped something in Holman's glass of sherry."

Police Constable Saunderson brought in the coffee.

Dover welcomed the refreshments with his usual charm and grace. "Coffee? 'Strewth, it's a square meal I want, laddie!" He grabbed the stickiest-looking cake. "This muck wouldn't keep a fly going."

"Maybe I can get you some sandwiches, sir," said P.C. Saunderson as another cake plunged down the Chief Inspector's gullet.

"Sandwiches? With my stomach, laddie?" Dover shook his head and his face assumed a suitably solemn expression. "I've got to be careful, I have. Doctor's orders. I've got a very delicate stomach, you see, and—"

But MacGregor had no intention of letting Dover get started on the subject of his stomach. "I do think, sir, that we ought to finish off these interviews before lunch. We've kept these people waiting long enough already and they are pretty important men, you know. We don't want them to be making complaints."

"Let 'em try!" blustered Dover with the bravado of one

who'd had more complaints made against him than most of us have had hot dinners. "We're dealing with murder, not some bloomin' parking violation."

"That's what makes speed in the initial stages so important, isn't it, sir?"

Dover, after a pause for thought, decided that MacGregor hadn't the guts to try being cheeky. He helped himself to another cake.

"Er—have you got any theories yet, sir?"

Dover wiped a blob of cream off his lapel and slowly licked his finger. "Didn't care much for the look of that Marquis fellow," he admitted grudgingly. "Or the other one, come to that."

"The Honorable Gisbert, sir? No, he wasn't very impressive, was he? This Dr. Zlatt looks as though he might be a good possibility."

Dover nodded, his mouth full again.

"Actually, sir,"—MacGregor broached the subject with considerable care because Dover had a habit of reacting unfavorably to other people's ideas—"I was wondering about the Marquis of Arnfield myself. It's this business of Sir Holman not liking sherry, you see. Now, presented with a tray of glasses, wouldn't he be likely to take the one that was *least* full? The Marquis could have poisoned one glass and then only half filled it—"

"You don't have to spell it out in words of one syllable!" snapped Dover, indicating that he was ready for his second cup of coffee by shoving the saucer noisily across the desk.

"It was just a suggestion, sir."

"And a damned stupid one!" snarled Dover as he stuffed the last cake in his mouth. "Anyhow, I thought of it myself hours ago."

"Yes, sir," sighed MacGregor.

Dover dropped six lumps of sugar in his cup and started stirring it with a silver swizzle stick that he'd come across in the Marquis of Arnfield's box. The gentle exercise appeared to give him pleasure and for some minutes he swizzled away. MacGregor and P.C. Saunderson stood in bemused silence until the Chief Inspector at last raised his head. "Well, what are you waiting for? Bring the next one in!"

Vice-Admiral Jonkett-Brown had bright blue mariner's eyes, a red face, and a nasty temper. In spite of this he very nearly became Dover's friend for life when he stormed in declaring that he would make no statement and answer no questions without the professional advice of his solicitor.

"Very wise!" approved Dover, most of whose attention was currently devoted to thumbing through a little address book he'd found. "Pity there aren't a few more like you. Get the next one, MacGregor!"

The Admiral was a little taken aback. "It's not that I want to obstruct your inquiries," he explained awkwardly.

"Of course not," agreed Dover, delicately moistening a finger before he turned over the next page.

"But you must admit we've all been placed in a deuced sticky position."

Dover's face was beginning to ache with the effort of sustaining an encouraging smile. "You can't be too careful," he mumbled.

"Not that I've anything to hide," the Admiral went on. "Damn it, I only exchanged a couple of words with Holman before he went down as though he'd been felled with a marlinespike." Without thinking he sat down in the chair and the last traces of benevolence faded from Dover's countenance. "So, you see, I couldn't have killed him, even if I'd wanted to. Poor old devil! What a rotten way to go, eh? Still, one of us four must have done it. There's no getting away from that. Well, luckily I'm not the sort of man who flinches in the face of unpleasant facts. Now, let's have a look at the rest of the field, shall we? What about the Marquis of Arnfield for a start? I daresay you've formed a few opinions of your own about him but I'd just like you to listen to a little theory of mine."

Dover reached for a watch from the Honorable Gisbert's box, wound it up, and placed it ostentatiously on the desk.

The Admiral beamed. "Good! I'm glad to see you're a man after my own heart. Be brief and keep to the point—that's what I used to tell my young officers. I can't tolerate chaps who ramble on and on without ever saying anything. I've been accused of being a trifle too blunt in my time, but nobody's ever called me a shilly-shallier. Thirty years in the Navy's taught me a thing or two—and keeping my eyes open is one of them. And using the old brain. I haven't been wasting my time sitting out there, you know. I've been thinking and in my opinion the Marquis of Arnfield might well be your man. And I can give you a lead as to how he did it, too."

To Dover's patent dismay the Admiral settled back comfortably in his chair and crossed one immaculately trousered leg over the other. "As soon as he'd poured out the sherry, Arnfield dashed across the room and caught poor Holman over by the window. They were talking together for quite a while, discussing Arnfield's chances of being re-elected to the board, I shouldn't wonder. Still, that doesn't matter at the moment. What does matter is that Arnfield is congenitally incapable of speaking to any of us members of the lower orders without waving that damned handkerchief of his about like a distress signal. You must have noticed him. It's a damned dirty habit, if you ask me, and dashed distracting, too. With that flapping about in your face you could have a ton of bricks dropped in your sherry and never even notice."

MacGregor caught Dover's eye and correctly interpreted the finger being drawn grimly across the Chief Inspector's throat as an indication that somebody's patience was becoming exhausted. Vice-Admiral Jonkett-Brown, however, was not a man who let himself be interrupted lightly and MacGregor's half-hearted attempts were sunk without a qualm.

"Mind you, the Marquis of Arnfield isn't the only one you ought to be keeping your eye on. There's our Herr Doktor Zlatt, too. I've always thought he was a deuced sight too clever by half. Ambitious, you know. Sort of blighter who'd stop at nothing. Well, now"—the Admiral uncrossed his legs and glanced expectantly up at Dover— "there's a couple of pointers for you to follow up."

Dover's eyes had been closed for some time and they didn't open now.

The Admiral, his ears already beginning to steam a little, turned brusquely to MacGregor in search of enlightenment. "The fellow's not gone to sleep, has he?" he demanded.

"Of course not, sir!" MacGregor's attempt to pass off a tricky situation with a gay laugh was not helped by the faint bubbling sound which started to come from Dover's lips. "Er—what about the Honorable Gisbert Fittsarthur, sir?"

"He happens to be a very old friend of mine," said the Admiral coldly, as though that settled the matter.

"But that doesn't mean that he isn't capable of murder, does it, sir?" asked MacGregor.

"It makes it dashed unlikely!"

"He did hand the sherry round, sir."

"True." The Admiral pursed his lips. "But we were all watching him very closely. He dropped the tray last month. He's beginning to show his age, you know. Getting doddery and more than a bit potty, too. He's got this bee in his bonnet about how poor he is. Well,"—the Admiral's red face creased in a frown as he tried to be fair—"I don't suppose he's worth a penny more than half a million these days but that's no excuse for some of the things he does. I mean, we've all got to tighten our belts a bit but there's no need to go writing your letters on the blank pages torn out of library books, is there?"

"I suppose not, sir," said MacGregor.

"And the way he goes on at these board meetings! It's a positive disgrace for a fellow of his breeding. Filling his fountain pen out of the chairman's inkwell, purloining pencils and sheets of paper, downing as much free sherry as he can get his hands on! I've warned him about it. 'Never you mind about finishing up in a pauper's grave,' I told him. 'It's the loony bin you're heading for.' I might as well have saved my breath because he went through the whole rigmarole just the same this morning. Jolly poor show, you know, with people like Zlatt looking on. Gives 'em an entirely false impression of British aristocracy."

By the time Dr. Benjamin Zlatt settled himself with bland composure in the suspects' chair, Dover had had more than enough. His stomach was rumbling like a jumbo jet at takeoff. Dr. Zlatt suddenly found himself at the tail end of Dover's fury.

"I'm thinking of charging you with murder!" snarled the Chief Inspector.

Dr. Zlatt didn't turn a hair. "In that case, my dear sir, I can only advise you to think again."

"You have access to poison!" roared Dover, determined now to make somebody pay for all the trouble he was being put to. "You'll be the next chairman of this bloomin' board and you could have slipped the poison into Sir What's-his-name's sherry when you were showing him those papers."

"Ah!" Dr. Zlatt nodded his head wisely. "Means, motive, and opportunity! Luckily I can demolish your hypothesis without much difficulty."

"Oh, can you? Well, take it from me, mate, if there's any demolishing to be done round here I'll do it!" Dover, suiting his actions to his words, raised his fists and clenched them threateningly. It would have been more impressive if they hadn't looked like a couple of rather dirty, pink, over-stuffed cushions.

Dr. Zlatt merely smiled. "May I be permitted to deal with your accusations one at a time? First, the question of the poison. I agree—nobody in that boardroom could have got hold of whatever poison may have been used more easily than I. But, please, give me credit for some intelligence. Should I ever contemplate committing murder, poison is the last means I should choose. It would point the finger of suspicion at me immediately."

"It's the old double bluff," said Dover. "You used poison because you thought I'd think you'd be too clever to use poison."

There were thirty seconds of respectful silence while everybody, including Dover, dissected the cunning logic of this statement.

"And then," Dr. Zlatt continued calmly, "we come to my presumed motive. No doubt the chairmanship of the Sewell and Vallotton board will be offered to me but that doesn't mean that I shall accept it. In fact, I shall not. I am an extremely rich man, my dear sir, and my time is already fully occupied with much work. You will have to take my word for it, but I can assure you that I simply am not interested in becoming Sir Holman's successor."

Dover was now regarding Dr. Zlatt with the utmost loathing. "You'd have to say that!"

"I turned down the chairmanship of another company only last week and the fees were nearly double what I would get here."

Dover turned green with envy and fished out his last ace. "You were the only one with the opportunity to poison the glass of sherry."

Dr. Zlatt trumped the ace. "Now that, my dear sir, is just not true. All the others were in the near vicinity of Sir Holman and had just as much chance as I did. Even more, I would imagine."

"They weren't waving papers all over the place to distract his attention."

Dr. Zlatt leaned back rather gracefully in his chair. "I'm afraid you have been slightly misinformed. I did talk to Sir Holman for several minutes and I did wave papers about. I was showing him the plans for a new research laboratory which Sewell and Vallotton are thinking of building. However, at that time, Sir Holman's glass of sherry was not in his hand."

Collapse of stout party. "Waddery'mean?" gabbled Dover.

"Before looking at the plans Sir Holman quite naturally put his glass down so that he could have both his hands free. He stepped across to the boardroom table and left his glass by the things in front of his chair. You know about his habit of draining his glass at one gulp just before he opened the meeting?"

"Oh, damn and blast!" said Dover and retired from the interrogation in a sulk.

Dr. Zlatt proved that he could manage quite well without him. "I wonder if you would permit me to offer you a small suggestion, Sergeant?" he said, turning to MacGregor. "It's this problem of motive. Sir Holman wasn't the sort of man who had murderous enemies, certainly not among his fellow directors. On the other hand we are all of us interested in money. Now, as soon as the stock market gets wind of Sir Holman's death, Sewell and Vallotton shares will drop like a plummet of lead. Somebody with prior knowledge could, if you will excuse the expression, make a killing."

MacGregor looked up from his notebook. "You mean by buying up shares in the hope they'll rise later, sir?"

"That's one possibility, but I was thinking of another manipulation. Selling short. A man contracts to sell at some future date shares which he doesn't yet possess. He hopes, of course, to be able to buy the shares meanwhile at a lower price and thus make a profit."

"Ah"—MacGregor had recently bought himself a paperback on the art of investing and reckoned he knew his way around the corridors of high finance—"you mean a bull, sir?"

"Well," said Dr. Zlatt kindly, "it's a bear, actually, but you've got the right idea."

Dover sniggered and got a reproving glance from Dr. Zlatt.

"We'll have to look into this, sir," said MacGregor thoughtfully.

"I should get your Fraud Squad people on to it. They know their way around the City. You see, if somebody in that boardroom did deliberately kill Sir Holman so that the Sewell and Vallotton shares would drop, he certainly wouldn't have used his own name in his financial dealings. You'll probably need an expert to unravel all the complications."

"And what," asked Dover, removing a fat cigar from Vice-Admiral Jonkett-Brown's pigskin case, "do you think you're doing?"

MacGregor paused in mid-dialing. "I was just getting on to the Yard, sir."

"Wafor?"

"I thought we should follow up Dr. Zlatt's suggestion, sir, and see if anybody has been playing the market with Sewell and Vallotton shares."

"'Strewth!" said Dover, his piggy little eyes gleaming contemptuously through a cloud of richly aromatic smoke. "You don't half like to do things the hard way."

MacGregor dropped the telephone back onto its stand. "Well," he said with as much patience as he could muster, "I really don't see what other line we can pursue at the moment, sir." He glanced in some despair at his notebook. "Our questioning of the four obvious suspects doesn't seem to have got us very far, does it? We can't do much about checking up where the poison came from until we know exactly what it was and it may be hours before the lab comes up with the answer. And as far as I can see from the rather muddled picture we've got of what happened immediately prior to the murder, any one of the four men could have put the poison in Sir Holman's glass of sherry."

MacGregor waited politely while Dover draped himself over the edge of the desk and coughed his heart up. "Actually I was wondering, sir, if perhaps we oughtn't to try staging a reconstruction of the crime. I don't know about you, sir, but I don't feel I've got a very clear idea of what people's movements really were. Of course," added MacGregor rather bitterly, "it would perhaps have helped if we'd examined the boardroom first."

Dover, strangely enough, was no longer coughing. He was laughing. Uproariously, triumphantly, and quite obviously at MacGregor's expense.

MacGregor, his jaw locked, counted up to ten. "Sir?"

"Reconstruction of the crime!" spluttered Dover. "'Strewth, you'll be the death of me yet!"

MacGregor hoped so from the bottom of his heart, but he was inhibited by police discipline from voicing his desire aloud.

"We'll make the arrest after lunch," said Dover, rubbing it in.

"Arrest, sir? But—who are you going to arrest?"

Dover picked up his bowler hat and screwed it on his head. "What's-his-name—that Australian fellow."

Australian fellow? MacGregor almost sagged with relief. The old fool had gone clean off his rocker at last. Or did he mean Austrian? "Dr. Zlatt, sir?"

"No, not Zlatt, you damned fool! He wasn't Australian, was he?" Dover dragged himself to his feet and tapped the ash off his cigar onto the lush carpet. "The one who kept saying 'coo-ee.' What's his name?" He looked at the labels on the little boxes. "Fittsarthur. The Honorable Gisbert."

"The Honorable Gisbert Fittsarthur, sir?" echoed Mac-Gregor incredulously. "But you can't arrest him!"

"Oh, can't I?" scowled Dover. "You just wait and see, laddie!"

MacGregor wrung his hands and tried an appeal to reason and common sense. "Sir, you can't just charge a man with murder because you don't like the look of him. You have to have *evidence*. You can't run in a man of his standing as though he was just some smelly old tramp. He'll kick up the most frightful shindy, sir, and you'll be—"

"I've got evidence," Dover broke in crossly. "What do you think I am? An idiot?"

It was not a question that MacGregor dared to answer. "You've got evidence that the Honorable Gisbert Fittsarthur murdered Sir Holman, sir?"

"As good as," muttered Dover, showing a belated sense

of caution. "All it wants is a bit of checking. Motive and the like."

"A bit of checking? I see, sir. Well, would it be asking too much to inquire of what it consists?"

The ironic tone was not lost on Dover. His face twisted up into a scowl. "Don't you start coming the old sarcastic with me, laddie!" he snarled. "I was solving crimes when you were still in diapers and don't you forget it! Here"—he grabbed the old-fashioned fountain pen out of the Honorable Gisbert's box and chucked it across at MacGregor—"there's your blooming evidence!"

MacGregor turned the fountain pen over doubtfully in his hands and tried to fathom out where it could possibly fit into the murder. Of course, the Chief Inspector was probably as far off the beam as he usually was but you could never be sure. Once in a blue moon the bumbling old idiot did manage to make two and two add up to four and, when he did, MacGregor was never allowed to forget it.

Luckily Dover wasn't prepared to postpone his lunch one second longer than was absolutely necessary. "That's what he carried the poison in, nitwit!"

Light dawned and MacGregor could have kicked himself. Of course! Oh why, oh why hadn't he spotted it first? It was so childishly obvious when you knew. "The Honorable Gisbert filling his fountain pen from the chairman's inkwell!" he gasped.

Dover gave a withering sniff. "My God, it's taken you long enough to see it! You're that busy scribbling down every blooming word in your little book that you miss what's sticking right up under your nose. When this Gisbert joker went to fill his fountain pen with ink, Sir What's-his-name's glass of sherry was next to the inkwell on the boardroom table, wasn't it?"

MacGregor agreed eagerly that it was. "Dr. Zlatt told us

that Sir Holman had put his glass down there—"

"And somebody else mentioned Gisbert filling his fountain pen."

"Vice-Admiral Jonkett-Brown."

"But when I tried to use the pen there was no bloomin' ink in it! I couldn't get the damned thing to write at all."

MacGregor, prompted by the most unworthy of motives, clutched at a final straw. He unscrewed the cap of the fountain pen and tried it. It didn't write. He wiggled the little lever on the side hopefully, but it was no good: the fountain pen was empty.

"Of course, sir," MacGregor said, "this doesn't *prove* that the Honorable Gisbert squirted poison into Sir Holman's glass of sherry while pretending to fill his fountain pen from the inkwell."

"'Strewth!" roared Dover, heading for the door and his lunch. "You want it with jam on, you do. I've told you what happened, laddie. I've done my bit. The rest is up to you."

—1970

Dover and the Dark Lady

"'Strewth!" puffed Chief Inspector Wilfred Dover, grinding to an exhausted halt on the half landing. "You'd think they'd put a ruddy lift in, wouldn't you?"

Detective Sergeant MacGregor, although by no means incapacitated by the ascent of one short flight of stairs, paused and watched with well-concealed exasperation as his lord and master propped himself up against the hand-rail. Fat old pit!

"Besides," said Dover, who would have made the Garden of Eden ring with his complaints if he had chanced to be there before the Fall, "having to look at dead bodies before breakfast turns my stomach."

Somewhere in the distance a church clock wheezily struck ten.

"Or after!" snarled Dover furiously.

Sergeant MacGregor managed to force an encouraging smile. "It's only up these next few steps, sir," he said, and got a malevolent scowl for his pains.

Higher up, outside the closed door of Flat 2, a young policeman impassively observed the sluggish progress of his betters. Although he had never seen him before, he recognized Dover without the least hesitation. That ungainly bulk, clothed in its shabby overcoat and topped by a ridiculous bowler hat, could belong only to Scotland Yard's most unwanted detective. The young constable, not believing for a moment that the old devil could be as awful as police gossip painted him, nevertheless braced himself.

"You waiting for a bus, laddie?"

The snarl with which these words were uttered was so unnecessarily vicious that it took the wind out of the young policeman's sails. "No, sir," he gulped and was mortified to find himself turning pink. The hand which he had been about to snap up to the brim of his helmet now dangled uselessly in midair. With an effort he pulled it down and flung the door open.

Dover shouldered his way past. "Fool!" he growled.

Inside the flat the scene of intense professional activity which met Dover's eyes was not calculated to ruffle his ill humor. Work in any shape or form was anathema to him and the sight of all those solemn-faced men measuring, photographing, and puffing out little squirts of fingerprint powder was enough to upset him for the rest of the day.

A uniformed Inspector came hurrying across from the far side of the large sitting room. He was bustlingly full of his own importance and stepped nimbly over the sheet-covered corpse which lay in the middle of the carpet.

The formalities were soon dispensed with. They usually were with Dover who was already looking around for somewhere to take the load off his feet.

The Inspector, cut short before he'd got more than a couple of words out, suggested the bedroom and the two of them, trailed by MacGregor, picked their way across the sitting room.

"Ooh, that's more like it," sighed Dover, sinking gratefully onto the bed. "My feet are crippling me!" He didn't let his relief get the better of him, though. He glared up at the somewhat disconcerted Inspector. "Well, come on, spit it out, man! I haven't got all day to waste sitting around here, if you have."

"Er—no, sir."

Dover blew impatiently down his nose. "Who's the stiff?"

The Inspector shot a bewildered glance at MacGregor but he got no help there. "George Andrew Willoughby, sir." The Inspector stopped as he became aware that Dover was concentrating most of his attention on unlacing his boots. Dover looked up.

The Inspector gave a nervous smile and continued. "Age, forty-three. Divorced. Living here alone. Death was the result of a gunshot wound in the left temple, fired at close quarters. We found a German Luger on the floor beside the body, and it would appear that was the weapon used."

Dover abandoned his bootlaces and looked up with a smile actually wreathing his pasty face. "Suicide," he announced with every appearance of satisfaction.

The Inspector failed to hide his dismay. "Oh, I think that's a little premature, sir."

"Who's interested in what you think?"

"There are one or two points which—"

"Somebody else's fingerprints on the gun?"

"There are no fingerprints on the gun, sir."

"So, there you are!" trumpeted Dover. "Suicide!"

The Inspector was one of those men who never know when they're beaten. Against all odds he still thought that reason, common sense, and cold hard logic would prevail. "The gun had been wiped clean, sir. It didn't even have Mr. Willoughby's fingerprints on it. And then there's the woman's handkerchief we found under the body and the fact that the front door was—"

"Here, hold on!" Dover's face had already slipped back into its habitual sullen expression. "One ruddy thing at a time! What's this about a handkerchief?"

The Inspector was gratified by such a display of interest. "It's in the next room, sir. I'll get it, shall I?"

Dover didn't bother to wait until the Inspector had closed the door behind him. He sneered, then swung round to vent his spite on his sergeant. "What's the matter with you?" he inquired. "Lost the use of your legs or something?"

MacGregor had turned the other cheek so often it's a wonder his head hadn't come unscrewed. "No, sir," he said meekly.

"Well, get out there and start having a look round, you blockhead! If we're not careful we'll have that oaf solving the case under our blooming noses."

"Yes, sir."

The paths of MacGregor and the uniformed Inspector crossed in the bedroom doorway. Each carefully avoided catching the other's eye.

The handkerchief which had been found under the dead man's body had been sealed in a transparent envelope. Dover examined it sourly. "It's got some initials on it," he said, making the statement sound like an accusation.

"Yes, sir. T.H., we think, but of course with these fancy monograms you can't always be sure."

Dover dropped the handkerchief negligently onto the bed. "Girl friend?"

"Well, that's just the point, sir." The Inspector took a couple of steps forward in his eagerness. "There is definitely a woman connected with the case. The spare bedroom, sir, is—"

One of Dover's hobbies was to cut people down to size. He now choked the Inspector off without a qualm. "Which side of the head did you say he shot himself in?"

"The left, sir." The Inspector raised his left hand and pointed the fingers like a gun at his temple.

Dover regarded him morosely. "Left-handed, was he?"

The Inspector almost wept with relief. He'd begun to think Dover was congenitally incapable of putting two and two together. "Not as far as we can ascertain, sir. The way his possessions are arranged on his desk and in the bathroom would seem to indicate—"

"How long since he snuffed it?"

A lesser man would have lost heart and even the Inspector was beginning to feel mauled. At the very minimum he felt he had the right to be treated with common courtesy. After all, this crime, whatever it was, was none of his business. He'd simply come along with the advance party just to keep an eye on things until—God help us!—the experts arrived on the scene.

The uniformed Inspector wasn't a detective and, if the specimen lolling in front of him like a hippopotamus in a mud hole was an example, he was damned glad he wasn't. He'd done his best to be helpful because he knew that speed was extremely important in the early stages; but if his assistance wasn't going to be appreciated—

"Cat got your tongue?"

The Inspector gritted his teeth. "The police surgeon thinks he's been dead about twelve hours, sir. Say somewhere between nine o'clock last night and one this morning. He may be able to narrow it down when he's done the postmortem. Would you like to have a word with him, sir?"

"Not bleeding likely," said Dover. He plumped up his pillows and yawned an enormous yawn. "And you can push off, too."

"You don't require me any longer, sir?"

"Never," observed Dover as he let his eyelids droop over

his piggy eyes, "wanted you in the first place."

But there is no rest for the wicked. Less than ten minutes after the Inspector had departed, Sergeant MacGregor came bursting in, bubbling over with an enthusiasm that made Dover's bones ache.

MacGregor tactfully ignored the fact that his noisy entrance had awakened Dover from a refreshing doze. "Sir, I really think we have a case of murder here!"

"Is that so?" said Dover bleakly. Trust MacGregor to put a blight on things.

"It's the way he was shot, sir. If he'd done it himself, he'd have had to use his left hand and—"

"Queen Anne's dead!" growled Dover unpleasantly.

"Eh? Oh, I see, sir." MacGregor counted slowly up to ten under his breath and tried again. After all, a crime had been committed and somebody had to cajole Dover into trying to solve it. "I think, sir, that there may be a woman involved."

Dover screwed his face up in disgust.

"And it's not only that lady's handkerchief, sir. Have you heard about the other bedroom?"

"What about it?" asked Dover cautiously.

"It's a woman's room, sir. Full of frocks and dresses and there's make-up and ladies' shoes and frou-frou and everything. The late Mr. Willoughby must have had a steady girl friend."

Dover scowled. "Who found the body?"

"Oh, that was Willoughby's ex-wife, sir. Apparently she called round this morning and—"

"Where is she?"

MacGregor was more than a little surprised at this sudden display of interest but he was anxious to encourage any spark of initiative Dover might show. "She's in the flat opposite, sir. They thought it'd be better for her to wait in there until you were ready to see her. She's pretty upset, I gather."

"Gerumph!" said Dover.

MacGregor tried to translate this into some expression of human desire. "Shall I fetch her in here, sir?"

Dover, however, wasn't as big a fool as he looked and, where his own comfort was concerned, he could weigh the pros and cons with amazing speed. He was not the one to go to the mountain if there was the faintest hope that the mountain could be brought to him; but he was also an astute student of human nature. Here was a shocked and distressed woman being looked after by kindly neighbors. The least the neighbors could do was offer the poor soul something in the way of light refreshment.

With a grunt Dover heaved himself to his feet and settled his bowler hat firmly on his head. "No, we'll go and see her, laddie."

Mrs. Thelma Lucian had, indeed, been extremely shaken by the gruesome discovery of her former husband's body and nobody raised any objection when Dover suggested that further supplies of cakes and coffee would be a great comfort. As soon as they arrived Dover began tucking in happily while MacGregor led Mrs. Lucian carefully through her story.

"Now, madam, you say you arrived at Mr. Willoughby's flat at about nine o'clock this morning. Were you calling by appointment or was it just a casual visit?"

"Well, both, really," said Mrs. Lucian, twisting a sodden handkerchief nervously in her fingers. "You see, Will—that's what everybody calls him—Will rang me up last night and said he wanted to see me right away. Well, I was absolutely dumfounded, you see, because I don't think I've seen him more than twice since we were divorced ten years ago. I'm surprised he even knew where to find me."

"What time was this?" asked MacGregor.

"Oh, about ten o'clock last night, I think." Mrs. Lucian passed a hand wearily across her forehead. "It was quite late."

"Why did he want to see you?"

"Well, he didn't say. I asked him, of course, but he just said it was terribly important and I simply must come over and see him right away."

"So you did?"

Mrs. Lucian was a pretty woman in her middle thirties with large dark eyes. She opened them wide now. "No, I didn't. I kept trying to tell Will that I didn't think I could but he just wouldn't listen. I mean, it was such a surprise, you see, after all these years. And, then, I was in the house by myself—my present husband's abroad at the moment—and frankly I simply didn't feel like turning out in the middle of the night and trailing halfway across London on my own just because Will had taken it into his head to snap his fingers."

MacGregor nodded his head sympathetically. "Did Mr. Willoughby seem distressed when he phoned you?"

"You mean, did he sound as though he was going to commit suicide?" Mrs. Lucian was not unintelligent. "No, I wouldn't say so. He was certainly extremely worked up about something, but he sounded—well—angry more than anything else. I couldn't make him out at all, really."

Out of the corner of his eye MacGregor saw Dover reaching for another slice of fruit cake. "And this morning?"

Mrs. Lucian sighed. "Well, in the bright harsh light of day I began to feel a bit guilty. I mean—" She shrugged delicately. "Anyhow, I decided to come round. I rang the bell several times but there was no answer. Then I knocked."

"Yes?"

"My knocking pushed the door open. It wasn't locked. I called Will's name but there was no reply, of course, so I went in and found him lying there on the floor."

"Was the light on?" MacGregor put the question casually but that didn't make it unimportant. Even Dover stopped munching to listen to the answer.

"No."

Dover's nose twitched in annoyance. Even he knew that suicides virtually never killed themselves in the dark. He took another large bite of the fruit cake. Just his blooming luck!

MacGregor went smoothly on with his questions. "Did you touch him?"

"No. I knew he was dead." Mrs. Lucian shuddered. "His eyes were open. Then I saw the gun on the floor beside him and I realized he must have shot himself. It was horrible. I felt I was to blame though I couldn't really see why." She struggled to control her feelings. "I picked the phone up and dialed 999 and then I waited outside on the landing until the police came."

"Do you know if your ex-husband owned a gun?"

"Yes, he did. A German one he brought back from the war. I think he had some ammunition, too. I tried to persuade him to get rid of it, but he never would."

"I see." MacGregor leaned back. "Well, I think that will do for the moment, madam, unless you have anything else you want to tell us." MacGregor remembered his manners just in time and turned to Dover. "Have you any further questions, sir?"

Dover pointedly ignored his sergeant and addressed himself to Mrs. Lucian. "What's your first name?"

"Thelma."

Dover inserted a podgy and none-too-clean finger into his mouth and dislodged a currant which had got stuck behind his upper denture. "And your maiden name?"

"Hamilton."

Dover examined the excavated currant dubiously before shoving it back in his mouth and consuming it. He searched round in his pockets, apparently without success. "Where's that damned handkerchief?"

"Here you are, sir."

Dover snatched the envelope from MacGregor's hands and tossed it across to Mrs. Lucian. "That yours?"

Mrs. Lucian examined the handkerchief unhappily. "I'm not sure. I don't think—"

"Got your initials on it!" barked Dover, signaling to MacGregor that he was ready for another cup of coffee.

"Well, yes—my initials before I was married," admitted Mrs. Lucian, "but I haven't used my maiden name for over ten years. I may have had some embroidered like this but it's all so long ago—"

"How do you explain your handkerchief being found under your husband's corpse?" demanded Dover.

Mrs. Lucian began to get flustered. "Well, I can't. I certainly didn't put it there. Maybe Will still had it."

"Kept it as a memento of you?" sneered Dover, who enjoyed bullying defenseless women. "Very romantic! What happened? You leave him for somebody with a bit more money?"

"No, I didn't," retorted Mrs. Lucian angrily. "Not that it's any business of yours, but my present husband happens to earn a good bit less than Will does—did. And I didn't meet him until several months after my first marriage was as dead as a dodo."

Luckily Dover didn't feel quite ready for a full-scale confrontation so early in the morning, so he sank back sulkily while MacGregor took over and calmed things down.

"Just a couple more questions, if you don't mind, Mrs.

Lucian," he said, smiling fetchingly so that she'd realize that not all members of the Metropolitan Police were that disagreeable. "What did Mr. Willoughby do for a living?"

"He was an income-tax consultant," said Mrs. Lucian, sparing time to flash a glance of pure hatred at Dover, "and a very successful one."

"Do you know if he had any business worries?"

"I'm afraid I don't. I told you, I haven't seen him for ages and I know practically nothing about his affairs. Judging by the way his flat was furnished, though, I wouldn't have thought he was short of money. In any case, Will just wasn't the type to get himself into financial difficulties."

MacGregor frowned. "He never married again?"

"No."

"Do you know if he had a girl friend?"

"I should imagine he's had several over the years," said Mrs. Lucian indifferently.

When MacGregor came back after having escorted Mrs. Lucian out, he found Dover staring moodily at the trayful of empty crockery which lay on the table.

"I've told Mrs. Lucian we'll send somebody round later to take a formal statement, sir."

If MacGregor had hoped to impress the Chief Inspector with his efficiency he was destined to be disappointed. Dover had weightier problems on his mind. "Got a cigarette, laddie?" he asked.

MacGregor was strongly tempted to say no, but he lost his nerve at the last moment. Resentfully he got his cigarette case out and passed it over.

"I reckon she did it," said Dover, who was a great believer in hedging his bets. "Ninety-nine times out of a hundred it's the wife. Or the ex-wife," he added as he saw MacGregor's mouth open. "You mark my words, she came round here last night and croaked him. Then she turned up this morning, all innocent-like, to discover the body and clean up any clues she may have left."

MacGregor had learned long ago not to be surprised at anything Dover did; but even he found this about face too mercurial to be let past without comment. "I thought you were inclined to the suicide theory, sir."

Dover ignored that. "You'd better clear off and interview a few of the neighbors, hadn't you? Ask 'em if they spotted Mrs. What's-her-name sneaking up here last night."

"Well, as a matter of fact, sir, I've just been having a word with the old couple who live here. They're a pretty nosey pair and they seem to have kept their eyes open where Willoughby is concerned. I think they may know something about his lady friend."

"Wheel 'em in," said Dover. "And then you shove off."

MacGregor's face fell. "Don't you think it would be better, sir, if I stayed and took—?"

"No," said Dover nastily, "I don't."

Mr. and Mrs. Grey were a retired couple who were extremely anxious that Dover shouldn't think they spent their entire time spying on their next-door neighbor.

"It's just," explained Mrs. Grey with a complacent smile, "that occasionally one can't help noticing things."

"Noticing things," echoed Mr. Grey with an approving nod.

Dover recognized the signs and bestirred himself to get a question in before he was overwhelmed by a flood. "Did you hear a shot last night?"

For some reason, known only to the Greys, this was classified as man's talk and Mr. Grey spoke up boldly. "Not with these walls," he said, proudly slapping the nearest one. "None of your prefabricated jerry-building here! This is solid, good old-fashioned workmanship. You'd not hear a bomb going off in the next room, never mind a pistol."

"Besides," put in Mrs. Grey, "we had the television on."

Dover slumped back in his chair and rested his head wearily on one hand. "All right," he rumbled, "what do you know?"

"That woman was there last night," said Mrs. Grey, her mouth settling into a disapproving line. "'The dark lady,' my hubbie calls her, though in my opinion she's far from being what I call a lady and she changes the color of her hair more often than he changes his socks. Blonde one day, brown the next, and a redhead the week after. All wigs, of course. You can always tell."

"I thought it was different women at first," chuckled Mr. Grey.

His wife jerked her head emphatically. "I didn't! It takes more than a change of hair to fool me. I should have liked to have told Mr. Willoughby that, just to let him know, but of course I didn't. Well, it was none of our business, really, was it? Actually, she was quite unmistakable once you got used to her. Tall and a bit on the broad-shouldered side. Like Joan Crawford. Big feet, too. Like Greta Garbo. Of course, what her face was like, that I can't tell you because she always took very good care never to let me get a proper look at her. Very furtive, she was."

"Very furtive," agreed Mr. Grey.

"You never," Mrs. Grey continued with hardly a pause for breath, "so much as laid eyes on her until it had gone dark. Never. She used to come creeping in and out like a thief in the night, turning her head away as soon as she saw you and only nodding when you said good evening. And those stairs outside are terribly badly lit, you know. My husband has written several times to the landlord about them."

"Several times," confirmed Mr. Grey.

Dover was getting impatient. "What about last night?"

"I was just coming to that," said Mrs. Grey. "It was when I was putting the milk bottles out. That'd be about ten o'clock, wouldn't it, dear?"

"About ten o'clock," said Mr. Grey.

"She used to come and go at all sorts of different times," Mrs. Grey went on, "but her little subterfuges didn't deceive us. Oh, dear me, no! We were just a bit too clever for her, weren't we, my love?" Mrs. Grey received her husband's affirmative nod and turned back to Dover. "We could hear her coming along the pavement past our window, you see. She didn't know that. Her step"—Mrs. Grey smiled smugly to herself—"was quite unmistakable."

"Quite unmistakable."

Reluctantly Dover made an effort to get the facts clear. "So last night you saw this woman going into Mr. What's-his-name's flat at ten o'clock?"

"That's right," agreed Mrs. Grey.

"Right," said her husband.

"See her leaving?"

Mrs. Grey was sorry but, no, she hadn't.

Mr. Grey was sorry, too.

"Any idea who she is? Her name? Where she comes from?"

Alas, the woman's identity remained a complete mystery—though not, Mrs. Grey managed to imply, through any want of their trying. "Her clothes were very good," she added, anxious to be helpful. "She was always dressed in the height of fashion. I dread to think how much she spent on them. She was wearing a lovely black and white check coat last night and a red silk head scarf."

"Is that so?" said Dover. "Well, you can give my sergeant a full description." He postponed getting to his feet a bit longer though, God knows, he'd had more than enough of Mrs. Grey. "This ex-wife woman you had in here?"

"Mrs. Lucian?"

"Could she be What's-his-name's nocturnal visitor?"

And it was with Mrs. Grey's tinkling laugh at the sheer absurdity of such an idea jarring in his ears that Dover finally retreated in search of a bit of peace and quiet. He loathed these first few hours of a criminal investigation with everybody rushing around like scalded cats and no place a chap could sit and think and call his soul his own. However, from long experience Dover knew that, once the initial hullabaloo was over, the quietest place was frequently in the eye of the storm.

He lumbered up to the young constable still on guard outside Mr. Willoughby's flat. "Anybody still in there?"

"I'm afraid they've all gone, sir."

"Good," said Dover. "Well, I'll be able to pursue my own investigations now." He fixed the constable with an eagle eye. "And I don't want to be disturbed by anybody at all for the next hour. Understand?"

"Yes, sir."

"You'd better. Oh, and I shall want some lunch laid on, so start organizing it. A couple of bottles of beer, a pie or two, some sandwiches, and a few cakes. Nothing elaborate."

The young policeman nodded, saucer-eyed.

Once inside the flat Dover proceeded to subject each and every room to the most meticulous search. Sergeant MacGregor would have been dumfounded if he had witnessed such thoroughness and such reckless expenditure of energy. It was, however, all to no avail. Dover couldn't find a single cigarette in the place.

He was not in the sunniest of moods when he flung the front door open again.

The young policeman jumped halfway out of his skin.

"Got any cigarettes on you, laddie?"

"I'm sorry, sir. I don't smoke."

"That's no bloody excuse!" snarled Dover. "You could carry some for other people, couldn't you?" He underlined his extreme displeasure by slamming the door as hard as he could.

That left only food. Dover waddled back to the kitchen and glumly surveyed the shelves. Corn flakes. Tins of sardines. Baked beans. Eggs. A couple of lamb chops on a plate in the fridge. 'Strewth, was the fellow on a blooming diet or something? In the end Dover grabbed a bottle of pickled onions and took it back with him to the sitting room where he collapsed onto the settee and thankfully put his feet up.

The dead body had already been removed to the mortuary but Dover wouldn't have minded if it had still been lying there on the floor beside him. He helped himself to a pickled onion and gazed idly round the room. Blimey, What's-his-name did himself jolly well! Leather armchairs, sporting prints and antique dueling pistols plastered all over the walls, color television . . .

Sergeant MacGregor, being only human, wasn't in any hurry to get back and report his progress. Grateful to be let off the leash even for a short while, he concentrated on doing an unspectacular but conscientious job. He interviewed all the other occupants of the block of flats and refused to become disheartened when his efforts went unrewarded. One could hardly expect everybody to be as genteelly inquisitive as the Greys.

Indeed, Mrs. Grey was lurking discreetly on the landing when MacGregor came down the stairs and he was obliged to go back into her flat and take her statement. Then, armed with a detailed description of the unknown woman, he commandeered the Greys' phone and began to organize his reinforcements.

Whether the late Mr. Willoughby's girl friend lived within walking distance of his flat or farther afield, inquiries could be made. From local residents and from taxi drivers. Although there was an underground station nearby and a bus route only three minutes' walk away, MacGregor thought that the taxi drivers would be the best bet to start with. According to Mrs. Grey's evidence, the woman sometimes visited Willoughby long after the buses and tubes had stopped.

In fact, MacGregor was rather intrigued by the hours the woman kept and he wondered if she was unmarried. Married women usually confine their extramarital activities to the hours when their husbands are safely away at work. Was this woman married to a man on the night shift or had she, perhaps, a job of her own? Willoughby himself, of course, wouldn't be free until the evenings but his girl friend did seem to keep some very late hours, though Mrs. Grey claimed to have seen her leaving the flat as early as eight o'clock on a couple of occasions.

Still, the extensive inquiries necessary to track the woman down were best left to the local police division. So, after he had set them in motion, MacGregor went off to find Dover.

MacGregor and lunch arrived on the scene of the crime at exactly the same moment. Dover opened one disconsolate eye and belched as MacGregor set the tray down. It is no part of a Detective Sergeant's duties to play nursemaid to his superior officer but MacGregor was a kindly man and didn't think it fair to expose the young policeman to the trauma of seeing Dover at feeding time.

Dover dragged himself into a sitting position and belched again. "Damn pickled onions!" he grumbled, gesturing with a flabby hand at the bottle which was now three-quarters empty. "They play hell with your guts."

MacGregor immediately became busy opening Dover's beer and placing the pile of sandwiches near to hand. Diversionary tactics were essential because, if Dover got started on the vagaries of his stomach, there was little hope of ever stopping him.

"Find out anything?" demanded Dover suspiciously as he came up for air with a foam mustache superimposed on his own.

"Not really, sir." Out of habit MacGregor pulled out his notebook and began turning over the pages. "One or two of the other residents have seen Mrs. Grey's 'dark lady' but they don't know anything more about her. The descriptions are, as usual, inconclusive." He read from his notebook. "'Above average height and well built.' I'm having the usual house-to-house inquiries made in the neighborhood, sir, and we're questioning taxi drivers. Of course"— he removed Dover's dirty plate and substituted another on which squatted a greasy pork pie—"she may turn up of her own accord when she finds out what's happened."

"And pigs might fly!" scoffed Dover, catching a dribble of jelly before it dropped off his chin onto his overcoat. "She's the one we're after, you know."

MacGregor noted with resignation that yet another unhatched chick was being counted. "Yes, sir."

"Stands out a mile," insisted Dover as he sensed that his previous statement hadn't exactly bowled MacGregor over. "Lovers' tiff. What's-his-name gets fed up and gives her her marching orders. She cuts up rough—you know what women are like—accuses him of tossing her aside like an old glove and shoots him. Bang!"

MacGregor chewed his bottom lip. "With his gun, sir?"

"Why not? She's been shacking up with him for years, hasn't she? She'd know about the gun and where he kept it. Then all she has to do is wipe the fingerprints off, let herself out quietly, and disappear into the night. Nobody knows who she is or where she lives or anything."

"Oh, steady on, sir!" MacGregor tried to soften the implied criticism of Dover's methods by offering the plate of cakes. "We've hardly started our investigations yet. There may be dozens of people who know all about her and her association with Willoughby."

"Such as?"

"Well, his friends and business colleagues, for example. Or relatives. Just because a total stranger like Mrs. Grey doesn't know everything, it doesn't mean—"

"Bet you!" said Dover sulkily. His temper was not being improved by the piece of seed cake he had just gobbled down. He seemed to have been digging those blasted bits out of his dentures for days!

"In any case, sir," MacGregor continued, "if she'd really intended to make a run for it, she'd hardly have left a roomful of clues behind her, would she? If we get no joy anywhere else, we'll probably be able to trace her through all those clothes and things."

Dover scowled and brushed ineffectively at the crumbs and beer he had spilt down his lapels. "She could hardly take 'em with her, could she?" he objected. "'Strewth, she'd need a bloomin' truck to move that lot! Besides, I don't reckon there was anything premeditated about this crime. She just saw red and let him have it. No time for elaborate plans." He gazed sullenly at the beer MacGregor was pouring out for him. "Is that the last of it?"

"I'm afraid so, sir." MacGregor, ever hopeful, pushed the bill for one pound and sixpence into what he trusted was Dover's line of vision. Dover looked clean through it. MacGregor sighed. "Would you like a cigarette, sir?"

Dover's mean little eyes narrowed. "Why?"

"I just thought that while you were letting your lunch

settle, I might go and have another look round that spare bedroom."

Dover was too old a hand to be caught like that. Give this young pup an inch and he'd be clapping the hand-cuffs on the murderer before you had time to catch your breath! With a nimbleness that only pure bloody-minded-ness could inspire, the Chief Inspector jumped up off his settee. "I'll come with you," he announced and had the exquisite satisfaction of seeing an expression of acute cha-grin pass over MacGregor's face. He didn't hesitate to rub the salt in. "Just in case you miss something, laddie."

In the spare bedroom Dover, with his cigarette, estab-lished his command post on the bed and directed opera-tions from there. MacGregor started with the wardrobe and began carefully and methodically to remove all the dresses and coats from their hangers. The frocks were pret-ty and very feminine but not one of them contained a maker's label. There were three coats, one of fur. MacGre-gor went through the pockets before returning them to the hangers. He turned to Dover and shook his head.

"No labels anywhere, sir. They've all been removed."

Dover was not disheartened. "Try the shoes."

But the shoes, apart from the fact that they confirmed the rather large size of their owner's feet, gave no indica-tion of their provenance, either.

"I suppose," said MacGregor doubtfully, "that we could get some experts in. They might be able to identify the manufacturers. Of course, if she just bought them over the counter in a chain store somewhere and paid cash—" He sighed and turned his attentions to the dressing table and the highboy. Handbags—all empty. Stockings, frilly nylon underwear, gloves, handkerchiefs, negligees.

"No laundry marks?" asked Dover, reclining like a sated pasha on his divan.

MacGregor dropped a pair of shocking-pink panties back in the drawer. "These are the sort of things a woman would wash by hand, sir."

"Well," said Dover, "faint heart never won fair lady. Get cracking!"

MacGregor slowly completed his search of the room, looking under the furniture and behind the pictures. He even got a bit of his own back when he obliged Dover to transfer to a chair while he stripped the bed.

"Oh, dear," said MacGregor as he pulled the pink satin bedcover back into place. "You'd think there'd be something that'd give us a lead, wouldn't you, sir? Even those wigs are ready-made ones, bought off the peg."

Dover grunted, most of his attention being engaged in climbing back onto the bed. "That gabbling old cow in the other flat—didn't she mention what the woman was wearing last night?"

Nothing was guaranteed to spur MacGregor on to greater efforts than the lively fear that, by some miracle, Dover had spotted something he'd missed. "I believe she did, sir," he agreed, searching his excellent memory at top speed. He had Mrs. Grey's statement in his notebook but he didn't want to admit even a partial defeat by referring to it. "Yes, she said that the woman was wearing a black and white check coat and a red silk head scarf." MacGregor hesitated and then leaped for the wardrobe. "Oh, of course, sir. You think this coat—?" He pulled the black and white coat off its hanger. "And"—he rushed over to the highboy—"this head scarf—?"

"It's a possibility."

MacGregor creased his forehead into a worried frown. "She changed her clothes before she left?"

"Must have. She'd have never left without a coat at this time of year."

"But—why?"

"Search me." Dover was making it plain that he had no intention of doing all the work but he did proffer one suggestion. "Maybe it started raining and she put a mac on."

MacGregor shook his head. "No, it didn't rain last night, sir." He examined the coat again. "Perhaps she got blood on it . . . No—no blood."

"She wouldn't have left bloodstained clothing behind, you nitwit!" snapped Dover. "She was trying to make it look like a suicide, wasn't she? A bloodstained coat left behind would soon have knocked that idea on the head."

MacGregor, who even after years of working with Dover, still had his pride, objected to being called a nitwit. "If she really was trying to make it look like suicide, she didn't do a very good job of it, did she? She shot him on the wrong side of the head and she wiped the fingerprints off the gun. And then what about that handkerchief she left under the body? That was obviously meant to direct our suspicions towards Mrs. Lucian. Well, you don't try to incriminate somebody else for murder if you're trying to fool the police into thinking it's suicide."

"Maybe she's a nut," said Dover drearily. His stomach was beginning to rumble in a most peculiar way. Could that pie have been spoiled?

"The handkerchief!" MacGregor slapped himself on the side of the head. "Just a minute, sir." He crossed over to the dressing table and pulled out the top drawer. There were a dozen handkerchiefs but he unfolded them all before turning to Dover with a grin of triumph. "Look at that, sir!"

Dover directed a jaundiced eye at the handkerchief being held out to him. It was similar to the one found under Willoughby's body and had the same two initials embroidered on it.

MacGregor was like a dog with two tails. He waved the handkerchief in Dover's face. "These initials belong to the unknown woman, sir. It's just a coincidence that they happen to fit Mrs. Lucian's maiden name as well."

As soon as Dover perceived that his sergeant was coming round, more or less, to his point of view, he changed it. "I still haven't crossed that ex-wife off my list," he said stubbornly and relished MacGregor's wince. "Her story's got more holes in it than a pauper's winding sheet."

MacGregor turned away and began to fold up the handkerchiefs. It gave him something to do with his hands and probably saved Dover from getting the punch in the nose he so richly deserved. He didn't resume the discussion until he was sure he'd got his voice under control. "Really, sir?"

"Yes, really, sir!" Dover as usual made a hash of mimicking his sergeant's accent. "What about that cock-and-bull story she spun us about a mysterious telephone call and him begging her to come round and hold his hand after ten years?"

"I don't think that is incompatible with a tentative suspicion of the missing girl friend, sir," objected MacGregor. "Perhaps Willoughby had been having trouble with the girl friend earlier and she threatened him. Willoughby got frightened and felt that he had to turn to somebody for help."

"And he turned to his ex-wife?" yelped Dover. "You're wasting your time in the police, laddie. You ought to be writing blooming fairy tales."

MacGregor was spared more samples of Dover's heavy-handed wit by the noise of scuffling and the sound of raised voices coming from the sitting room outside. He went across and opened the door to find the young policeman, helmet askew, grappling with a plump middle-aged man. "What," he demanded in a voice of thunder that might have come from Dover himself, "the hell is going on here?"

The combatants disentangled themselves and stood looking sheepishly at each other.

The young policeman adjusted his helmet. "This chap was trying to run away, Sergeant," he said breathlessly. "He came up the stairs and then, as soon as he caught sight of me, he turned on his heel and—"

"Nonsense!" interrupted the plump man indignantly. "I just changed my mind, that's all." He pulled his coat straight. "And I wish to register my objection to the brutal and entirely unwarranted manhandling I have just received."

Dover appeared in the doorway and the plump man forgot his complaints and goggled. MacGregor quickly took advantage of this hiatus to dismiss the young policeman and get everybody else sitting down calmly.

"Now, sir," he began sternly, "may I ask what you are doing here?"

The plump man was staring at the rough chalk outline in the middle of the carpet. He looked up. "I came to see Mr. Willoughby. Look, what's been happening here?"

MacGregor had the typical detective's habit of never answering questions. "Are you a friend of Mr. Willoughby's, sir?"

The plump man nodded. He was looking at the chalk outline again. "Is he dead?"

"Why should you think that, sir?"

The plump man gazed round helplessly. "Well, it's pretty obvious, isn't it? The constable on the door—and I suppose you are a policeman, too?"

"I am Sergeant MacGregor, sir, and this is Chief Inspector Dover."

"Oh," said the plump man, rather inadequately. "Er—how do you do?"

Dover had been showing signs of restlessness for some time and now he exploded. "'Strewth!" he spat—at Mac-Gregor, of course. "Can you get a move on? We're supposed to be investigating a murder case, not holding a ruddy tea party!"

"*Murder?*" The plump man's mouth dropped open. "You don't mean Will's been *murdered?*"

Now that Dover had let, if not the cat, at least a fair-sized kitten out of the bag, MacGregor tried to remedy the situation. He got his notebook out and assumed his most official air. "Your name, sir?"

"Crump. Charles Anthony Crump."

"And what are you doing here, sir?"

"I told you," said Mr. Crump, still staring in awed fascination at Dover. "I came round to see Will."

On the settee Dover roused himself again. "At this time of day?" he demanded incredulously. "What made you think he'd be here?"

Mr. Crump cringed visibly and ran a pink tongue over his lips. "I rang his office and they said he hadn't come in this morning. I thought he might be unwell or something."

Dover had many shortcomings but his ability to spot a victim was unerring. He squinted at Mr. Crump like a somewhat overweight stoat sizing up a juicy rabbit. "Very considerate," he sneered.

Mr. Crump tried to fight back. "It's just that Will has been extremely upset and worried recently and I was afraid—well, I was afraid he might do something silly."

"You mean, commit suicide?" asked MacGregor, who always found Dover's antics acutely embarrassing.

Mr. Crump nodded. "I must admit the possibility

crossed my mind. He had a gun, you know."

"Do you know what he was worried about, sir?"

"Oh"—Mr. Crump squirmed uneasily in his chair—"things, you know. Middle age. Life turning a shade sour in general."

"Women?" That was Dover sticking his oar in once more.

"Women?" Mr. Crump started nervously and again flushed to the tips of his ears. "Well, I—I don't know."

"You knew about his popsie though, didn't you?"

"His popsie?"

Mr. Crump's obvious distress was meat and drink to Dover and he gave the screw another twist by appealing mockingly to MacGregor. "Just like a little parrot, ain't he?"

"Now, look here"—Mr. Crump apparently thought he had a few human rights left—"I must protest against being spoken to like that! I am perfectly willing to help in any way I can but I will not"—he made the mistake of catching Dover's eye—"be browbeaten," he concluded feebly.

"Then stop messing about and answer a simple question when you're asked," roared Dover. "What about What's-his-name's bit of fluff?"

"I know nothing about her," wailed Mr. Crump.

"How long have you known What's-his-name?"

Mr. Crump bit his lip to stop it trembling. "Eight or nine years, I suppose."

"Been to this flat before?"

"Of course I have."

"And you didn't know anything about that love nest in there?"

"No!" screamed Mr. Crump.

"Liar!" bellowed Dover.

"Oh, God!" Mr. Crump's voice broke into a sob and he buried his head in his hands.

Dover's pasty face split into a grin of pure delight. Exerting himself above and beyond the call of duty he got up off the settee and bore down on the unfortunate Mr. Crump, seizing him by two greedy handfuls of coat and yanking him to his feet. "You're hiding something, you miserable little runt," he howled, shaking Mr. Crump to and fro like a ragdoll. "Well, I'm going to find out what it is if I have to break every bone in your body!"

Still rattling Mr. Crump backward and forward, Dover turned to MacGregor. "This is the joker we've been looking for, laddie! We've got our murderer!"

MacGregor knew that he ought to say something, if only goodbye. It was not as if the sight of Dover beating a confession out of a perfectly innocent member of the public was any great novelty. MacGregor had witnessed it several times before and knew there was little he could do to induce Dover to substitute brains for brawn. Still, the effort had to be made, if only because one day the worm might turn and MacGregor would find himself involved in the ensuing scandal.

"Er—easy on, sir."

For a man who had just found his fourth solution to a crime in less than three hours, Dover proved remarkably amenable to the warning. Or, maybe, it was just that his arms were getting tired. In any case he slung an exhausted and terrified Mr. Crump back into his chair. Mr. Crump's ordeal, however, was by no means over.

Very deliberately Dover rested his hands on the arms of Mr. Crump's chair and advanced his face until he and his prey were virtually nose to nose. "Where," he asked, breathing heavily and menacingly, "were you last night?"

The wretched Mr. Crump raised a trembling hand and eased his collar. "I had nothing to do with Will's death," he protested hoarsely. "I swear I didn't."

Dover raised a meaty fist. "Where were you?"

"I stayed on at the party. I stayed on for hours after Will had left, honestly I did. I can prove it, too. Anybody there will vouch for me. I didn't leave until one o'clock this morning."

Dover straightened. "What party?" he demanded. If there was one thing Dover disliked almost as much as work it was a surprise.

"Just a party," hedged Mr. Crump, looking shifty.

Dover refrained from battering out further details. He had other fish to fry. "And What's-his-name was at it?"

Mr. Crump nodded his aching head.

"Last night?"

"Yes."

"Well, I'll be damned!" Dover, thoroughly disgusted with this unwelcome complication, retired to his settee and let MacGregor sort things out.

MacGregor moved in with a will and under his shrewd questioning it emerged that the dead man had, indeed, spent his last evening in this vale of tears at a party. There had been some sort of row or quarrel—Mr. Crump was not forthcoming about it and for the time MacGregor didn't press him—and Willoughby, considerably wrought up, had left at about half-past nine.

"How long would it take him to get back here?"

Mr. Crump shrugged helplessly. "Half an hour at that time of night, I should think."

MacGregor glanced at Dover to see if the significance of this had sunk in. It hadn't. Puzzled, MacGregor went over and whispered in Dover's ear. "Willoughby must have got back here last night, sir, at almost the same time as Miss X."

"So what?"

"Well, nothing, really, sir, except that it just struck me as odd. I mean, if he was expecting her to call, you wouldn't think he'd have gone out for the evening, would you?"

"God knows," said Dover irritably.

Since this appeared to be the only contribution the Chief Inspector was going to make to the discussion, Mac-Gregor returned to Mr. Crump and tried a new line of questioning. "Do you know Mr. Willoughby's ex-wife, sir? Mrs. Lucian?"

"No." Mr. Crump looked fractionally happier with the change of topic. "They were already divorced when I met him."

"What was the relationship between them?"

"I don't know how she felt about Will but he was very bitter about her. Especially when he'd had a few drinks. He used to claim she'd let him down and he blamed her and the breakup of his marriage for all his troubles."

"He had a grudge against her?"

"Well, yes, I suppose so. He could get to be quite a bore about it at times, threatening to get even with her one day and make her sorry for all she'd done to him." Mr. Crump looked anxiously at MacGregor. "It was all talk, you know."

"You can say that again," came from the settee. "Look, Sergeant, just get the names and addresses of the people who were at this party and then we can start busting this creep's phony alibi."

With MacGregor's attention momentarily distracted by the dulcet tones of his master's voice, Mr. Crump misguidedly decided to make a run for it.

He didn't get very far.

MacGregor brought him down with a flying tackle before Crump even reached the door, and Dover, staggering up when all the excitement was over, joyfully extinguished the dying sparks of resistance with his boot.

It was a sadder and sorer Mr. Crump who eventually recovered sufficiently to resume his place on the hot seat. "I simply can't give you the names and addresses," he moaned, with the tears trickling down his cheeks. "I simply can't!"

"Want a bet?" chuckled Dover, bunching his fist and flourishing it under Mr. Crump's nose.

"But they'll just deny they were there!" sobbed Mr. Crump. "I know they will."

Dover scowled. "What sort of party was this, for God's sake?"

In the end, when Mr. Crump had been forcefully persuaded that further silence would certainly result in his nose being bloodied, his eyes blacked, and his teeth smashed down his throat, he resolved to reveal all. "It was a dressing-up party," he whispered in a barely audible voice. "Just a bit of harmless fun, you know."

He got his handkerchief out and blew his nose with considerable pathos. "Cross-dressing, we call it. Men dressed up as"—he choked on the word—"women."

Dover gasped.

MacGregor was more sophisticated. "You mean it was a transvestite party?"

"Yes," murmured Mr. Crump. "We meet around once a fortnight. Or"—he added miserably—"we did. I suppose this'll be the end of it now!"

MacGregor was beginning to see the light. "Willoughby was a transvestite?"

"One of the best. He used to brag that he could pass for a woman anywhere."

"I see! So all those women's clothes in the spare bedroom are his?"

"He spent a fortune on them," sighed Mr. Crump enviously.

"And last night he changed into drag here in the flat and traveled to and from your party in women's clothes?"

Mr. Crump brightened at the memory. "He looked quite, quite beautiful."

"Well, there we are, sir," said MacGregor, tossing a triumphant smile at Dover. "We needn't waste any more

time searching for the elusive Miss X. 'She' was Willoughby himself."

"He called himself Rosina when he was dressed,"
explained Mr. Crump helpfully. "I'm Betsy—though, of
course, I'm not in Will's class by any means. I wouldn't
dream of taking the risks he did."

"When we want any more of your reminiscences,"
snapped Dover, "we'll ask for 'em!" Having cowed Mr.
Crump into silence Dover gave MacGregor a piece of his
mind. "All you've established so far, clever devil, is that
What's-his-name was as kinky as a dog's hind leg. You still
haven't proved how he came to be dead."

MacGregor nobly forbore to point out that this was supposed to be Dover's job. " I think we've got the general picture now, sir," he said smugly. "I imagine Willoughby
found this transvestite business was beginning to be dangerous. After all, it's a pretty risky pastime, isn't it? He must
have been scared stiff the whole thing would come out."

"Oh, it's a terrible strain," agreed Mr. Crump feelingly.
"Will had wanted to stop for ages, but he just couldn't. He
was terribly ashamed of himself, really. Then one of the
other 'girls' said something bitchy to him last night and it
all came pouring out. How he hated them and their silly
primping and preening and how he hated himself for
being like them. I thought he'd really come to the end of
his tether this time but he stormed out before anybody
could stop him."

"And came back here," said MacGregor, "changed into
his pajamas and shot himself."

Dover was looking far from pleased. "In the wrong side
of the head?" he objected. "Without leaving fingerprints
on the gun? And in the dark?"

"Oh, I think that was all a rather silly attempt to throw
the suspicion of murder on Mrs. Lucian, sir. That's why he
phoned her and used her handkerchief to wrap around the

gun. Mr. Crump says he blamed her for all his troubles. If she had turned up last night as Willoughby planned she should, we would certainly have had plenty of questions to ask her."

Dover was never one to face facts gracefully. "Nobody ever told me that he was wearing pajamas," he groused.

"Oh, I'm sorry, sir," apologized MacGregor, tongue in cheek. "I thought you'd looked at the body."

Dover sniffed angrily. Much more of young MacGregor's lip and he'd— "Where did that handkerchief come from, then?"

"Left behind by Mrs. Lucian when she and Willoughby split up, don't you think, sir? A couple of handkerchiefs are easily overlooked."

"Hm." Dover sighed deeply. "I said it was suicide right from the first," he pointed out pugnaciously.

"Indeed you did, sir." MacGregor looked at his watch. "Well, I think I'd better call off the search for Miss X and then I'll start getting the formal statements and begin on the report, shall I, sir? Unless"—he bethought himself rather naughtily—"you'd prefer to do it yourself, sir?"

Dover stored that up for later retaliation. "I've got plenty to keep me busy here," he said, as much for Mr. Crump's benefit as for MacGregor's. "And on your way out tell that young copper I'm ready for my tea!"

—1972

Dover Does Some Spadework

"You're supposed to be a detective, aren't you?"

Chief Inspector Dover—unwashed, unshaved, still in his dressing gown and more than half asleep—stared sullenly across the kitchen table at his wife. The great man was not feeling at his best. "I'm on leave," he pointed out resentfully as he spooned a half pound of sugar into his tea. "Supposed to be having a rest."

"All right for some," muttered Mrs. Dover crossly. She slapped down a plate of bacon, eggs, tomatoes, mushrooms, sausages, and fried bread in front of her husband.

Dover had been sitting with his knife and fork at the ready but now he poked disconsolately among the goodies. "No kidney?"

"You want it with jam on, you do!"

Dover responded to this disappointment with a grunt. "Besides," he said a few minutes later when he was wiping the egg yolk off his chin with the back of his hand, "I'm Murder Squad. You can't expect me to go messing around with piddling things like somebody nicking your garden tools. Ring up the local coppers if something's gone missing."

"And a fine fool I'd look, wouldn't I?" Mrs. Dover sat

down and poured out her own cup of tea. "My husband a Chief Inspector at Scotland Yard and me phoning the local police station for help! And I told you, Wilf—nobody stole anything. They just broke in."

Dover considerately remembered his wife's oft-reiterated injunctions and licked the knife clean of marmalade before sticking it in the butter. Well, it didn't do to push the old girl too far. "It's like asking Picasso to decorate the back bedroom for you, you see," he explained amid a spray of toast crumbs. "And if there's nothing actually missing . . ."

"Two can play at that game, you know." Mrs. Dover sounded ominously like a woman who had got all four aces up her sleeve.

A frown of sudden anxiety creased Dover's hitherto untroubled brow. "Waddaryemean?" he asked nervously.

Mrs. Dover ignored the question. "Have another piece of toast," she invited with grim humor. "Help yourself. Enjoy your breakfast. Make the most of it while it's here!"

"Oh, 'strewth!" groaned Dover, knowing only too well what was coming.

Mrs. Dover patted her hair into place. "If you can't do a bit of something for me, Wilf," she said with feigned reasonableness, "you may wake up one of these fine days and find that I can't do something for you. Like standing over a hot stove all the live-long day!"

"But that's your job," protested Dover. "Wives are supposed to look after their husbands' comfort. It's the law!"

But Mrs. Dover wasn't listening. "I wasn't brought up just to be your head cook and bottle washer," she claimed dreamily. "My parents had better things in mind for me than finishing up as your unpaid skivvy. Why"—she soared off misty-eyed into the realms of pure fantasy—"I might have been a concert pianist or a lady judge or a TV personality, if I hadn't met you."

"And pigs might fly," sniggered Dover, being careful to restrict his comment to the range of his own ears. "Well," he said aloud and making the promise, perhaps a mite too glibly, "I'll have a look at the shed for you. Later on. When the sun's had chance to take the chill off things a bit."

Mrs. Dover was too battle-scarred a veteran of matrimony to be caught like that. "Suit yourself, Wilf," she said equably. "Your lunch will be ready and waiting for you . . . just as soon as you come up with the answer." She began to gather up the dirty crockery. "And not before," she added thoughtfully.

"So that," snarled Dover, "is what I'm doing here! Since you were so gracious as to ask!"

Detective Sergeant MacGregor could only stand and stare. Almost any comment, he felt, was going to be open to misinterpretation.

But even a tactful silence gave no guarantee of immunity from Dover's quivering indignation. "Cat got your tongue now, laddie?"

MacGregor suppressed a sigh. He didn't usually come calling when his boss was on leave, having more than enough of the old fool when they were at work in the normal way; but he needed a countersignature for his Expenses Claim Form and, since most of the money had been dispensed on Dover's behalf, it was only fitting that his uncouth signature should grace the document.

So when, at eleven o'clock, the sergeant had called at the Dovers' semidetached suburban residence, he had been quite prepared to find that His Nibs was still, on a cold and foggy December morning, abed. What he had not expected was Mrs. Dover's tight-lipped announcement that her better half was to be found in the tool shed at the bottom of the garden. It had seemed a highly improbable state of affairs but, as MacGregor was now seeing for himself, it was true.

Dover, arrayed as for a funeral in his shabby black overcoat and his even shabbier bowler hat, was sunk dejectedly in a deck chair. He glared up at his sergeant. "Well, don't just stand there like a stick of Blackpool rock, you moron! Come inside and shut that damn door!"

Even with the door closed the tool shed was hardly a cosy spot, and MacGregor was gratified to notice that Dover's nose was already turning quite a pronounced blue. "Er—what exactly is the trouble, sir? Mrs. Dover wasn't actually very clear about why you were out here."

Dover cut the cackle with the ruthlessness of desperation. "She's got this idea in her stupid head that somebody bust their way into this shed during the past week and borrowed a spade. Silly cow!"

"I see," said MacGregor politely.

"I doubt it," sniffed Dover. "Seeing as how you're not married."

"A stolen spade, eh, sir?" For the first time MacGregor turned his attention to his surroundings and discovered to his amazement that he was standing in the middle of a vast collection of implements which, if hygiene and perfect order were anything to go by, wouldn't have looked out of place in a hospital operating theater. As MacGregor's gaze ran along the serried ranks of apparently brand-new tools he wondered what on earth they were used for. Surely not for the care and maintenance of that miserable strip of barren, cat-infested clay which lay outside between the shed and the house? Good heavens, they must have bought the things wholesale!

The walls were covered with hoes and rakes and forks and spades and trowels, all hung on special hooks and racks. A couple of shelves groaned under a load of secateurs, garden shears, seed trays, and a set of flower pots arranged in descending order of size, while the floor was almost totally occupied by wheelbarrows, watering cans, and a well-oiled cylinder lawn mower. MacGregor only tore his mind away from his inventory of sacks of peat and fertilizer when he realized that the oracle had said something. "I beg your pardon, sir?"

"I said it wasn't stolen," snapped Dover. "It was only borrowed." The lack of comprehension on MacGregor's face appeared to infuriate the Chief Inspector. "That one, you idiot!"

MacGregor followed the direction of Dover's thumb which was indicating the larger of two stainless-steel spades. He leaned forward to examine the mirror-like blade more closely. "Er—how does Mrs. Dover know it was—er—borrowed, sir?"

Dover blew wearily down his nose. "Why don't you use your bloomin' eyes?" he asked. "Look at it all!" He flapped a cold-looking hand at the tools on the wall. "They're all hanging on their own hooks, aren't they? Right! Well, every bloody Tuesday morning without fail Mrs. Dover comes down here and turns 'em all round. Get it? Regular as ruddy clockwork. One week all these spades and trowels and things have got their backs facing the wall and then, the next week, they've got the backs of their blades facing out to the middle of the shed. Follow me?"

"I understand perfectly, thank you, sir," said MacGregor stiffly.

Dover scowled. "Then you're lucky," he growled, "because it's more than I do. She reckons it evens out the wear, you know. Silly cow! Anyhow!"—he heaved himself up in his deck chair again and jerked his thumb at the spade—"that thing is hanging the wrong way round. Savvy? So that means somebody moved it and that means, since this shed is kept locked up tighter than the Bank of England, that somebody must have broken in to do it."

He sank back and the deck chair groaned and creaked in understandable protest. "Mrs. Dover's developed into a very nervous sort of woman over the years."

MacGregor's agile mind had already solved the problem. "But, if you'll forgive me saying so, sir, the spade *isn't* the wrong way round." He moved across to the appropriate wall so as to be able to demonstrate his thesis in a way that even a muttonhead like Dover could understand. "All the tools are currently hanging with their backs turned towards the shed wall, aren't they? With the prongs and the—er—sharp edges pointing outward towards us. Right? Well, the spade in question is hanging on the wall in just the same way as all the other tools, isn't it? So, it's *not* hanging the wrong way round, unless of course"—he ventured on a rather patronizing little chuckle—"Mrs. Dover has got a special routine for that particular spade."

Dover didn't bother opening his eyes. It would be a bad day, he reflected, when he couldn't outsmart young MacGregor with both hands tied behind his back. "She killed a spider with it last week," he explained sleepily. "When she was in doing a security check. God knows what a spider was doing in this place, apart from starving to death, but there it was. On the floor. Mrs. Dover's allergic to spiders, so she grabbed that spade and flattened the brute."

"I see, sir," said MacGregor who had not, hitherto, suspected that Mrs. Dover was a woman of violence.

"Then," said Dover, pulling his overcoat collar up closer round his ears, "the spade had to be washed, didn't it? And disinfected, too, I shouldn't wonder." He tried to rub some warmth back into his frozen fingers. "Well, nobody in their right senses, it seems, would dream of hanging a newly washed spade with its back up against a shed wall.

In case of rust. So Mrs. Dover broke the habit of a lifetime and replaced the spade the wrong way round so that the air could circulate freely about it."

"I see," said MacGregor for the second time in as many minutes. "Our mysterious borrower, when he returned the spade, then understandably hung it back on its hook in the same way that all the other implements were hung—with their backs to the wall. Yes"—he nodded his head—"a perfectly natural mistake to make."

" 'Strewth, don't you start!"

"Sir?"

Dover wriggled impatiently in his deck chair. "Talking as though this joker really exists. He damn well doesn't!"

"Then how do you explain the fact that the spade is hanging the wrong way round, sir?"

"I don't!" howled Dover. "I wouldn't be sitting here freezing to death if I could, would I, dumbbell?"

There was a moment's pause after this outburst. By rights MacGregor should have emulated Mrs. Dover's way of dealing with pests by seizing hold of the nearest sufficiently heavy instrument and laying Dover's skull open with it; but the Metropolitan Police do too good a job on their young recruits. MacGregor swallowed all his finer impulses and concentrated hard on trying to be a detective. "Are there any signs of breaking in, sir?"

There was a surly grunt from the deck chair. "Search me!"

MacGregor crossed the shed and opened the door to examine the large padlock which had been left hooked carelessly in the staple. It looked as though it had recently been ravaged by some sharp-toothed carnivore.

Dover had got up to stretch his legs. He squinted over MacGregor's shoulder. "I had a job getting the damn thing open."

Oh, well, it wasn't the first time that Dover had ridden roughshod over what might have been a vital clue, and it wouldn't be the last. Just for the hell of it, MacGregor gave Dame Fortune's wheel a half-hearted whirl. "I suppose you didn't happen to notice when you unlocked the padlock, sir, if—"

Dover was not the man to waste time nurturing slender hopes. "No," he said, "I didn't."

MacGregor closed the door. "Well, presumably our chappie knows how to pick a lock. That's some sort of lead."

"Garn," scoffed Dover, "they learn that with their mother's milk these days." He began to waddle back to his deck chair. "Got any smokes on you, laddie?" he asked. "I'm dying for a puff."

MacGregor often used to bewail the fact that he couldn't include all the cigarettes he provided for Dover on his swindle sheet but, as usual, he handed his packet over with a fairly good grace. He waited patiently until Dover's clumsy fingers had extracted a crumpled coffin nail and then gave him a light.

"Fetch us one of those plant pots," ordered Dover. "A little one."

A look of horror flashed across MacGregor's face. A plant pot? Surely Dover wasn't actually going to—

"For an ashtray, you bloody fool!" snarled Dover. "Mrs. Dover'll do her nut if she finds we've made a mess all over her floor."

MacGregor felt quite weak with the relief. "I've been thinking, sir," he said.

"The age of miracles is not yet past," snickered Dover.

MacGregor turned the other cheek with a practiced hand. "We can deduce quite a bit about our Mr. Borrower."

"Such as what?" Dover leered up suspiciously at his sergeant.

MacGregor ticked the points off on well-manicured fingers. "The spade must have been purloined for some illicit purpose." He saw from the vacant look on Dover's face that he'd better watch his language. "If the fellow just wanted a spade for digging potatoes or what-have-you, sir, he'd have just asked for it, wouldn't he? Taking a spade without permission and picking a padlock to get at it must add up to some criminal activity being concerned, don't you agree, sir?"

Dover nodded cautiously, unwilling to commit himself too far at this stage. "You reckon he nicked the spade to dig something up?" he asked, eyes bulging greedily. "Like buried treasure?"

"I was thinking more along the lines of him wanting to hide something, actually, sir. By concealing it in the ground. He returned the spade to the shed, you see. Surely, if he was merely digging up buried treasure, he wouldn't have gone to the trouble of putting the spade back carefully in its place?"

"*Burying* buried treasure?" Dover, dribbling ash down the front of his overcoat, tried this idea on for size.

"Or a dead body, sir," said MacGregor. "That strikes me as a more likely explanation."

Dover's heavy jowls settled sullenly over where his shirt collar would have been if he'd been wearing one. For a member (however unwanted) of Scotland Yard's Murder Squad, dead bodies were in his mind inextricably connected with work, and work always tended to bring Dover out in a cold sweat. He tried to concentrate on an occupation more to his taste: nit-picking. "How do you know it's a 'he'?" he demanded truculently. "It could just as well be a woman."

MacGregor was so anxious to display his superior powers of reasoning and deduction that he, perhaps, showed

insufficient regard for Dover's slower wits. "Oh, I doubt
that, sir! I don't know whether you've noticed, but Mrs.
Dover had two spades hanging on the wall. The one that
was 'borrowed' and a smaller one which is called, I believe,
a border spade. You see? Now, surely if our intruder were a
woman, she would have taken the lighter, more manage-
able border spade?"

Dover's initial scowl of fury was gradually replaced by a
rather constipated expression, a sure indication that his
thought processes were beginning to swing into action.

MacGregor waited anxiously.

"A *young* man!" said Dover at last.

"Sir?"

"You'd hardly find an old-age pensioner nipping over
garden fences and picking locks and digging bloomin'
great holes big enough to take a dead body, would you?
'Strewth, what you know about the real world, laddie,
wouldn't cover a pinhead. We've had a frost out here for
weeks! The ground's hard as iron."

MacGregor's unabashed astonishment at this feat of
unsolicited reasoning was not exactly flattering, but
Dover, the bit now firmly between his National Health
teeth, didn't appear to notice.

"And I'll tell you something else, laddie," he went on, "if
our joker borrowed my missus's spade to bury a dead body
with, I'll lay you a pound to a penny that it's his wife!"

MacGregor perched himself gingerly on the edge of a
wheelbarrow, having first inspected and then passed it for
cleanliness. Mrs. Dover certainly ran a tight garden shed.
There was another deck chair stacked tidily in a corner but,
since it was still in its plastic wrapper, MacGregor didn't
feel he could really make use of it.

Having settled himself as comfortably as he could, Mac-
Gregor gave his full attention to putting the damper on

Dover's enthusiasm. "Oh, steady on, sir," he advised.

"Steady on—nothing!" Dover had his fixations and he wasn't going to have any pipsqueak of a sergeant talking him out of them. In Dover's book, wives were always killed by their husbands. This was a simple rule of thumb which had more than a little basis in fact and saved a great deal of trouble all round—except for the odd innocent husband, of course, but no system is perfect. "A strapping young man with a dead body to get rid of, nicking a neighbor's spade. Use your brains, laddie, who else could it be except his wife?"

MacGregor retaliated by taking a leaf out of Dover's book and, instead of dealing with the main issue, quibbled over a minor detail. "A *neighbor's* spade, sir? I don't think we can go quite as far as—"

Dover went over his sergeant's objection like a steamroller over a cream puff. "Well, he didn't bloomin' well come over by Tube from Balham, did he, you nitwit? Twice? Once to get the bloody spade and once to put it back? Of course he comes from somewhere round here. He wouldn't have known about our tool shed otherwise, would he?"

Without really thinking about it, MacGregor had pulled his notebook out. He looked up from an invitingly blank page that was just aching to be written on. "Actually, sir, I have been wondering why anybody would pick on this particular tool shed to break into in the first place."

Dover had no doubts. "Spite!" he said.

"There must be dozens of garden sheds round here, sir. Why choose this one?"

Dover belched with touching lack of inhibition. His exile was playing havoc with his insides. "Could be pure ruddy chance," he grunted.

"He had to prize open a good-quality padlock to get in

here, sir. There must be plenty of sheds that aren't even locked."

Dover turned a lackluster eye on his sergeant. "All right, Mr. Clever Boots, so what's the answer?"

"It's because Mrs. Dover's tools are all kept so spotlessly clean, sir, and in such immaculate order. I'm sure our unwelcome visitor thought he'd be able to take the spade and return it without it ever being noticed that it had so much as been touched. You see, if the shed were dirty and dusty and untidy and covered, say, with cobwebs, it would be virtually impossible to borrow a tool and put it back without disturbing something. Do you follow me, sir? He'd be bound to leave a trail of clues behind him. But here"—MacGregor swept an admiring hand round the shed—"our chap had every reason to believe that, as long as he cleaned the spade and replaced it neatly on the wall with all the others, no suspicions would ever be aroused."

"He was reckoning without my old woman," said Dover with a kind of gloomy pride. "Like a bloodhound. More so, if anything." He shook off his reminiscent mood. "Anyhow, what you're saying just goes to show for sure that this joker is living somewhere round here. That's how he knows this is the cleanest garden shed in the country."

He broke off to stare disgustedly around him. "She got all this lot with trading stamps, you know. It's taken her years and years. Never asks me if there's anything *I* want, mind you," he mused resentfully, "though they've definitely got long woolly underpants because I've seen 'em in the damn catalogue."

"I agree our chap probably does live near here, sir," said MacGregor, who'd only been debating the point just to keep his end up. "It's hard to see how he could have known about the tool shed or the tools otherwise. On the other hand, he must be something of a newcomer."

Dover snapped his fat fingers for another cigarette and used the time it took to furnish him with one in trying to puzzle out what MacGregor was getting at. He was forced to concede defeat. "Regular little Sherlock Holmes, aren't you?" he sneered.

Privately, MacGregor thought he was a jolly sight smarter than this supposed paragon, but he wasn't fool enough to confide such an opinion to Dover. "Our Mr. Borrower would hardly have come breaking into this particular tool shed, sir, if he'd known that you were a policeman. A Chief Inspector from New Scotland Yard, in fact."

Dover, almost invisible in a cloud of tobacco smoke, mulled this over. He was rather taken with the idea that all the barons of the underworld might be going in fear and trepidation of him. "He might be potty," he observed generously. "Otherwise he'd know he couldn't hope to pull the wool over the eyes of a highly trained observer like me."

Another thought struck him and he flopped back in his deck chair, suffering from shock. "'Strewth," he gasped, "it's only a couple of hours since I first heard about this crime, and look at me now! I've solved it, near as damn it! All we've got to do is find a young, newly married villain who's recently moved into the district. And I'll lay odds he's living in that new block of flats they've built just across the way. They've got the dregs of society in that place.

"So, all we've got to do now is get onto the local cop shop and tell 'em to send a posse of coppers round to make a few inquiries. Soon as they find somebody who fits the bill, all they've got to do is ask him to produce his wife. If he can't—well, Bob's your uncle, eh? And that," added Dover, seeing that MacGregor was dying to interrupt and being determined to thwart him, "is why he had to borrow a spade in the first place! Because people who live in flats don't have gardens, and if they don't have gardens they don't have gardening tools, either!"

MacGregor put his notebook away and stood up. "Oh, I don't think our man is living in a flat, do you, sir?"

Dover's eye immediately became glassy with suspicion, resentment, and chronic dyspepsia. "Why not?"

"He'd have nowhere to bury the body, sir."

Dover's scowl grew muddier. "He could have shoved it in somebody else's garden, couldn't he?" he asked, reasonably enough.

MacGregor shook his head. "Far too risky, sir. Digging a hole big enough to inter a body would take an hour or more, I should think. Now, it would be bad enough undertaking a job like that in one's own garden, but in somebody else's—" MacGregor pursed his lips in a silent whistle and shook his head again. "No, I doubt it, sir, I really do. I think we must take it, as a working hypothesis, that—"

"He could have planted her in the garden of an empty house," said Dover doggedly and, as a gesture of defiance against society, dropped his cigarette end into the empty watering can.

"Well, I suppose it's a possibility, sir," said MacGregor with a sigh, "and I agree that we ought to bear it in mind. The thing is, though, that you're hardly in the depths of the country out here, are you? I mean—well, everywhere round here does tend to be a bit visible, doesn't it?"

There are plenty of suburban mortgage holders who would have taken deep umbrage at such a damaging assessment of their property, but Dover was not cursed with that kind of pride. He simply reacted by nodding his head in sincere agreement. "Too right, laddie!" he rumbled.

"There's another point that's been puzzling me, sir," MacGregor said. "Why did our chap go to all this trouble to *borrow* a spade? The way he broke into this shed may carry all the hallmarks of a professional job, but he was still running a terrible risk. Anybody might have seen him and blown the whistle on him."

"He'd do it after dark," said Dover, "and, besides, you don't go in for murder if you aren't prepared to chance your arm a bit. And what choice did he have? With a dead body on his hands and no spade? He could hardly start digging a hole with a knife and fork."

"He could have bought a spade, sir."

"Eh?"

"He could have bought a spade," repeated MacGregor, quite prepared for the look of horror that flashed across Dover's pasty face. The Chief Inspector regarded the actual purchasing of anything as a desperate step, only to be contemplated when all the avenues of begging, borrowing, and stealing had been exhaustively explored. "It wouldn't have cost all that much, sir, and it would have been a much less hazardous operation."

Dover wrinkled up his nose. "The shops were shut?" he suggested. "Or he didn't have any money?"

"A professional villain, sir? That doesn't sound very likely, does it? And if he's going to nick something, why not nick the money? A handful of cash wouldn't be as compromising, if something went wrong, as Mrs. Dover's stainless-steel spade would be."

Dover shivered and shoved his hands as deep as they would go in his overcoat pockets. The shed wasn't built for sitting in and there was a howling gale blowing under the door. The sooner he got out of this dump and back into the warmth and comfort of his own home, the better. "That's why he didn't buy a spade!"

"Sir?"

"Put yourself in the murderer's shoes, laddie. You've just knocked your missus off and you're proposing to get rid of the body by burying it in a hole. Sooner or later people are going to come around asking questions. Well, I'd have said the last thing you wanted was a bloomin' spade standing there and shouting the odds. No, borrowing the spade and putting it back again shows our chap has a bit of class about him. He's somebody who can see further than the end of his nose. An opponent," added Dover with a smirk, "worthy of my steel. Well"—he raised a pair of moth-eaten eyebrows at his sergeant—"what are you waiting for? Christmas?"

"Sir?"

Dover sighed heavily and dramatically. "It's no wonder you've never made Inspector," he sneered. "You're as thick as two planks. Look, laddie, what's a detective got to do if he wants to be everybody's little white-haired boy, eh?"

MacGregor wondered what on earth they were supposed to be talking about now. "Well, I don't quite know, sir," he said uncertainly. "Er—solve his cases?"

"'Strewth!" snarled Dover, giving vent to his opinion with unwonted energy. "Look, you know what they're like, all these Commissioners and Commanders and what-have-you. They're forever yakking about a good detective being the one who goes out and finds his own cases, aren't they?"

"Oh, I see what you mean, sir."

"Well, look at me!"

"Sir?"

"I'm on leave, aren't I?" asked Dover, warming gleefully to the task of blowing his own trumpet. "But I don't go around sitting with my ruddy feet up! On the contrary, from the very faintest of hints—the sort any other jack would have brushed aside as not worth his attention—I've uncovered a dastardly murder that nobody else even knows has been committed."

Too late MacGregor saw the danger signals. "But, sir—"

"But, nothing!" snapped Dover. "With the information I'm giving 'em, the local police'll have our laddie under lock and key before you can say Sir Robert Peel!"

"But we can't go to the local police, sir," said MacGregor, breaking out in a sweat at the mere idea. "After all, we've only been theorizing."

Dover's face split into an evil grin. "Of course *we* are not going to the local police, laddie," he promised soothingly. "Just you!" There was a brief interval while the old fool laughed himself nearly sick. "Ask for Detective Superintendent Andy Andrews and mention my name—clearly! Tell him what we've come up with so far—that we're after a young, agile newlywed villain who's just moved into a house in this area. A specialist in picking locks."

"Oh, sir!" wailed MacGregor.

"There can't be all that many jokers knocking around who'd fit that bill," Dover went on. "And, if there are, Andrews will soon spot our chap because he'll be the one with a newly turned patch of soil in his garden and no wife. Or girl friend. You never know these days."

MacGregor tried to believe that he was just having a nightmare. "You're not serious, sir?"

"Never been more serious in my life," growled Dover. "And I've just thought of something else. If they're newcomers to the district, that's why nobody's reported the wife missing. She won't have had time to establish a routine yet or have made any close friends. Her husband will be able to give any rubbishy explanation for her absence." He realized that MacGregor was still standing there. "What's got into you, laddie? You're usually so damn keen they could use you for mustard!"

"It's just that I don't feel we're quite ready, sir."

But Dover wasn't having any argument about it. He cut ruthlessly through his sergeant's feeble protests. "And stick to old Andrews like a limpet, see? Don't move from his side till you've got the handcuffs on our chummie—I don't want Andrews stealing my thunder. I've solved this case and I'm going to get the glory for it. Well"—he glared up at a very shrinking violet—"what are you waiting for now? A Number Nine bus?"

MacGregor answered out of a bone-dry throat. "No, sir."

"Leave us your cigarettes," said Dover, not the man to get his priorities mixed. "You'll not be having time to smoke."

Reluctantly MacGregor handed over his pack of cigarettes and even found a spare packet of matches. When, however, he'd got his hand on the door handle he paused again. "Er—you're staying here, are you, sir?"

In all the excitement Dover had not overlooked his own personal predicament. "Call in at the house on your way out and tell Mrs. Dover that I've solved the problem of her bloody spade and that you're off to arrest the bloke for murder. I'll give you five minutes' start, so she's got time to digest the good news, and then I'll follow you. And I don't mind telling you, laddie"—he surveyed the scene of his exile with a marked lack of enthusiasm—"I'll be glad to get back to my own armchair by the fire." He waggled his head in mild bewilderment. "Do you know, she's never let me come in here on my own before. Funny, isn't it?"

Long before the allotted five minutes was up, however, Dover was infuriated to discover that Sergeant MacGregor was coming back down the garden path at the double. Extricating himself from his deck chair, he dragged the door open and voiced his feelings in a penetrating bellow of rage. "That damn woman! Is she never satisfied?"

MacGregor glanced around nervously, although the silent, unseen watchers weren't his neighbors and he really didn't care what they thought about the Dovers. "It's not that, actually, sir."

"Then what is it, *actually?*" roared Dover, mimicking his sergeant's minor public-school accent.

"It's a message from Mrs. Dover, sir."

Dover knew when he was being softened up for the breaking of bad news. "Spit it out, laddie," he said bleakly.

MacGregor grinned foolishly out of sheer embarrassment. "It's just that she's remembered she turned the spade round herself, sir. Mrs. Dover, I mean. It had quite slipped her mind, she says, but she popped down to the shed before she went to church on Sunday morning to count how many tie-on labels she'd got and the spade being hung the wrong way round on the wall got on her nerves, she says. And since she reckoned it must have dried off after having been washed, she—"

"You can spare me the details," said Dover as all his dreams of fame and glory crumbled to dust and ashes in his mouth.

"Mrs. Dover was going to come down and tell you herself, sir, when she'd finished washing the leaves of the aspidistras."

Dover seemed indifferent to such graciousness. "You didn't get in touch with Superintendent Andrews, did you?"

MacGregor shook his head. "There didn't seem much point, sir. As it was Mrs. Dover who changed the spade back to its proper position, well"—he shrugged—"that did rather seem to be that. Nobody broke into the shed to borrow the spade and, if nobody borrowed the spade, that means there was no dead body to be buried. And if there's no dead body to be buried, that means we haven't got a wife murderer and—"

But Dover had switched off. He had many faults, but

crying over spilt milk wasn't one of them. He was already lumbering out through the shed door, his thoughts turning to the future. He tossed a final question back over his shoulder.

"Did she say what she was giving me for my dinner?"

—1976

Dover Goes to School

Detective Chief Inspector Dover was a creature of habit. Whenever he entered a room he made a point of selecting the most comfortable-looking seat and heading straight for it. On this occasion, as he waddled across the threshold of the large old-fashioned bathroom at Skelmers Hall College, he was not embarrassed by choice. The rim of the bath was definitely out and he didn't fancy the three-legged stool. That left only one place where 241 pounds of flab could be safely deposited, and the Chief Inspector sank gratefully onto the oval of polished mahogany. That flight of stairs up from the ground floor had taken it out of him.

Two other men entered the bathroom. One was the young and handsome Detective Sergeant MacGregor, Chief Inspector Dover's long-suffering assistant; the other was an older man in uniform, Inspector Howard. He was the representative of the local police force whose unenviable job it was to put these two clever devils from Scotland Yard in the picture.

It was Inspector Howard's first encounter with members of the prestigious Murder Squad and he was understandably somewhat diffident. Still, a man had to do what a man had to do. He cleared his throat. "Er—excuse me, sir."

Dover's mean little eyes opened slowly and balefully. "What?"

"Your—er—feet, sir."

"What about 'em?"

"They're resting on the—er—body, sir."

Dover glanced down and with ill grace shifted his boots back a couple of inches from the corpse that lay sprawled, in pajamas and dressing gown, over the bathroom floor. "Thought you were supposed to be telling us what's happened," he observed nastily.

Inspector Howard swallowed. "Oh, yes, I am, sir."

"Well, get on with it, then! I don't want to sit here all morning gawping at a stiff!" Dover's pasty face twisted in a grimace.

Not surprisingly, Inspector Howard's account of the murder which had taken place in the bathroom at Skelmers Hall College was somewhat incoherent. Shorn of his stammerings and splutterings, and expurgated of Dover's increasingly obscene interjections, the story ran something like this:

Skelmers Hall College was an Adult Education Centre where members of the general public could attend courses on subjects of interest to them. The course which had been planned for that weekend was on icons and half a dozen enthusiasts had assembled just before supper on the previous evening, Friday. After supper they had been treated to an introductory lecture by the visiting expert, Professor Ross, and had then dispersed to their various bedrooms for the night. It was in the early hours of Saturday morning that one of the students, a young woman named Wenda Birkinshaw, had discovered the body.

"What's his name?" asked Dover, giving the corpse a poke with his boot.

"Er—Rupert Andrews, sir. Quite a well-known building contractor, I understand, and a County Councillor too."

"How was he croaked?"

"Ah, now that's rather interesting, sir." Inspector Howard's boyish enthusiasm didn't find much echo in his audience. "He was knocked unconscious, then strangled with the cord of his own dressing gown. This was probably one of the weapons, sir."

"This" proved to be a sausage-shaped object, about two feet long, still lying where it had been found on the floor by the washbasin.

Dover inspected it from a safe distance. "What the hell is it?"

"It's a draft excluder, sir. Mrs. Crocker, the Warden's wife, made it herself. It's just a tube of cloth some three inches in diameter filled with sand. You stretch it out along the windowsill to keep the draft out. There are several more of them about the Hall. These old houses generally seem to have badly fitting windows, don't they? This particular draft excluder weighs several pounds, sir, and would make a highly efficient cosh. It belongs here in the bathroom."

Dover had slumped back until his spine rested comfortably against the wall. "You always this bloody long-winded?" he asked unpleasantly. "Or is it just for my benefit? And don't," he added as poor Inspector Howard produced yet another prize exhibit, "bother telling me what that is because I know. It's a bath brush."

"It's another murder weapon, sir," explained Inspector Howard. He glanced for sympathy at Sergeant MacGregor, but that young gentleman was prudently keeping his head well down over his notebook. "The handle of the bath brush, sir, was inserted into the dressing-gown cord and used like a tourniquet to tighten it round the neck of the unconscious victim. The victim was a middle-aged man, sir, but quite strong. In the doctor's opinion quite a frail person could have killed him using this method."

"When I want the bloody doctor's opinion," grunted Dover who really worked at being ungracious, "I'll ask for it. Anything else?"

"I don't think so, sir," replied Inspector Howard miserably.

"What about bloody suspects?"

"Oh, yes, well, virtually everybody in the house last night is a suspect, sir." Inspector Howard shifted uneasily from one foot to the other. Things weren't going at all as he'd expected. Where was that friendly cooperation between one copper and another? That professional camaraderie— That happy exchange of— He caught Dover's jaundiced eye and hurriedly took up the thread of his story. "The Hall is securely locked up at night, sir, and there's no sign of a break-in. Of course we can't definitely exclude—"

"Let's have a few names," growled Dover.

"Of the suspects, sir?"

Dover rolled his eyes toward the ceiling.

"Well, there's Brigadier and Mrs. Crocker, sir, the resident Wardens of the College, and—"

"Here," said Dover as the thought suddenly struck him, "do you have to pay to come to this dump?"

"Oh, yes, sir. Not very much, though. The students' fees, I understand, only cover part of the cost of running the place. The rest comes from the government."

"Bully for some!" grumbled Dover. "Well, get on with it!"

There were, it turned out, no less than eight possible murderers currently at the Skelmers Hall College for Adult Education—and Chief Inspector Dover's face fell at the news. Apart from the Crockers, they were in alphabetical order: Miss Wenda Birkinshaw (who had discovered the body), Miss Betsy Gallop, Mr. and Mrs. Mappin, Professor Ross (the lecturer), and Peter Thorrowgood.

Somewhat to everyone's surprise, Dover had actually been listening. "No Mrs. Anfield?" he demanded indignantly.

"Anfield, sir?"

Sergeant MacGregor was more accustomed to the great man's idiosyncrasies. "I think you mean Andrews, sir," he said, looking up from his notebook. "The dead man was named Andrews."

"What I said!" snarled Dover before turning again on the shrinking Inspector Howard. "So where's his wife?"

Inspector Howard gave up trying to understand. "I gather he was divorced, sir."

"Pity," said Dover, sinking back into lethargy.

"Sir?"

In an untypical flush of generosity Dover tossed one pearl of his investigatory wisdom to this poor provincial bluebottle. "If Mrs. Ashford had been on the scene, laddie, we could just have arrested her and all gone home." He sensed that Inspector Howard needed something more. "Husbands, laddie," he added, disgruntled at having thus to gild the lily, "are always murdered by their wives. And vice versa."

Inspector Howard, to his eternal credit, took his courage in both hands. "Always, sir?"

"Near as damn it!" grunted Dover, hauling himself to his feet and stepping clumsily over the dead body. "It's a law of nature." He headed for the door. "If anybody wants me I'll be downstairs." As he passed MacGregor he fired off a valedictory behest in a voice that carried just far enough to do the most damage. "And get rid of *him!*"

Whether it was Dover's sensitive ears that had caught

the clink of bottles or his delicate nostrils that had picked up the aroma of good malt whiskey at 150 paces, the world will never know. Suffice it to say that he made his way unerringly downstairs and straight into the small parlor that served Skelmers Hall College as a bar just as Brigadier Crocker raised his tumbler to his lips.

Caught red-handed, there was nothing a retired officer-and-gentleman could do but reach for another glass. The Brigadier introduced himself. "You look," he said, erroneously attributing Dover's habitual pallor to shock, "as though you could do with this."

"It wasn't a pretty sight," agreed Dover, reaching out an eager paw.

The Brigadier proposed a toast. "Absent friends!"

Dover emptied his glass and prudently got a refill before putting the boot in. "Pal of yours, was he?"

The Brigadier's indignation nearly sobered him. "Good lord, no! I never set eyes on the bounder before last night."

"Bounder?" queried Dover, who liked seeing people squirm.

"Well, what would you call a chappie of fifty who attends a weekend study course on icons accompanied by his teenage popsie?"

Dover mulled it over. "You sure?"

"Of course I'm sure. Him and Miss Birkinshaw—well, you only had to see them together to realize precisely what was going on."

Dover slowly examined his surroundings. "Bloody funny setup for a romantic weekend," he commented.

"It's a jolly sight cheaper than a hotel," the Brigadier pointed out, replenishing the drinks with an unsteady hand. "And he'd be less likely to run into any of his business chums. County Councillor, indeed!" He stared sullenly into the depths of his glass. "I should have a good look at Miss Birkinshaw, if I were you, Chief Inspector. She found Andrews, you know, and in my opinion—"

There might have been further revelations if it hadn't been for the arrival of a very tall, very thin man who moved with the preternatural leisureliness of a giraffe.

"Ah, Professor Ross!" Brigadier Crocker accompanied his greeting with legerdemain which had the bottle of whiskey out of sight before you could say "usquebaugh."

"I simply want to know how much longer I'm supposed to keep on," bleated Professor Ross. "I've just finished my lecture on Iconography, Part One, but it's hard going. They're hardly a very receptive audience."

"Business-as-usual was my idea," the Brigadier told Dover proudly. "Takes their minds off the tragedy, keeps 'em out of your hair, *and* stops 'em asking for their money back." He addressed Professor Ross again. "What are they doing now?"

"Having their coffee break," whined the Professor. "That's what's on the timetable."

The Brigadier emerged reluctantly from behind his bar. "I'd better go and give the lady wife a hand before she starts feeling put upon, what? I'll bring you your coffee back here."

Left alone, Dover and the Professor eyed each other moodily. In the end it was Dover, his tongue no doubt loosened by the strong drink, who cracked first.

"You don't look like a professor to me," he said, just to be rude.

Professor Ross's face turned scarlet. "Well, actually," he admitted hoarsely, "I'm not, really."

Dover leered in evil encouragement.

"No," confessed the unfortunate academic with an agonized grimace. "It's just that people have got into the habit of calling me one."

Dover removed his bowler hat the better to scratch at his head. "And you didn't stop 'em?"

Professor Ross (as we may as well continue to call him) murmured, "Well . . ."

"Here," yelped Dover, almost overwhelmed by the audacity of his imagination, "did Ainsworth know about this?"

"Ainsworth?"

"The dead man!" screamed Dover. "Did he know you were sailing under borrowed plumes?"

"Good heavens, no!" wailed the Professor. "The loud-mouthed bully was unpleasant enough to me without that! Oh, *dear!*" Too late—far, far too late—Professor Ross clamped a restraining hand over his mouth.

The only thing left in life that gave Dover real pleasure was bullying the weak and helpless. Naturally he preferred pushing widows and orphans around but, failing them, Professor Ross would do. It wasn't long before the whole story poured out.

It had happened during Professor Ross's introductory lecture, given on the previous evening immediately after supper. Professor Ross had been guilty of a couple of slips of the tongue and Councillor Andrews had pounced on them with unconcealed relish. Professor Ross realized with dismay that he'd encountered every lecturer's nightmare—an expert in the audience. And there were eight more sessions to get through!

"I *knew*," whimpered Professor Ross, "that I was showing them a Hodegetria Mother of God, and I can't think *why* I called it Glykophilusa. It was just a momentary mental aberration."

Dover grunted. It was all Greek to him.

"And then, when I was talking about the metal covers, he pulled me up again. I was simply trying to keep things simple. I know there's a *technical* difference between a riza and an oklad, but really the terms are—"

Dover's threshold of boredom could be measured in microns, so it was fortunate that the Brigadier chose this moment to return with coffee and biscuits. Mrs. Crocker came bustling in behind him. She was one of those women who are always busy.

"You forgot the sugar, Tom." The empty whiskey glasses on the bar counter caught her eye and her routine wifely exasperation turned to real fury. "Oh, for God's sake, you've not been at the booze already, have you?"

Her husband grinned sheepishly at his male companions. "Just a quick snifter to speed poor old Andrews on his way, m'dear."

If this reference to the dear departed was an attempt to inhibit Mrs. Crocker's wrath, it failed. "Poor old Andrews?" she repeated incredulously. "That's not what you called him last night, my lad. Last night you couldn't find words bad enough for him. I don't know when I've seen you in such a blind temper."

She was so absorbed in rinsing out glasses and wiping the bar top down that she failed to notice her husband's frantic signals, and went blithely on, "I'm surprised you need reminding, Tom, that 'poor old Andrews' is the same bloody interfering swine who was going to get us both turned out into the streets without a penny to our name."

Brigadier Crocker glanced at Dover to see if he was paying any attention to this tirade. Strangely enough, he was. "Nonsense, old girl," said the Brigadier desperately. "Andrews hadn't that much influence. He wasn't God Almighty, y'know."

"He was chairman of that special committee the Council set up for slashing local government expenditures," snapped Mrs. Crocker, draping her towel over the beer pump. "And he's not the only one who thinks Skelmers Hall College is a waste of public funds. He just happens to be the most influential and dangerous one we've come across to date."

The arrival of MacGregor to announce that the body had been removed interrupted this heated exchange of views.

Dover hoisted himself to his feet. "About bloody time!"

"They'll let us have the postmortem report as soon as possible, sir," said MacGregor as he followed Dover upstairs. "And then I was wondering if you'd like to examine Andrews's room now, sir. He only brought one small suitcase, of course, but—"

Dover marched straight into the bathroom and locked the door firmly behind him.

When he emerged five minutes later, he was not pleased to find Professor Ross waiting for him on the landing. The Professor jerked into life and caught Dover by the sleeve. "Remember the old adage," he advised hoarsely. "*Cherchez la femme!*"

Dover tried to brush him off but the Professor was tenacious.

"It's the fair sex you ought to be looking at, Chief Inspector. That Mappin woman for a start."

Dover progressed, carrying Professor Ross with him as he went. "And who's she when she's at home?"

Having twined himself right round Dover, Professor Ross was now able to whisper confidentially in his ear. "She's a student of the course. With her husband. Not that that's cramping her style. They arrived early last night, like Councillor Andrews. You should have seen the pair of them in the bar—Mrs. Mappin and Andrews. Getting on like a house on fire! Flirting. Making suggestive remarks. Saying things with double meanings."

"What was her husband doing?" asked Dover, trying without success to break Professor Ross's wrist.

"Oh, he was maintaining a very low profile. Most of the time he wasn't even there. No doubt he's used to it, but if it had been my wife carrying on like—"

"I'll bear it in mind," promised Dover. "Jealous husband."

"No, no," moaned Professor Ross frantically. "The *wife*, not the husband."

Dover was trying to use his feet. "Eh?"

"*Mrs.* Mappin!" said the Professor. "Don't you understand? She thought she'd made a conquest. But she hadn't. He was just passing the time until Miss Birkinshaw turned up."

Something stirred in Dover's subconscious. "The girl who found the body?"

"That's right. She arrived just before supper and the minute she arrived on the scene Andrews dropped La Mappin like a hot potato."

"Hmm," said Dover.

Professor Ross was an experienced teacher and he knew that you couldn't repeat a thing too often for some people. "Hell," he announced, "hath no fury like a woman scorned."

MacGregor looked round as Dover burst into the bedroom and slammed the door shut behind him.

"Find anything, laddie?"

"Nothing of any significance, I'm afraid, sir."

"No cigarettes?"

"Andrews was a nonsmoker, sir."

"Trust him!" Dover's bottom lip protruded. "You sure you haven't got any, laddie?"

"You smoked all mine on the way down, sir."

Dover crossed over to the bed and flopped down on it

sulkily. "You could have brought some more," he pointed out. "And what's that you're holding?"

"It's a tie, sir."

"I can see that!" snarled Dover before sinking back and closing his eyes.

MacGregor gazed nostalgically at the dazzling blue-and-silver stripes. "Councillor Andrews must have been a Butcher's Boy, sir."

"Eh?" Unlike his sergeant, Dover had not had the advantage of a Public School education, and further elucidation was required.

"Oh, that's what we used to call the chaps who went to Bullock's College, sir," said MacGregor. "Bullock, you see, sir—and the blue-and-white stripes. Like a butcher's apron."

"So what?"

"Well, so nothing, actually, sir." MacGregor draped the tie back over the mirror. "Just that we used to play them at cricket and rugger. Annual events, you know." MacGregor chuckled softly to himself. "We usually beat 'em too!"

Dover wallowed luxuriously among the pillows. "Are you claiming you knew this Ambrose, laddie?"

"Andrews, sir." MacGregor made the correction without much hope. "No, he'd be years before my time."

"Pity," grunted Dover. "I was hoping we'd be able to chuck our hands in, seeing as how you were personally involved with the deceased."

MacGregor had given up counting to ten years ago. Nowadays he found it took 30 or even 40 to get his passions under control. "Shouldn't we start interviewing the suspects, sir?" he asked eventually.

Dover really fancied a preprandial nap but his superiors at the Yard had been hounding him a bit recently. "Oh, all right," he grumbled. "Wheel 'em in."

"We've got the use of a room downstairs, sir."

But Dover had reached the end of his concessions. "Here, laddie, here."

Miss Wenda Birkinshaw, as befitted her status as finder of the body, was the first victim and MacGregor fought to keep his eyes fixed on her face as she undulated, in a miasma of cheap scent, over to the chair which had been placed ready for her. She even got Dover sitting bolt upright and taking notice, but this was only because her first action, after provocatively crossing her legs, was to produce her cigarettes and ask if anyone minded. MacGregor broke the world record with his lighter, and Dover was only fractionally behind with the begging bowl.

"Keep the packet," said Miss Birkinshaw grandly, and thereby insured that, whoever stood before the bar of British Justice to answer for the murder of Rupert Andrews, it wouldn't be she.

She rattled off her story with admirable economy. "I work in the typing pool at County Hall and me and Randy—that's what he told me to call him—have been friends for a couple of months. This awful weekend was his idea. Well, you didn't think I was interested in holy pictures, did you?" Miss Birkinshaw uncrossed her legs.

"Mr. Andrews booked separate rooms for you?" said MacGregor from a tight throat.

"There's elections coming up and he didn't want any filthy talk till they were over. Last night he was supposed to wait till everybody'd got settled down and then nip along to my room. Well, I got cheesed off with waiting, didn't I? Mind you, I was in two minds. The way he'd been chatting with that old Mappin woman, the silly cow! I soon put a stop to that, I can tell you. 'If you're going in for geriatrics nowadays, Randy,' I told him, 'just let me know because I can easily fix myself up elsewhere.' What, dear? Oh, last night? Well, like I said, I went looking for him, didn't I? I saw the bathroom door was half open and the light on, so I popped my head round and—ugh. It was terrible!"

"What did you do then, Miss Birkinshaw?" asked Mac-Gregor apologetically.

"Screamed the bleeding place down, dearie, and why don't you call me Wenda?"

"Er—were you and Mr. Andrews intending to get married?"

Miss Birkinshaw blinked her enormous baby-blue eyes. "What for?"

"Do you know anybody who'd want to murder Councillor Andrews?"

"Only just about everybody he ever met, dearie! Let's face it, he could be a right pig. He was on the outs with half the people here before I even arrived on the scene. And the other half after I got here."

Dover lit another of Miss Birkinshaw's cigarettes. "Anybody in particular?"

"Well"—Miss Birkinshaw didn't lose much sleep over the ethics of the situation—"there was that young lad, Peter Thorrowgood, for a start. Wet behind the ears? You wouldn't believe! Randy went over him like a bloomin' steamroller."

"Why?"

"Because of me, dearie! Randy thought he was trying to make time with me, though anybody could see the kid didn't know how many beans make five. Here"—Miss Birkinshaw changed the subject abruptly—"do I have to keep going to these damn old lectures? It's worse than school. I mean, *icons*—who cares?"

Dover graciously excused Miss Birkinshaw and said she could watch the telly instead. MacGregor barely managed to clear up a couple of minor points before the nubile young woman went on her way rejoicing. No, she'd never been to Skelmers Hall College before. No, she hadn't heard anything suspicious before she went out to look for Councillor Andrews, and finally she thought that Councillor Andrews had booked their places on the course about a month ago.

"What was that all about?" asked Dover after Miss Birkinshaw had departed. His mood had been much improved by the intake of nicotine.

"If the murder was premeditated, sir, the murderer would have had to apply for the course *after* Andrews did."

"Garn," said Dover, his mood not being as rosy as all that, "this murder wasn't premeditated! Stands out a mile—the joker just grabbed whatever was to hand and used it. How could he know in advance there'd be a bath brush and that sausage thing all ready and waiting?"

"He could if he'd attended a course here before, sir. That's why I asked Miss Birkinshaw if this was her first visit."

"'Strewth," said Dover, gazing fondly at his packet of cigarettes, "you're not suspecting that poor little girl of anything, are you?"

"The doctor did say no great strength would be required, sir. And who better than Miss Birkinshaw to catch him unawares?"

Dover had no intention of wasting his time on theoretical and unpalatable discussions. "Fetch that lad in she mentioned!" he commanded and playfully punched his fist into the palm of his other hand. "Let's see if we can't bash a nice free and voluntary confession out of him!"

Peter Thorrowgood, being immature, weedy, and extremely nervous, might have been tailor-made for Dover. He was so eager to cooperate that it wasn't necessary to lay a finger on him. He admitted that he was a frequent student on these weekend courses but insisted that this was his first visit to Skelmers Hall. He wasn't particularly interested in icons—nor in medieval monasticism or pottery for beginners, if it came to that. No, he attended these courses in order to make friends and meet people. Like young ladies of the opposite sex.

Dover sniffed.

Mr. Thorrowgood went pale and launched himself hurriedly into the rest of his *curriculum vitae*. Although currently training to be a shoe-shop manager, he didn't really consider he had as yet found his true vocation. He felt he would prefer a job which brought him more into contact with people. Like young ladies of the opposite sex. Young ladies of the opposite sex were, Mr. Thorrowgood confided, a bit thin at the moment. "Sometimes," he added, "I wonder if it's me."

Had he ever met Councillor Andrews before?

"No, never." Mr. Thorrowgood squared his shoulders. "And if you're going to ask me about that scene at the supper table, I'm quite prepared to admit that I did feel like murdering him—for a moment. He deliberately set out to humiliate me in front of everyone, you know. How was I to know that Miss Birkinshaw was some kind of special friend? In any case, all I did was indulge in some polite conversation. From the way Mr. Andrews went on, you'd have thought I'd tried to— Well, it was all very unpleasant and embarrassing. I'd be a hypocrite if I said I was sorry Mr. Andrews is dead, but that doesn't mean I killed him. Because I didn't."

And from this position young Mr. Thorrowgood refused to budge. Even Dover couldn't shake him. MacGregor took over the questioning as Dover sank back, sullen and exhausted, on the bed.

Mr. Thorrowgood was willing but unhelpful. He'd neither seen nor heard anything out of the ordinary last night. He'd never met any of his fellow suspects before and his application for the course had been sent in at least six months ago because you never knew if these things booked up and, no, he couldn't think of anybody who would have wanted to murder Mr. Andrews except— well—

Young Mr. Thorrowgood paused and licked his lips.

MacGregor exuded encouragement.

Sneaking seemed to be endemic at Skelmers Hall.

"Miss Gallop was getting pretty uptight."

"She's a fellow student?"

Mr. Thorrowgood nodded. "I thought she was going to scratch Councillor Andrews's eyes out at one point."

"Why?"

Mr. Thorrowgood didn't know. "She sort of railed against him as soon as she realized who he was. Something to do with donkeys. And goats. I couldn't make head nor tail of it. Anyhow, whatever it was, Miss Gallop claimed it was all Andrews's fault."

"When did this happen?"

"After the first lecture last night. Andrews had drawn a fair amount of attention to himself by having quite a heated argument with Professor Ross." Mr. Thorrowgood took time off to seize another straw. "That's somebody else you might have a word with—Professor Ross. He was looking pretty sick by the time Councillor Andrews had finished with him."

"Let's just stick to Miss Gallop," said MacGregor, who didn't want Dover getting all muddled up. "What was Mr. Andrews's reaction to her attack?"

"Oh, he gave back as good as he got." Mr. Thorrowgood was plainly envious. "Told her he hadn't got where he had in life by letting silly old maids like her push him around. Miss Gallop looked as though she was going to have a fit."

Dover and MacGregor were given lunch in a small room by themselves. As Mrs. Crocker explained, even before she'd seen Dover's table manners, it would be less embarrassing for all concerned.

"I don't suppose," she said as she put the soup on the table, "that they want to hobnob with you any more than you do with them. Not," she added as she watched Dover stuffing handfuls of bread down his gullet, "that one has much to complain about as far as this course is concerned. They're a fairly civilized lot. We've just had the one gentleman turning up for supper in an open-necked shirt, but then we've had nobody going around all day in bedroom slippers or parking their chewing gum under the chairs in the lecture room."

It was no good looking to Dover for polite conversation at feeding time, so MacGregor, raising his voice to be audible over the splashing and sloshing, did the honors. "I would imagine you get a pretty decent type here on the whole," he said politely.

"Yes, we do, really," agreed Mrs. Crocker, finding it hard to tear her eyes away from the spectacle of Dover eating. "We try to preserve the old country-house atmosphere, you know, and most people are very cooperative. Well, we're all starved for gracious living these days, aren't we? That's what makes it so depressing when somebody like Mr. Mappin lets the side down. It isn't"—she watched Dover mop up the last of his soup with the last of his bread—"as though he hadn't got a tie because he was wearing one when he arrived. Well, I'll fetch the next course, shall I? It's a beef casserole."

It would be absurd to pretend that Dover's drive, acumen, and general get-up-and-go weren't a little impaired after lunch. Two helpings of everything is hardly the formula for a dynamic afternoon.

The remaining interviews were held in the room in which the two detectives had had their lunch, and there is every reason to believe that Dover slept through the first one. This was no mean feat because Miss Betsy Gallop was a woman of strong character, loud voice, and a distinct aroma of goat.

"Never heard of Gallop Goats?" she said in disbelief. "You do surprise me. Thought everybody'd heard of Gallop Goats. S'why I got so enraged with the late unlamented. I mean, Gallop Goats are practically a national institution. Not," she added in a sour afterthought, "that they would have been much longer if Andrews had had his foul way."

MacGregor's pencil flew over the pages of his notebook as Miss Betsy Gallop let it all come gushing out.

"My small holding is on the edge of Donkey Bridge Wood," she confided. "That rotter, Andrews, bought up a chunk of land about a quarter of a mile away on which he proposed to build a housing tract. Planning permission? A mere formality, dear boy! He was on the Council, wasn't he? That bunch of pusillanimous sycophants would have given him the moon if he'd asked for it. You can see where that left yours truly, can't you? Right up the creek and without a paddle!"

MacGregor raised the shapeliest eyebrows in Scotland Yard, policewomen not excepted.

"Approach roads, dear boy!" explained Miss Gallop. "Scheduled to go right through the middle of my herd of pedigreed beauties! It would have put the kibosh on my whole way of life. Don't just breed goats, you know. See this trouser suit I'm sporting?"

MacGregor nodded. He'd been wondering about that trouser suit.

"Hair from my own goats!" claimed Miss Gallop proudly. "Woven by a chum of mine. That"—her brown eyes filled with tears—"was what Andrews was going to destroy, the philistine. Well, somebody's cooked his goose for him!"

The elegant MacGregor eyebrows rose again.

Miss Gallop's scowl wouldn't have looked out of place on Dover's face. "Certainly not me!"

"What happens to the housing scheme now?"

Miss Gallop turned a grubby thumb downward. "No other builder's got the pull Andrews had with the Council. I'll be able to disband my little action committee."

MacGregor turned to other aspects of the case. Was Miss Gallop interested in icons?

"No jolly fear! Just happens this is the only weekend I could get a goat-sitter. It's not everybody who can stand it, you know. When did I book? Oh, a couple of months ago. I generally give myself a little break at this time of year." She started fishing in her hip pocket. "Can give you the exact date, if you—"

MacGregor said it didn't matter.

Miss Gallop was equally forthright when it came to the events of Friday night. "Didn't hear a thing, dear boy! Dead to the world as soon as my head touches the pillow. Even the screams didn't wake me," she added. "Had to be wakened specially."

And that was that. The closing of the door must have roused Dover and there was a great deal of snorting and puffing.

MacGregor tried to put his superior in the picture as tactfully as possible. "Well, at least Miss Gallop didn't try to pin the murder on somebody else."

"Gerrumphahugh!" said Dover. He smacked his lips. "'Strewth, I could do with a cup of tea."

"Tea's ordered for four o'clock, sir, and we've only got Mr. and Mrs. Mappin left to see. Just enough time. We've got on quite well, all things considered."

"People don't realize what a strain it all is," said Dover through a yawn. He extracted another of Miss Birkinshaw's cigarettes and waited for MacGregor to give him a light. "Well, fetch 'em in," he growled. "The sooner we start, the sooner we finish."

"Shall we take the lady first, sir?" asked MacGregor, sensibly striking while the iron was lukewarm.

He'd reckoned without Dover's cunning. "We'll see 'em both together, laddie! It'll be quicker."

Harold and Cynthia Mappin approached their ordeal with understandable apprehension. MacGregor ran an experienced eye over them as he invited them to sit down. Mrs. Mappin was well into her middle forties in spite of fighting every day of the way. From the way she was dressed MacGregor surmised that a hefty proportion of the family income finished up on her back. Mr. Mappin was older, grayer, and shabbier. He was in a sober, badly cut suit which he had tried to enliven by permitting a tantalizing glimpse of his hairy chest to peep through the open neck of his shirt.

Dover opened the proceedings. "You can smoke if you want to."

He was out of luck. The Mappins didn't.

Dover washed his hands of the pair of 'em.

MacGregor soon found out that it was Mrs. Mappin who did the talking, answering not only her own questions but her husband's. She had a quick and decisive mind and the preliminaries were soon dispensed with. Her husband was an assistant bank manager, this was their first visit to Skelmers Hall College, and Mrs. Mappin was the one who was passionately "into" icons. Neither of them had ever heard of Councillor Andrews before.

MacGregor cautiously broached the question of the alleged flirtation between Mrs. Mappin and the deceased and was not surprised to be presented with a version which differed considerably from the one supplied by Professor Ross. Mrs. Mappin modestly pictured herself as the innocent target of a lascivious brute's unbridled lust. "I simply couldn't get rid of him," she complained. "Could I, Harold? He just wouldn't leave me alone. And his hands, Sergeant, were *everywhere!*"

MacGregor avoided catching anyone's eye.

"You've no idea what a relief it was when that girl finally turned up," Mrs. Mappin went on, twisting her lips in a sneer. "Such a cheap-looking little thing! Still, she no doubt would provide *exactly* what Councillor Andrews was looking for."

MacGregor tried to draw Mr. Mappin into the conversation but, once again, it was Mrs. Mappin who was quicker on the draw.

"Jealous?" she echoed with an unpleasant laugh. "Harold? You must be joking, Sergeant! My precious husband wouldn't so much as bat an eyelid if he saw me being attacked on the hearthrug at his feet. Councillor Andrews wasn't the first man to make a pass at me, and I doubt if he'll be the last. I've learned to protect myself and not rely on Harold's strong right arm—if any."

An uncomfortable silence followed, during which Harold Mappin grinned vaguely at nothing in particular.

MacGregor addressed the voluptuous Cynthia again. "Did you hear anything suspicious last night?"

Mrs. Mappin shook her head in a drumroll of oversize earrings. "I was so upset I took a sleeping pill."

"Because of Councillor Andrews's unwelcome attentions?"

"That," said Mrs. Mappin with a spiteful glance at her husband, "and other things."

"How about you, Mr. Mappin?"

Harold Mappin jumped. "Oh, no, nothing! I—er—sleep very soundly."

"Like a log," agreed his wife.

"Er—twin beds?" asked MacGregor, never very happy when having to deal with such intimate matters.

"What else?" queried Mrs. Mappin.

MacGregor let them go.

"Well, that's that, sir," he said as he resumed his seat. "We've seen all the people who were in the Hall last night."

"Moldy lot," grumbled Dover. "Could have been any one of 'em."

"I'm afraid it could, sir. Anybody could have guessed that Andrews would be creeping along to Miss Birkin-shaw's room as soon as things were quiet. It'd be easy enough to lie in wait for him, strike him down with the draft excluder, drag him into the bathroom, and strangle him. No,"—MacGregor tucked his pencil away in his pock-et—"we're going to have our work cut out to crack this one. It'll probably take weeks."

Work? Weeks? "I fancy that last joker," Dover said desperately.

"Harold Mappin, sir? To avenge his wife? Oh, I hardly think so. From the looks he kept giving her, I think he'd more likely murder *her*."

Dover didn't care for being crossed. "He had the opportunity!" he snarled.

"They'd *all* had the opportunity, sir."

Dover scowled. It was rapidly becoming a point of honor to drop a noose round Harold Mappin's scrawny neck. Neck? Dover was reduced to clutching at any straw. "That's why he's not wearing a tie!"

One day, MacGregor promised himself, he really would pick up the nearest blunt instrument and— "Andrews was strangled with the cord of his own dressing gown, sir, not by a necktie."

But Dover was nothing if not a whole-hogger. "Says who? Look, What's-his-name ambushes Who's-your-father and garrotes him with his tie. See? But, since he's not a complete idiot, he doesn't leave the corpse lying there with his tie round its neck. No, he removes the tie and sub-stitutes the dead man's own dressing-gown cord. What's wrong with that?"

"Mr. Mappin simply has no motive, sir."

"He's jealous of his wife." Dover looked his sergeant up and down before forestalling his objection. "I mean, you're no flaming expert on married life, are you?" Mac-Gregor's carefree bachelor status never ceased to irritate.

MacGregor retreated to his notebook. "Practically every-body in Skelmers Hall has a better motive than Mappin, sir. The Crockers were in danger of losing their jobs here, and Professor Ross was in much the same boat. Miss Gallop might have been turned out of her goat farm and—"

"What about Wenda Birkinshaw?" demanded Dover, who could remember names perfectly well when he want-ed to. "Or that reedy young man?"

"Miss Birkinshaw could have had a hundred reasons for killing Andrews," retorted MacGregor. "As for Mr. Thor-rowgood—well, he admitted he could cheerfully have murdered him, given half a chance."

Dover wasn't listening. "Fetch him back!"

"Mappin, sir?"

Dover grinned. "We'll have a confrontation!" Raising his arm he managed to get a couple of wiggles out of the fat over his biceps. "I'll soon clout the whole story out of him. And if you don't like it, laddie," he added contemptuously, "try looking the other bloody way!"

MacGregor knew that he should have put up more of a fight, but there was nothing like years of close association with Dover to knock the heroics out of Dover's assistant.

Mr. Mappin returned to the interview room alone, looking even more henpecked without his wife than he did with her.

Dover acknowledged that the burden of this particular examination rested solely on his own shoulders. He opened the proceedings with typical finesse. "Where's your bloody tie?"

Mr. Mappin clutched at his throat. "My—my tie?"

Dover grew bored with all this fencing about. "You killed What's-his-name!" he roared.

To MacGregor's eternal disgust these tactics worked.

"I knew I'd never get away with it," said Mr. Mappin bitterly. "Not with my luck." He looked up and appealed to Dover. "I'm not unintelligent. I work hard. I'm honest. I've got my fair share of imagination. So why am I always a failure? Why me? Why am I the one who's passed over for promotion, left out of the first team? Damn it"—he banged his fist down on the arm of his chair—"I've only got her word for it that the boy's my son!"

It was no good expecting sympathy from Dover. "What did you do it for?"

"I knew Andrews would recognize me sooner or later. Bound to. After all, I knew him right away."

Dover blinked. "You knew Andrews?"

"Of course. We were at school together. He was the school bully and I was the school butt—a poor bespectacled little runt, no good at games, a coward . . . For three years he made my life hell on earth."

"'Strewth!" said Dover. "And you've been nursing a grudge ever since?"

"Not a grudge exactly," said Harold Mappin wearily. "More of a promise, I suppose. Or the inability to keep a promise."

"And that's as clear as mud!" snapped Dover.

"I'm sorry." Harold Mappin sighed and tried again. "It's just that when I was a kid I always promised myself that one day I'd be a tremendous success at *something*. I didn't know what. I just knew I'd finish up a field marshal or a multimillionaire or . . . something. It was the only thing that kept me going. Without a dream like that to hang on to, I'd have cut my throat. Well"—Harold Mappin shrugged helplessly—"I never made it. I'm an assistant bank manager and that's my limit. I've a wife who flaunts her unfaithfulness and a son who despises me. And I'm up to my ears in debt. I've no money, no friends, and no bloody hopes for the future. Andrews would have had a field day with me. He'd have put the clock back thirty years! Well, I couldn't face it. I kept out of his way as much as I could last night, but I couldn't hope to dodge him for the rest of the weekend."

Dover relaxed with a triumphant smirk at MacGregor. "So you strangled him with your tie."

Mr. Mappin seemed mildly irritated. "No, I used the cord of his dressing gown. Why should I use my tie? I may be unlucky but I'm not stupid."

Dover frowned. Damn it, even murderers started giving you cheek these days. "Look, mate," he snarled, "you arrived here last night wearing a tie. Right? And before supper you took it off and you haven't worn it since. Well, why—if it isn't the bloody murder weapon?"

"But I've explained all that!" protested Mr. Mappin. "I didn't want Andrews to recognize me. Damn it all, that's why I killed him."

Dover leaned across and caught Mr. Mappin by the lapels. "So?"

"So the tie I was wearing was my old school tie, wasn't it? My wife nagged me into putting the damned thing on. She thinks it impresses people. Well, Andrews may not have recognized my face right away, but he would have recognized that tie because it was exactly the same as the one he was wearing!"

MacGregor saw Harold Mappin in a new light. "So you're a Butcher's Boy too!" he cried with evident delight and held out his hand. "I was at St. Spyridon's, myself."

Dover, whose formative years had been spent at the Peony Street Mixed Infants, slumped back in his chair.

—1977

Dover Without Perks

"And this is where the body was found, sir."

Detective Chief Inspector Dover, having with difficulty been induced to leave the shelter of the police car, stood shivering inside his overcoat. He tossed an indifferent glance at the site before transferring his disgruntled gaze to his surroundings.

'Strewth, what a dump! Like the back of the bloody moon!

He was standing on a short stretch of access road which led from the busy dual carriage-way on his left to a new housing development, just beginning to spread its unloveliness over the hillside, on his right. From this distance the development was a jumble of unmade roads, scaffolding, patches of raw earth, and a few demoralized houses poking up like sore thumbs into the cold sky. Beyond, as far as the eye could see, lay acres of deserted, frost-bitten fields with only the occasional wind-swept hedge to break the monotony.

Such desolation made it all the more surprising that the access road proudly sported a brand-new pedestrian crossing, complete with black and white stripes and flashing orange beacons. It was here, some 50 yards before the access road swung round to glide into the dual carriage-way, that the dead man had been found at 5:25 that morning.

"Funnily enough, sir, it was his son-in-law who found him. He's a milk roundsman and he was cycling down to his depot. It was still dark then, of course, but he spotted the old chap in the light of the beacon." Even Inspector York, the local man who was doing the honors, was stamping his feet to warm them.

But Dover, who had been transported from London to the scene of the crime with what he considered unseemly haste, still hadn't got his bearings. "Where the hell are we?" he demanded crossly while his young, handsome, and long-suffering assistant, Detective Sergeant MacGregor, turned aside to hide his blushing.

Inspector York was a little disconcerted, too. It was his first encounter with Scotland Yard's famous Murder Squad and he didn't know quite what to make of it. Surely they couldn't all be like this? "Well, this is Willow Hill Farm Housing Estate, actually, sir," he said, indicating the miserable clutch of dwellings on the hillside. "Part of Bridchurch's slum-clearance scheme. Bridchurch is where you got off the train, sir. It's three miles away." He pointed down the dual carriage-way. "Someday, sir"—this time he made a generous, encircling gesture—"all this will be covered with houses. Meantime, it's all a bit isolated. Still, that should make our job a bit easier, shouldn't it, sir?"

Dover's response might have been a belch or it might have been an encouraging grunt.

Naively Inspector York plumped for the encouraging grunt. "There are not likely to be many people knocking about round here on a dark November night," he explained earnestly. "We've been working on the hypothesis that the murderer has some connection with the housing estate. In fact, he probably lives there. We found a lump of dried mud not far from the body and it probably came off the car that hit him. Now, we're pretty certain that the mud came from the housing estate—it's a proper quagmire when it rains, as you can imagine. It hasn't, however, rained for a fortnight. Well, if our chappie was on the estate a fortnight ago, the odds are that he lives there. Or, at the very worst, he's a frequent visitor."

Dover's habitual scowl deepened appreciably. "If it's a local case, why the hell fetch us into it?"

Inspector York quailed before such naked fury. "Our Chief Constable thought the Yard would want to handle it themselves, sir, since the dead man was one of yours."

"One of ours?"

"Malcolm Bailey, sir. He was an ex-Metropolitan policeman. We thought there might be—well—ramifications."

"Ramifications? Was he Special Branch or what?"

"No, sir." Inspector York wished the Chief Constable was there to do his own dirty work. "His last job before retirement was court usher at Ealing actually. Since then he's had fifteen years with the Corps of Commissionaires in the West End. He was a Londoner, you see. Nothing to do with Bridchurch at all."

But Dover's butterfly mind had already moved on to weightier problems. The murder of obscure superannuated coppers could wait. "Here," he said, trying to disappear into the depths of his overcoat, "where've you set up the Murder Headquarters? I'm getting bloody frozen out here. Got us a nice cosy pub, have you?"

To date, unfortunately, there were no pubs on the Willow Hill Farm Estate. Nor were there any shops, cinemas, or other amenities.

"We were going to use a caravan, sir, but it hasn't arrived yet. I've been trying to chase it up but—"

But Dover was already stumping back to the comparative warmth and shelter of the police car. After a moment's hesitation MacGregor and Inspector York followed him.

Once they were all in the car, MacGregor took charge of things since Dover appeared to have lost all interest and was sitting slumped in a corner with his bowler hat pulled well down over his eyes. If it hadn't been completely unthinkable, Inspector York might have been tempted to conclude that old Mastermind was having a bit of a snooze.

"If Bailey was a Londoner," said MacGregor, resting his notebook awkwardly on his knees, "what was he doing down here?"

"He'd come for a few days' holiday with his daughter. He only arrived yesterday."

"That's the daughter who's married to the milkman who found the body?"

"Yes. They're named Muldoon. Apparently, last night, the dead man decided to go out for a drink. Like I said, there aren't any pubs on the Estate, so he had to catch a bus out there on the main road and go into Bridchurch."

"The Muldoons didn't go with him?"

"No. They don't go out much at night in the middle of the week because of him having to be up so early in the morning."

MacGregor pondered. "The Muldoons didn't raise the alarm when Bailey failed to return home at a reasonable hour?"

"They didn't know. It's this milk business again. Both Muldoon and his wife go to bed early, about half-past nine, they say. Last night they simply gave Bailey a key and told him to let himself in when he got back. They'd no idea, they claim, that he wasn't fast asleep in the spare room until Muldoon himself practically fell over the dead body on the pedestrian crossing."

Dover, roused by a crick in the back of his neck, joined in the conversation. "Damned fool place to stick a zebra crossing," he grumbled, massaging the offending spot. "Right out here in the back of beyond."

Inspector York risked a placatory smile. "It's supposed to be a mistake on the part of the Highways Department, sir. It should have been erected on another housing development on the other side of town."

"'Strewth!" said Dover and surrendered himself once more to torpidity.

Inspector York, a novice at Dover-watching, waited to see if any more pearls of wisdom were going to drop from beneath that moth-eaten little black mustache, but luckily MacGregor knew a snore when he heard one.

"What about the medical evidence? Have we got a time of death yet?"

Inspector York dragged his eyes away. "Er—oh, yes, sorry, Sergeant! Time of death? About eleven last night. That fits with the supposition that Bailey would be on the last bus from Bridchurch which would drop him out there on the main road just before eleven. He wouldn't hang about on such a cold night and I reckon he simply walked from the bus stop to where he was found and was killed there. He wasn't robbed, by the way."

"And the cause of death?"

"Head bashed in with a blunt instrument. However"— Inspector York leaned forward so as to deliver his *bonne bouche* with maximum effect—"before that he'd been knocked down by a car. The doctor's absolutely sure about it. Bailey was severely bruised all down the left side, though it's unlikely the car was damaged. Still, you see what it means, Sergeant?"

"Oh, I think so," said MacGregor with a patronizing smile, the local bobby not having yet been born who

could catch him napping. "It means that Bailey was probably knocked down by a car which was coming *from* the
housing estate." He flapped a languid hand. "If Bailey got
off the bus at that stop, he'd walk down there and cross
this road here at the crossing with his left-hand side
towards the housing estate. Interesting."

Inspector York suppressed an unworthy longing to sink
his fist up to the wrist in a certain smug young face, then
reminded himself that it was his job to be helpful. He got
a couple of sheets of paper out of his pocket. "Luckily," he
said, "there aren't many people on the estate who can
afford to run a car these days. It takes some of 'em all they
can manage to pay the bus fares. Anyhow"—he passed one
sheet of paper over—"there's a list of those who have got
cars. And here"—he held out the second sheet—"is a real
bonus!"

"You don't say!"

Inspector York gritted his teeth. Much more of this and
he'd leave the pair of 'em to stew in their own juice! "It's
the name and address of an old lady who may narrow the
field down even further. My lads had a chat with her earlier on and she seems bright enough. However, she's no
chicken, so you'll have to use your own judgment."

"Your lads seem to have been very busy," said MacGregor as he accepted the second sheet.

Inspector York let some of the bitterness show through.
"My lads," he muttered angrily, "could have had this case
tied up a couple of hours ago if they hadn't been told to
hang back and wait for you lot."

Mrs. Alice Golightly was 84 years old and still fighting
back in spite of the fact that she had been sentenced to vir-
tual solitary confinement by a caring community. The sheltered housing, into which she had been moved, was miles
away from all her friends and relations and consisted of a

drab row of two-roomed units built halfway up a steepish hill and fronting onto a block of communal garages.

"Bloody motor cars!" quavered Mrs. Golightly. "I'd ban 'em if I was prime minister, straight I would." She leaned across and gave Dover a poke in the paunch to gain his attention. "Nasty stinking things! They're more bloomin' bother than they're worth."

MacGregor smiled a kindly smile.

Mrs. Golightly leered back. It had been a long time since she'd had two fine chaps like this hanging on her every word. "There's that young punk up at the back," she went on. "You know—What's-his-name." She rummaged around in her memory. "Miller—that's him! Woke me up at ten past seven this morning trying to start his car—grind, grind, grind! Well, that meant I had to go to the toilet, didn't it? I'd hardly got sat down when—damn me!—he finally gets it going and all these stinking, smelly petrol fumes come pouring in through the bathroom window where there's gaps you could drive a corporation bus through. It's a public scandal! There isn't a bloody window in this whole bloody row that fits proper."

Dover roused himself to recall his hostess to a sense of what was fitting and proper. "Don't you," he bellowed at her, "usually have a cup of coffee about this time, missus? And a butt and a few biscuits?"

Mrs. Golightly was not amused and MacGregor rushed in before she could start expressing her opinion of those who attempted to sponge on old-age pensioners. "Er—does this Mr. Miller often wake you up starting his car?"

"He'd better not! Next time I'll have the law on him. Bloody motor cars!" She looked up. "I remember when it was all horses," she boasted. "Not but what they hadn't got some disgusting habits, but at least they didn't go messing your telly up!"

"Ah," said MacGregor with heaven-sent inspiration, "your television, Mrs. Golightly! Is that how you know when the cars use the garages opposite?"

Mrs. Golightly nodded grimly. "They break my picture up something cruel," she grumbled. "Every last one of 'em! And don't talk to me about suppressers! They've all had 'em fitted and it doesn't make a ha'porth of difference. I've had them Post Office engineers round here," she went on savagely. "Endless. Nothing but kids, most of 'em, and about as much use as my old boot. I have to keep a bloody record for 'em now, you know." She snatched a small writing pad off the table and waved it contemptuously. "Like I told her from the Welfare—it's coming to something when a lady's word isn't good enough!"

MacGregor tried to unravel things, just in case Dover was still listening. "You keep a note of every time there's interference with your television picture," he said, "and that means every time a car enters or leaves those garages opposite."

Mrs. Golightly's sniff acknowledged that this was so.

"And you watch television all evening?"

"I watch it all day," came the forthright answer. "And so will you when you're my age, sonny! I'd have it on now if you lot weren't here putting me through the third degree."

"And last night?"

"None of them cars went in or out after six o'clock. Well, they never do on a Thursday, do they?"

"Don't they?"

"Everybody's skint on a Thursday." Mrs. Golightly appreciated a bit of company but you could have too much of a good thing. "Friday's payday. Nobody's got any money left to go gallivanting on a Thursday. I should have thought even you'd know that."

Dover heaved himself to his feet. Although, to the untutored eye, his role in the interview may have appeared completely passive, some information had evidently filtered through. "I'll just go and have a look at that toilet," he said.

MacGregor tried to pass the time in small talk, but Mrs. Golightly's aged ears didn't miss a thing. Eventually she raised her voice over the sound of rushing water. "That fellow who's been killed—"

"Malcolm Bailey?" asked MacGregor.

"I saw him when he arrived," said Mrs. Golightly. "A fine figure of a man." She paused spitefully to underline her point. "What I call a *real* policeman!"

So, if old Mrs. Golightly's evidence was to be believed, none of the cars habitually kept in the block of garages could have been involved in the murder.

"And that, actually, sir, leaves us with only three suspects." MacGregor gazed unhappily around at the wilderness of builders' rubbish and half-finished houses. "The people who own cars but who leave them parked out on the road. Always assuming, of course, that Bailey was killed by whoever knocked him down. I wonder what the motive was. It can't be anything to do with his past life, surely? He's been retired for ages and he doesn't seem to have been exactly a ball of fire when he was in the Force. On the other hand, he's hardly been down here long enough to make enemies. Less than twenty-four hours and this was his first visit." MacGregor sighed. "I think we'll have to have a good long look at this daughter and her husband."

Dover was not the man for idle speculation. "For God's sake, let's get out of this bloody wind!" he growled. "It's enough to freeze a brass monkey!"

MacGregor, being MacGregor, knew where he was going. "Azalea Crescent, sir," he said as he led the way into a slightly curving, potholed stretch of road. "Mr. Jarrow lives here. And that, I imagine, is his car." Ever mindful that Dover's eyesight was something less than keen, Mac-Gregor indicated an enormous black Humber parked by the curb and sparkling magnificently in the pale sunlight.

Sparkling?

"*Stop that!*" MacGregor leaped forward and screamed like a banshee.

The man with the soft duster jumped back as though stung. "Eh?"

"You're destroying evidence!"

"What?"

"Didn't the police tell you we might want to examine that car?"

The unfortunate perfectionist shook his head. "A couple of 'em had a good look at it earlier on," he said lamely.

"Didn't they tell you not to touch it?"

Bill Jarrow gesticulated feebly with his duster. "I was just passing the time, like."

It was Dover—he of the aching feet and the rumbling stomach—who moved the proceedings indoors. Bill Jarrow put his duster away and called to his wife to put the coffee on. He thus insured that, unless the evidence was *very* strong to the contrary, he'd be able to get away with murder where Dover was concerned. He further endeared himself by keeping his answers short and to the point, seemingly knowing by instinct that Dover valued brevity well above truthfulness.

Mr. Jarrow proved to be a taxi driver and the car he had been polishing belonged to the company for whom he worked. Most weekday evenings, when business was slack, he was allowed to bring the car home with him and answer any calls from his house. "It saves 'em keeping the office open," he explained.

"Did you get called out last night?"

"No. Me and the missus sat watching telly till it was time for bed."

"So your wife is the only witness?"

Bill Jarrow didn't seem unduly perturbed that his alibi was being questioned. "You can check the mileage, if you like. They'll have a note at the office of what it was yesterday evening when I left. You can soon see if it doesn't tally."

Since Dover had got his National Health Service dentures inextricably sunk in Mrs. Jarrow's homemade treacle cake, MacGregor carried on with the questioning. "There's no meter on the taxi?"

"Not this one. We use this one for funerals, you see," said Mr. Jarrow, passing Dover's cup through the kitchen hatch for a refill. "Folk don't like to see a meter clicking away when they're following their loved ones to the crematorium."

MacGregor examined Bill Jarrow thoughtfully. "Anything to stop you getting a call, doing the job, altering the mileage reading, and pocketing the fare?" he asked pleasantly.

For the first time Mr. Jarrow's occupational antipathy to the police showed through. "Trust you bloody cops!" he said disgustedly. "Look, mate, I've been a taxi driver for twenty years. I wouldn't last five minutes if I started pulling tricks like that. What do you think my boss is, stupid or something? Petrol consumption alone'd be a dead giveaway. And suppose I had a smashup? Or somebody saw me?"

Bill Jarrow continued to wax indignant for some time but, eventually, he recovered his equilibrium sufficiently to direct MacGregor to Japonica Mount, their next port of call. It was so close at hand that even Dover didn't think it was worth demanding a police car.

"That chap might have run us there in his taxi," Dover observed sourly as he and MacGregor proceeded slowly on their way back past Mrs. Golightly's humble abode, "if you hadn't been so bloody rude to him. What got into you? Any fool could see he's too thick to be anything but honest."

MacGregor didn't agree. "You don't need much intelligence, sir, to alter a mileage reading. And he was giving that car a thorough cleaning. He could have been removing traces of incriminating evidence."

"Stuff!" puffed Dover, already finding the going hard. "Besides, where's the motive? He'd never even met What's-his-name."

"Bailey, sir." MacGregor was well used to Dover's inability to remember any name (including probably his own) for more than five minutes. "Besides, I don't think we're looking for that kind of motive."

"Oh, don't you?" sneered Dover in a poor imitation of MacGregor's refined accent. "Well, what kind of motive are we looking for, Smartie-boots?"

"I think the murder is tied up with the car accident, sir."

Dover paused to contemplate the young mountain which had suddenly loomed up in front of them. 'Strewth, if he'd realized that the "couple of hundred yards" was going to be straight up . . . "Of course it's tied up with the car accident," he growled, once he'd got his breath back. "The killer runs Whatd'yecall'im down and immobilizes him, and then gets out to finish him off with a tire lever or something. Gangsters in America are doing it all the time."

"It'll be just by that small red car, sir," said MacGregor, cringing away as Dover grabbed his arm and hung on. As a 240-pound weakling, the Chief Inspector wasn't fussy about who shared the burden. "I was thinking of a slight variation, actually," MacGregor went on, failing to appreciate that aching feet were now looming larger in Dover's mind than violent death. "I was wondering if the murder had to be committed *because* of the accident. That would fit Jarrow, you see. Suppose he had been doing a job without his employer's knowledge, and during the course of it accidentally knocks Mr. Bailey down. Well, to report the accident in the normal way would expose what he'd been doing and he'd get the sack. So"—even MacGregor was beginning to sound unconvinced—"he finishes Bailey off. I admit it sounds a bit thin, sir, but"—MacGregor cheered up—"plenty of murders have been done for less."

"This it?"

They had climbed almost to the top of the steep incline that was Japonica Mount and were now level with the small red car. According to its number plate it was fourteen years old and it was obvious why its owner wasn't paying out good money to rent a garage for it.

Dover turned thankfully through the little wrought-iron gate and waddled up the path. The curtains in the front room had twitched but he stuck his finger in the bell-push and rested his weight on it.

A woman opened the door and Dover was halfway inside before he discovered, to his undisguised chagrin, that it was the wrong house.

"No," said the woman, "I'm Mrs. Jedryschowski. The Millers live the next house down." She moved forward fractionally and pointed.

Dover's fury mounted as he realized that the Miller house was one they had already passed.

"You'll not find her there, of course," said Mrs. Jedryschowski, "but he's in. The police turned him back when he was going to work."

Dover wasn't prepared to let the matter rest there. It was MacGregor's fault for dragging him to the wrong address, of course, but this Mrs. Whatever-her-name-was must take some of the blame. "That his car?" he demanded, with menace.

"Mr. Miller's?" Mrs. Jedryschowski eyed Dover with some suspicion. "Yes, it's his car."

"Then why is it parked outside your house?"

Not for the first time MacGregor marveled at Dover's unerring ability to grasp at the inessential.

It was all one to Mrs. Jedryschowski, of course. "You might well ask," she said, leaning forward to stare at the vehicle in question. "He always leaves it there. We have spoken to him about it but it made no difference. He says it's something to do with saving his battery."

MacGregor, of course, understood perfectly. "Oh, you mean he starts it by letting it run down the hill."

Mrs. Jedryschowski, something of an ignoramus where the internal combustion engine was concerned, nodded. "Something like that. If he leaves it outside his own front door, he doesn't get a long enough run or something." She watched her visitors go back halfway down the path before closing the door on them.

Henry Miller was a livelier character than his next-door neighbor, though not by much. He welcomed Dover and MacGregor into a house that was clearly lacking a woman's touch. Dover realized there was a fat chance of being offered any decent light refreshments here. He shoved a bundle of old socks out of the most comfortable-looking armchair and flopped down. This was going to be a bloody short interview.

Mr. Miller cleared a couple of dirty plates off another chair for MacGregor. "Bit of a mess," he mumbled in apology. "What with the wife being away—"

"Not ill, I hope?" asked MacGregor politely as he got his notebook out.

"Not exactly." Mr. Miller perched himself on the arm of the settee and looked hunted. Like everybody else on the housing estate, he knew all about the murder. He didn't, however, know Mr. Bailey or his daughter and her husband. "People keep themselves to themselves round here," he explained. "We don't want to impose. And this time of year you don't want to leave your own fireside, do you?"

Mr. Miller paused in the hope that somebody else might like to say something, but they didn't. "I work as a groundsman," he volunteered. "At Bridchurch Central Junior School. The police stopped me when I was driving off to work this morning and said I was to stay at home till somebody came and took a statement off me or something. They had a look at my car, too."

There was another pause. Mr. Miller mopped his brow. This time, however, MacGregor took pity on him and tossed a question.

Mr. Miller was grateful but unhelpful. "No, I didn't. I got back from work about four o'clock and I didn't leave the house again till this morning."

Even MacGregor was obliged to swallow a yawn. Dover, of course, wasn't even pretending to listen and was now resting his eyes against the light.

"You're alone in the house?"

Mr. Miller blinked. "Yes. With the wife being away like."

MacGregor looked at the layer of burnt crumbs which covered one corner of the table. "Has she been away long, sir?"

Mr. Miller sighed. "Only three days. I'm afraid I've been letting the housework slip a bit."

Having been given MacGregor's solemn word that the home of the last car owner could be reached in three minutes and that it was downhill all the way, Dover reluctantly consented to walk.

Since it really was downhill, the Great Detective had breath to spare for an in-depth discussion of the case so far. "That milksop?" he questioned incredulously. "You must have lost your marbles! He couldn't say boo to a goose!"

"He hasn't got an alibi, sir."

"Innocent people never have alibis," retorted Dover, generously imparting the fruits of his many years of experience. "Besides, where's his motive? What's-his-name could hardly get *him* into trouble for driving his own blooming car."

"Miller might have come up against Bailey in a professional capacity, sir. Bailey might have nabbed him for something and this is a revenge killing."

"A revenge killing?" Dover's uninhibited hoot of mirth sent the seagulls winging up from a nearby field. "'Strewth, you've been at those detective-story books again! Revenge—on a clapped-out copper from Ealing who's been retired for twenty years?" Dover, seeing that MacGregor was about to correct his figures, rushed raucously on. "That Miller pouf would still have been in his cradle when Who's-your-father was pounding the beat."

MacGregor quietly resolved to check whether Miller had a police record and if there was any possible earlier connection between him and the deceased. "Ah, here we are, sir."

They had just turned into Viburnam Avenue and the car this time was a huge and very ancient Ford, liberally decorated with anarchistic slogans, Mickey Mouse stickers, pictures of nude ladies, and rust. Inside the appropriate house they found the owner of this vehicle—Lionel Hutchinson. He was a moronic-looking, slack-mouthed teenager, the epitome of a petty, unsuccessful crook. Lionel's mother, having let Dover and MacGregor into the house while her ewe-lamb remained lolling full-length on the sofa, returned wearily to her ironing.

Young Lionel was uncooperative. "You must be joking!" He removed neither his eyes from his comic book nor the cigarette from his mouth. "Drive that jalopy out there? Watcher trying to do—trap me?"

"I was merely asking if you went out in it last night," said MacGregor.

"Not last night and not for months!" said Lionel. "Because why? Because it hasn't passed its M.O.T. test, it isn't licensed, and it's not insured. Damn, I should have thought even you punks knew it was a criminal offense to take a car like that on the bleeding road. Besides"—he chucked his cigarette stub vaguely in the direction of the fireplace and reached for the packet on the floor at his side—"I can't afford the petrol."

Mrs. Hutchinson spoke up. "He doesn't get hardly anything from Social Security."

Dover looked hopefully at the packet of cigarettes, but it was not handed round. That was the trouble with these working-class crimes—no bloody perks! Dover vented his disappointment on Lionel. "You took that car out last night, didn't you?"

Lionel turned over the page. "Negative, Fatso!"

"Just because it wasn't taxed and insured?" sneered Dover. "Try pulling the other one!"

Mrs. Hutchinson came galloping to the rescue again. "He's got to watch his step," she explained. "It's prison next time they catch him."

Lionel raised himself up and glared at his mother with less than filial affection.

Dover had another spot. "You took that car out last night and—"

"Stuff yourself!"

"—ran Bailey down because he was a copper and then —"

"Aw, get knotted!"

"—got out and finished him off as he lay there help-less."

Lionel Hutchinson struggled into a sitting position. "Without nicking his wallet?" Almost as exhausted by the effort as Dover would have been, he sank back. "I was home all evening. Ask my mum!"

Once they were safely outside, Dover waxed bolder. "I'll get that little bleeder!" he promised, looking fierce.

MacGregor took a more moderate line. "I doubt if he'd have the guts to kill a grown man, sir. Mugging old ladies for their pension books is about his limit."

"There's probably a gang of 'em," grunted Dover. He was bored, hungry, thirsty, and suffering from nicotine starvation.

"Perhaps forensic will turn up something on the murder weapon," said MacGregor hopefully. "And I think we must examine these cars again, too. I can't really believe that the car that knocked Bailey down would be completely unmarked."

They were walking slowly back up the hill and Dover was in no condition to contradict everything MacGregor said just for the hell of it.

"Oh, look, sir!" MacGregor pointed. "There's the caravan at last. Good! Now at least we'll have somewhere we can settle down to work in."

Dover shied like a nervous horse at the mere mention of work. "I want my lunch! I'm starving."

"Oh, there'll be coffee and sandwiches in the caravan for sure, sir."

By some miracle Dover found the puff to tell MacGregor what he could do with his coffee and sandwiches, interrupting his tirade only to stick his tongue out at old Mrs. Golightly who was peeping out from behind her curtains.

MacGregor hastened to make amends by giving her a cheery smile and raising his hat. "Poor old thing," he said when he could get a word in. "You'd think they could do something better for them than this, wouldn't you, sir? Sticking them out here miles away from anywhere and right on top of those noisy garages, to say nothing of having petrol fumes seeping in through your bathroom window. Good God!"

Afterward both MacGregor and Dover claimed to have spotted it first but, since Dover had fewer inhibitions about bawling his head off on the public highway, he tended to hog the glory at the time.

He stopped dead in his tracks. "But there shouldn't have been any petrol fumes!"

By great good fortune there they were, standing right on the spot. Branching off on the left as they went up the hill was the row of houses for the old-age pensioners. And running up even higher beyond them was Japonica Mount. Miller's small red car was clearly visible, not more than a couple of hundred feet away, still outside Mrs. Jedryschowski's house and still with its nose pointing down the hill.

Dover's brain nearly blew a gasket as he struggled to work it out. "How far," he panted, "on a cold morning would you have to let that car roll down the hill before you could start it?"

MacGregor was amazed at Dover's grasp of the technical problem involved. "Oh, right to the bottom, I imagine, sir. Certainly well past Mrs. Golightly's bathroom window."

"We've got him!" said Dover, and rested his case.

MacGregor felt they needed a little more than that.

"Miller could have started his car on the starter this morning for some reason or other, sir."

"Why the hell should he? And even if he did, the fumes still wouldn't get into that old biddy's bog, would they?"

"Not if the car was parked outside Mrs. Jedryschowski's house where it is now, sir," agreed MacGregor. "On the other hand"—his eyes narrowed as he took in the topography of the area—"if he started the car on the starter outside his own house, old Mrs. Golightly would certainly have got the full benefit of both the noise and the smoke. He'd be hardly any distance away as the crow flies."

Dover had had his fill of the Willow Hill Farm Housing Estate. "Come on," he said with unwonted enthusiasm, "let's go get him!"

MacGregor was appalled. "But there could be dozens of perfectly innocent explanations, sir," he bleated anxiously. "I think it would be a big mistake for us to go off half-cocked like this before we've—"

"You speak for yourself, laddie!" snorted Dover, already charging up the hill like a two-year-old tortoise. "Me, I've never gone off half-cocked at anything in my whole bloody life!"

It was fortunate for the Cause of Justice that Henry Miller was one of Nature's losers.

"I knew I'd never get away with it," he said dejectedly as Dover lay panting like a stranded whale in one of the armchairs and MacGregor, getting his notebook out, issued the formal caution. "Oh, I don't mind making a statement. Why not?"

"Keep it short," advised Dover, cursing himself for not having had his lunch first. He accepted a cigarette from MacGregor, unaware that it was offered with the sole aim of stopping his mouth up.

But Miller had never been much of a talker in any case.

"My wife left me a couple of days ago," he mumbled. "Just went. Late last night I got to wondering if she'd gone to stay with her sister. I thought I'd drive over and see."

"What time did you leave?"

Miller shrugged. "Latish."

"How did you start your car?"

"Like I always do—I let it roll down the hill."

"And you headed for the main road?"

"That's right. I wasn't going fast or anything. Then, just by the zebra crossing, he stepped out right in front of me and—bang!—I hit him. Not hard. I wasn't doing more than twenty. I stopped and got out. Well, he just lay there in the road, cursing me up hill and down dale. A right mouthful. Said I knocked him down deliberate on a pedestrian crossing and he'd have the Law on me.

"Said he'd charge me with dangerous driving and God knows what. I tried to calm him down a bit and ask if he was hurt, but he just kept on shouting. Said he was an ex-policeman and that he'd see me behind bars if it was the last thing he did. Well, he would have, wouldn't he? My word against his? I wouldn't have stood a chance. So I killed him."

"Just like that?" Dover didn't like to hear of policemen being disposed of so casually.

"I couldn't afford to be found guilty, you see," said Miller drearily. "Not on any charge. I've been in trouble before, you see."

"I'm not surprised," sniffed Dover. "Was it Bailey who nabbed you?"

"Oh, no, nothing like that. I didn't know Mr. Bailey from Adam."

"Then why kill him, for God's sake?"

Miller sighed heavily. "It was when I was still up north. I"—he cleared his throat and avoided looking at either of his two inquisitors—"well, it was sort of to do with sex."

"Oh, yes?" said Dover, on whom the mouth-stopping cigarette was not working too well.

Miller moistened his lips. "Children, actually," he muttered. "I got six months. But"—he raised his head with a faint show of defiance—"that was four years ago and I haven't been in trouble since. I pulled myself together, see? I moved down here and got myself a good job and got married and everything."

MacGregor understood. "You were afraid that if you were convicted on this motoring charge, your previous record would come out in open court?"

"They say they don't punish you twice for the same offense, but they do. I'd have lost my job straight off. I work at a school, you see. Kids everywhere. And then there's the wife. She'd have never come back if she knew I'd been in the nick for molesting kids. And then there's the neighbors." He appealed to the more sympathetic face confronting him. "You can see how I was fixed, can't you? I couldn't just do nothing and let him ruin my life. I didn't want to kill him, but he give me no choice. I hit him with the wheel brace."

But Dover's heart was not made of stone. He saw how distressed Miller was and was ready with solace. He addressed MacGregor. "Why don't you go and make us all a nice cup of tea, laddie?"

Miller raised his head. "There's a bottle of whiskey in the sideboard," he said shyly.

Dover beamed. "Even better! Where do you keep your glasses?"

Miller's statement was completed in an increasingly convivial atmosphere and he had to be asked several times about the parking of his car after the murder.

"Oh, that," he said. "Well, I forgot all about going after

the missus and I come rushing back here. All I wanted was to get out of sight as quick as possible. That's why I left the car right outside instead of driving it to the top of the hill and turning it around ready for the morning like I usually do."

"So, when you left for work today, you had to start the car on the starter?" MacGregor, of course, didn't drink on duty and was as sober as a judge.

"That's right. I had the devil of a job with it. It really needs a new battery but, what with one thing and another . . . Anyhow, I won't have to bother about that now, will I?"

"What did you do with the murder weapon?"

"It's under the coal in the shed. I was going to chuck it in the canal when things quietened down. Here"—for the first time Miller showed a flicker of curiosity—"how did you get on to me?"

"It was the break in the pattern, laddie!" said Dover, feeling he owed his host something for the whiskey. "If you'd turned your car and parked it like you always did outside the Jedryschowskis', you'd have got away with it."

MacGregor gawped. How on earth had the old fool managed to hang on to a name like Jedryschowski, for heaven's sake?

"You got cloth ears or something, laddie?"

MacGregor abandoned his disloyal speculations. "Sir?"

"I said, go and get somebody to take him away."

MacGregor hesitated. Leave Dover alone with a self-confessed murderer? "Will you be all right, sir?"

Dover winked wickedly and reached for the whiskey bottle. "Oh, I'll be fine, Sergeant!" he said. "Just fine now!"

—1978

Dover and the Smallest Room

"Grut," she said, adding in case there might be any doubt about it, "*Miss* Grut."

She waited, thin-mouthed and disapproving, while Detective Sergeant MacGregor carefully wrote it down in his notebook.

"And you were the one who found the deceased, Miss Grut?"

"I was."

"And you are the late Mr. Zandarowski's—er—house-keeper?"

"In a way."

Miss Grut, perched in deliberate martyrdom on a hard wooden stool, faced the two detectives from Scotland Yard with her chin up and her shoulders squared. Unable to overcome her life-long habit of never yielding an inch to any man, she was turning out to be a rather difficult witness. Not that her uncooperativeness was bothering the senior and fatter of the two policemen overmuch. Introduced at the beginning of the interview as Detective Chief Inspector Dover, he had unerringly spotted the most comfortable chair in the room and collapsed thankfully into it. Now, with paunch out and eyes closed, he was sitting well back, having unselfishly delegated all responsibility for the initial stages of the investigation to his young, handsome, and care-worn assistant.

"I'm part owner of this house," explained Miss Grut reluctantly. "My father left it jointly to my sister and myself. When she died, her son inherited her share."

"That's the late Mr. Zandarowski?" queried Sergeant MacGregor, who was a bit of a fanatic about getting the facts straight.

"My sister married a Pole, for all the good it did her. Still"—Miss Grut stiffened her backbone still further—"I did keep house for my nephew though our living quarters are entirely separate and in no way can it be said that we shared anything other than a common roof."

"Oh, quite!" agreed Sergeant MacGregor encouragingly. "Now, if you could tell us exactly what happened . . ."

Miss Grut tossed her head. "There's nothing much to tell. I came into the studio here at eight o'clock this morning to see why he hadn't come in to his breakfast and there he was." She indicated the chalked outline on the bare boards of the studio floor. "Dead as mutton with his shirt all covered with blood and that dratted gun tossed over there in the corner."

MacGregor was trained to pick up even the faintest nuances. "You'd seen the gun before?"

"Of course. They'd lent it to him—hadn't they?—to do that book jacket. And some real ammunition. Of all the stupid things to do! I knew no good would come of it." She saw that MacGregor was looking a little lost. "My nephew was a commercial artist. Freelance."

"Ah!" MacGregor did honestly feel he was beginning to get the hang of things. Speaking for himself, of course. How much was actually penetrating the thick skull and wax-filled ears of his somnolent superior was anybody's guess. "And how long had Mr. Zandarowski been in possession of this gun?"

"Since the day before yesterday. Saturday. He brought it back from London with him. As pleased as Punch that he'd got it in time for the party. Like a child with a new toy. Not," she added sourly, "that he was particularly child-like in any other respect. Far from it. That was his Polish blood, of course. He didn't get that sort of disgusting behavior from the Gruts."

MacGregor refrained for the moment from exploring this unsavory-sounding avenue. "You mentioned a party?"

"Sunday lunchtime," said Miss Grut with a shudder of distaste. "Wine and cheese. I was here for the first ten minutes or so, handing the food round. Then I left them to it, before things degenerated into the usual drunken orgies."

"Have you any idea what time the guests left?"

"Oh, they'd all gone by two. There's a limit to how much cheap wine you can drink at a sitting. And as for that cheese—well, I wouldn't have given it house room. Nasty, smelly, foreign muck!"

MacGregor stared dejectedly at his notebook. "It doesn't sound like a very enjoyable affair."

"It wasn't meant to be," said Miss Grunt tartly. "He was just paying back local hospitality as cheaply as possible. Catch him wasting his money on old bores like Dr. Horncastle."

"Mr. Zandarowski wasn't married?"

"Only in the eyes of God. Divorced. Years ago. She couldn't stand his lecherous habits any longer and ran off with a Canadian. I don't know if any good came of that, either, but I doubt it. Since then Peter's consoled himself with an endless succession of concubines—if you can call it a succession when he was carrying on with three or four of them at the same time. Filthy beast! Sex mad! No woman was safe within a mile of him."

MacGregor ignored all the rules about methodical progression in murder investigations and tried to take a short-cut. "Do you think that's why he was killed? By a jealous woman, perhaps?"

"Or a jealous husband," said Miss Grut, not without relish. "Carnality will be at the bottom of it somewhere. Why else should anybody shoot him down like a dog?"

"How about for the money?"

Both Miss Grut and MacGregor jumped. They had forgotten that there was a silent witness to their conversation—silent, that is, apart from the odd grunt that might have been a snore. Now, however, Chief Inspector Dover was apparently bursting into some semblance of life as he opened his eyes and actually spoke.

Miss Grut examined this marvel with justifiable caution. Of course, she'd been told that this was a high-ranking member of Scotland Yard's prestigious Murder Squad, but she hadn't believed it. Well, one only had to look at him! Fat, slovenly, pasty-faced—why, even his mustache was flaked with dandruff. And those clothes! Miss Grut squirmed. The least fastidious tramp would have jibbed at donning that filthy overcoat and that even filthier bowler hat. Oh, no, Miss Grut hadn't credited for one moment that this sullen, overweight, lethargic lump could possibly be a famous detective. Now, however, she wasn't quite so sure. Men were ever deceivers and maybe all this air of general stupidity and piggishness was just a clever camouflage, concealing the shrewd and penetrating brains underneath. Miss Grut decided to give Detective Chief Inspector Dover the benefit of the doubt.

"What money?"

Dover glared balefully. If there was one thing he couldn't stomach it was a woman who echoed his words like a bloody poll-parrot. "His money, of course!" He flapped a flabby hand to encompass the spacious and well-appointed studio in which they were sitting. "All this lot. Who stands to get it now that What's-his-name's kicked the bucket?"

For the first time in her life Miss Grut envisaged the possibility of defeat in the battle of the sexes. "Well, I suppose I do," she admitted uneasily. "As next of kin. He never made a will though I was always telling him he ought to . . ." Her voice trailed off.

Dover sank back in his chair, losing interest now that he'd solved the entire case with one cunningly searching question. He was a passionate believer in delegation and was more than content to leave the final dotting of the i's and the crossing of the t's to his long-suffering sergeant.

MacGregor in the meantime was doing all he could to avoid catching Miss Grut's bewildered eye. God knows, after all these years, he should have grown hardened to the—for want of a better word—peculiarities of his lord and master, but he hadn't. Dover's loutish behavior was still the source of the most excruciating embarrassment.

MacGregor cleared his throat. "Er—perhaps you could give me the names of the people who were at Mr. Zandarowski's party, Miss Grut," he said, clutching desperately at the first thing that came into his mind.

Miss Grut had her own theories about who had murdered her nephew. "That's where you'll find the guilty party!" she said, nodding her head approvingly. "Apart from anything else, they're the only ones who would know he'd got that gun and the ammunition."

MacGregor waited patiently with his pencil poised. He did wish that, just occasionally, members of the general public would refrain from trying to do his job for him.

Miss Grut, preferring not to notice that Dover had hooked a chair up and was now thankfully depositing his filthy boots on it, began to tick off the prime suspects on her fingers. "There was old Dr. Horncastle, but you needn't bother about him. He might feel like avenging his daughter's honor but his arthritis wouldn't let him. He wouldn't be able to pick that gun up, never mind fire it. His daughter was at the party, too. Perlita Horncastle. Peter used to be very friendly with her at one time. Then there was Betsy Norman. She's divorced, and one can well see why."

"Is she another of your nephew's friends?"

Miss Grut nodded grimly. "I told you—anything in skirts. Or trousers, as they mostly are these days."

"Anybody else?"

"Lady Tisdale. Known locally as the Merry Widow and about as much of a lady as my old boot. And the same goes for Joan Wisbey. She's single but still hoping. Then there was Rodney Chesshire and his wife. Her name's Muriel but she likes to be called Spooky—so you can tell what sort *she* is. Have you got all that down?"

MacGregor repressed a little sigh and nodded.

"Mrs. Barclay-Rhys, but without Mr. Barclay-Rhys. He was invited but couldn't come—whatever that may mean. Oh, and there was young Fabian Eastholm. He was there, too. That's the lot."

MacGregor ran his eye down the list of names. "Only three men," he commented.

"If you count young Fabian," agreed Miss Grut, "but he's only sixteen. I should cross him off, if I were you, because he couldn't have driven the car."

MacGregor's head came up. "What car?"

"The murderer's car."

"The murderer's car!" repeated MacGregor helplessly,

thankful for once that Dover was taking no part in the proceedings.

"It must have been," said Miss Grut. "It drove up here
at about half-past eight last night. Whoever it was didn't
stay more than ten minutes before driving off again. That's
more than long enough to shoot Peter dead and wipe your
fingerprints off everything."

"You mean you actually heard the shot?" demanded
MacGregor furiously, sheer exasperation overcoming his
natural courtesy. "Why in God's name didn't you say so
before?"

"No, I did not hear the shot!" snapped Miss Grut. "And
I'd be grateful if you'd kindly watch your language, young
man. This is, after all, a house of mourning. Now, if you'll
just listen for a minute, I'll explain. Last night a car drove
up the lane. The lane's a dead end and this is the only
house in it, so the car must have been coming here. I did-
n't hear the shot because I was watching one of those Wild
Western films on the telly and it was all shooting."

"Just a minute!" MacGregor had already been given a
good idea of the layout of the house and the desire to put
Miss Know-it-all Grut in the wrong sharpened his wits no
end. "Your sitting room is right at the back of the house. If
you were too far away to hear a revolver fired here in the
studio, how is it that you were able to hear a car driving up
in the first place?"

"I didn't say I heard it!" retorted Miss Grut.

"You saw it?"

"It made my television picture break up. The car engine
wasn't properly suppressed or whatever they call it. That's
against the law, of course, but for all the notice you policemen take . . . I was just sitting there watching this film
when, all of a sudden, the entire screen broke up into a

confusion of lines and squiggles and I don't know what. I looked at the clock to see what time it was because I should need that to put in my complaint. I was going to ask my nephew later who his visitor was so that I could report them to the Post Office or the B.B.C. or whoever it is. Well, the car engine was switched off and my television picture returned to normal, only to break up all over again when the car drove away some ten minutes later. Right, I thought to myself. Enough's enough! I'm not paying out a small fortune for a TV license every year just to have all my entertainment ruined by some selfish individual who won't spend a few pennies getting his car fixed properly. I know my rights!"

"But even if you're right," said MacGregor a trifle wearily, "and it was the murderer's car, it doesn't help us much. There must be thousands of cars running around that aren't properly suppressed."

Miss Grut's look of triumph was quite sickening. "This car belongs to somebody who was at Peter's wine-and-cheese party," she said firmly, brooking neither interruption nor argument. "There was precisely the same effect on my television picture when they were all driving away on Sunday afternoon. Precisely the same. One of the cars which had been parked outside this house yesterday afternoon wasn't properly suppressed."

"But there could easily be two unsuppressed cars," MacGregor pointed out when he was finally allowed to get a word in.

Miss Grut clamped her lips in an unyielding line and shook her head. "No. The pattern of the breakup was exactly the same in both cases. I was watching the cricket on Sunday afternoon," she added, as though that clinched matters. "So there you are! Find out which of my nephew's party guests is driving an unsuppressed car, and you've found your murderer. Of course, if that is a task beyond the capabilities of Scotland Yard I've no doubt I could track down the offending vehicle myself and thus do all your job for you."

MacGregor was beginning to feel that Miss Grut had got him pinned on the ropes, but help was at hand from a most unexpected quarter. Dover again bestirred himself. Apparently much refreshed and rested, he gazed almost benignly at the two protagonists. Miss Grut was the recipient of a most ingratiating leer as Dover made his most significant contribution to the investigation so far.

"How about a nice cup of coffee, eh?"

Miss Grut might have been expected to put up a stouter fight in the face of such blatant male piggery, but for some inexplicable reason she capitulated just like any ordinary, downtrodden, unemancipated female. "I'll go and get some," she said feebly.

"A few sandwiches wouldn't come amiss," Dover called after her. "And a bit of cake! We had an early start, you know." He turned his attention to MacGregor. "If you don't ask, you don't get," he explained with a grin.

"Really, sir."

Dover's grin widened. "She certainly made mincemeat out of you, laddie!"

"Silly old cow!" muttered MacGregor, and then felt ashamed of himself for descending to a level he had thought hitherto as fitting only for the Dovers of this world.

Dover surrendered himself to an enormous yawn. "It's not a bad theory," he said as his dentures clicked back into place.

"But not one, I'm afraid, sir, that would hold water for a minute."

"Says who?"

MacGregor tried not to sound too patronizing. After all, however low an opinion he held of Miss Grut as a detective, it was considerably higher than the one he held of

Dover in the same role. "Well, take the gun, sir. The guests at the wine-and-cheese party may have been the only ones to know there was a gun and live ammunition here in the studio, but what's to stop the murderer being somebody else entirely who just used the gun to shoot Peter Zandarowski because it was to hand?"

Dover scratched his head. "Sort of unpremeditated?"

"Perhaps. Or the murderer may have brought his own weapon with him, seen the gun, and realized it was a better bet."

"Hm," grunted Dover, who found all this theorizing very taxing on the brain.

"And there is, of course, sir, absolutely nothing to connect this car Miss Grut claims called here last night with the murder."

"Time's right," observed Dover. "According to what the police surgeon said."

MacGregor was surprised to find that Dover had actually been listening when the police surgeon made his report, but naturally he refrained from commenting on the point. "That was only a preliminary estimate, sir," he said. "The time of death could be considerably altered by the postmortem. You see, apart from the fact that Miss Grut might simply be lying, the only evidence for the existence of this car is the TV interference. Well, that could be caused by anything, couldn't it? Trouble at the transmitter or an airplane or a piece of faulty electrical equipment here in the house. I've known an electric razor to break up a television picture. There may well not have been any car at all, and certainly not one belonging to one of the guests at the wine-and-cheese party."

Dover, one ear cocked to the rumblings of his stomach, regarded his sergeant with loathing. Whatever MacGregor's opinion was of Dover, it was returned ten times and in spades. Self-opinionated little squirt! "It'll have to be checked," he warned.

"Oh, of course, sir!" MacGregor was nothing if not extremely conscientious. Well, in that unholy partnership it was as well that somebody was. "The whole story will have to be meticulously investigated."

Dover yawned again and scratched his stomach. "So you'd better get cracking."

"Sir?"

"I'll make your excuses to Miss What's-her-name," promised Dover happily, thus converting his mid-morning coffee break into quite a substantial meal as he munched greedily through MacGregor's share of the goodies.

Miss Grut herself didn't seem to have much of an appetite. They took their refreshments in the studio as Dover was not the man to indulge in unnecessary movement, so it may have been the presence of the chalked outline of her nephew's dead body that put Miss Grut off her food. On the other hand, it may simply have been the appalling spectacle of Dover with both feet in the feeding trough which turned her queasy.

However, all good things must come to an end—especially when they're being gulped down by one of Nature's gluttons—and it wasn't long before Dover was reduced to staring nostalgically at an array of empty plates and cups. He sighed deeply and turned to Miss Grut.

Miss Grut steeled herself to repulse the long-awaited assault on her innocence. She had now got Dover's measure. All this belching and lip-smacking, guzzling and gobbling—it was all part of an act designed to lull intended victims into a false sense of superiority. Well, Miss Grut had seen through it. Indeed, she was actually mildly contemptuous of the way Dover had been overplaying his hand during the coffee-and-cake episode. Now she was ready for anything.

Dover spoke—and the kid gloves came off with a vengeance. "You got a toilet down here, missis?"

Miss Grut was never the same woman again. In a stunned silence she conducted her unwanted guest to the downstairs loo and then returned to the studio. For the first time in her life she was unsure what to do next. Should she return to her own quarters at the back of the house? Phone for a solicitor? Or smash that damned coffeepot into smithereens on the floor?

It was some time before Dover emerged. "That's the bloody trouble with coffee," he observed chattily as he waddled back to his chair, "it goes right through you."

Miss Grut struggled to retain control over her shattered nerves. Dear heavens, she had thought her late nephew was the ne plus ultra of male chauvinism, but this nasty, unspeakable brute of a policeman . . . "Will you be needing me any longer?" she inquired distantly. "There are quite a lot of things that I ought to be . . ."

But Dover was in one of his gregarious moods and Miss Grut's company was marginally better than his own. "Artist, you said?" he queried conversationally while peering around to see if there were any cigarettes going begging.

"A commercial artist, yes."

"That's why he's got the walls of the bog out there all covered with picture postcards, is it?" asked Dover. "Sort of artistic?"

"Yes," said Miss Grut, who thought the décor of the downstairs lavatory little short of an abomination.

"Suppose it comes cheaper than wallpaper," mused Dover, sadly coming to the conclusion that Peter Zandarowski had been one of those skinflint nonsmokers who don't keep any for their friends. "Or tiles."

"I think it was meant to be some sort of Bohemian joke," said Miss Grut thinly.

Dover began to think about his lunch. "There's one missing," he observed idly as he tried to weigh up his chances of getting a postprandial drink out of Miss Grut. "It must have dropped off."

Miss Grut's face hardened. She might disapprove of the smallest room in the house being papered with picture postcards, but she disapproved even more strongly of it being disfigured. After all, the entire house was now her property. Without a word she turned on her heel and stormed off to investigate.

When she returned her face was black with fury. "It's sheer vandalism!" she raged. "Really, some people are beyond belief! It was somebody at that party, you know. Fancy prizing off a postcard like that, right in the middle of the back wall. It looks terrible. You see it missing the moment you enter the room. I shall have to find another one to replace it until I can get the whole room redecorated. I wonder if Peter kept any spare postcards in here . . ." She moved over to a filing cabinet and began rummaging through it.

"Saucy, was it?" inquired Dover with a leer. "One for the connoisseur, eh? I noticed some of the others were a bit on the naughty side."

"No, it wasn't!" Miss Grut was opening and shutting drawers with increasing speed. "It was a very pretty card and a most unusual one An Italian girl in peasant costume. The top of her was just an ordinary picture, but her skirt was made with real embroidery silk. It was lovely!" She tossed her head angrily. "Isn't that just like people? They choose the only really beautiful card in the entire room to vandalize. They couldn't take one of the ordinary cards, could they? Oh, no, they have to steal the best. That card must have cost the earth and it came all the way from Italy. I remember noticing the stamp."

Dover didn't usually waste his time on detective work but, caught in that unhappy No Man's Land between morning coffee and lunch, he'd nothing much else to do. "Can you remember who sent it?"

Miss Grut drew herself up to her full height. "I am not in the habit of reading other people's postcards!"

Dover's pasty face split into an evil grin. "Now pull the other one!" he invited.

"Well, it wasn't signed, if you must know," said Miss Grut, succumbing to the temptation to reveal all. "Well, only with a row of crosses, and we all know what they mean. Disgusting!"

Dover waited.

"The message was something like: 'Wish you were here! Especially at bedtime! Hope this finds you as it leaves me at present—in the pink!' Well, one doesn't have to be a university professor to work *that* out! Fancy sending such obscene filth through the post!" Miss Grut gave a *frisson* of exquisite horror, and abandoning her search for a replacement postcard, gathered up the dirty coffee cups. She then swept majestically out of the studio and left Dover to his own devices.

It was MacGregor who eventually woke him up.

Dover took a few seconds to recollect where he was and MacGregor was able to take advantage of this hiatus to make his report. Everything was naturally well in hand. The Traffic police had been alerted and were standing by, prepared to check the suppressers on any car that the men from Scotland Yard might designate. Most of the people who had attended the wine-and-cheese party had been contacted and told to hold themselves in readiness for a visit that very afternoon from no less a person than Detective Chief Inspector Wilfred Dover himself.

"'Strewth!" said Dover, apparently appalled at the prospect which lay before him. He made a gallant effort to gather his wits. "Here, what time is it?"

MacGregor's long and grueling association with Dover enabled him to find the correct answer to that question. "They've laid on a hot meal for us at the pub down the road, sir."

A repast consisting of tomato soup, steak and kidney pie with chips and two veg, a double helping of roly-poly pudding and custard, and cheese and biscuits is not, perhaps, the ideal foundation for an afternoon's cerebral work but, all things considered, Dover stood up to the ordeal quite well. Nobody was actually able to swear he wasn't just resting his eyes against the light.

As the afternoon wore on, MacGregor felt that his initial pessimism was being fully justified. They were getting nowhere fast. None of the suspects—if that's what they really were—showed the slightest sign of fulfilling every detective's dream by coughing up a nice full confession.

Old Dr. Horncastle was in such a state of decrepitude that one glance was enough to clear him of all suspicion of being either a car driver or a murderer. His daughter Perlita, on the other hand, was a Jehu of some local notoriety, but she was also a keen bridge player and could produce a solid alibi for the whole of Sunday evening. She managed to run quite a strong promotional campaign for Spooky Chesshire as the murderess on the grounds that that particular overblown tart was both a raving sexpot and the niece of a man who'd been put on probation once for persistent indecent exposure.

Dover held his fire until just before Perlita Horncastle closed the door on him and MacGregor. The answer he got to his question was accompanied by a short and bitter laugh. Holiday? Perlita Horncastle hadn't had a holiday for five years and probably wouldn't for the next five if she couldn't find somebody to look after her father while she was away.

MacGregor was still trying to work out what Dover was getting at as he confronted Mrs. Barclay-Rhys in the stronghold of her chintz-draped drawing room. On this occasion the lady was accompanied by her husband, and since he was an experienced and successful solicitor, her responses to MacGregor's questions were unhelpfully monosyllabic. She did once begin to hint that Miss Joanie Wisbey, having recently been dropped by Peter Zandarowski, might be the one they were looking for, but a steely glare from Mr. Barclay-Rhys shut her up smartly.

Dover's feet were beginning to hurt and he tried to prolong the interview by asking Mrs. Barclay-Rhys how she had got to the wine-and-cheese party. It emerged that she had come on foot.

"Don't you drive?"

Mr. Barclay-Rhys smoothly stuck his oar in. Yes, Mrs. Barclay-Rhys did drive, was an excellent driver in fact, but as Mr. Barclay-Rhys had just taken possession of a brand-new Jaguar . . . well, it was hardly a ladies' car, was it?

Lady Tisdale was the next on the list, and Dover was flagging. Lady Tisdale, too, had a husband in attendance, though he wasn't hers. She had, she announced, flashing a roguish eye at her three male suitors, a complete alibi for the whole of Sunday afternoon, evening, and night, but she would only produce it if actually confronted with the gallows. "In these enlightened days," said Lady Tisdale, "the least we women can do is behave like gentlemen."

Dover's sordid little attempt to cut this noble female down to size fell on particularly stony ground. You don't bring a blush to the cheeks of the Lady Tisdales of this world by asking them if they paid a visit to the loo during the course of Peter Zandarowski's wine-and-cheese party. Lady Tisdale had not paid such a visit, and said so without fear or favor.

"Oh, 'strewth," whined Dover as he limped down Lady Tisdale's garden path, "enough's enough!"

MacGregor was inclined to agree, especially after Dover's last contribution to the investigation, but he knew that speed was of the essence in murder cases. "Just one more, sir," he wheedled, "and then we'll stop for tea."

Regrettably, it soon became evident that the Chesshires weren't giving anything at all away, not even a pot of the brew that cheers but does not inebriate. They had seen nothing, heard nothing, and knew nothing. Frightfully sorry. Alibis? Well, to be perfectly honest, they'd both made a jolly early night of it, retiring to bed with hot-water bottles, Alka Seltzers, and sleeping pills.

"When we got back home after that wine-and-cheese party," confided Spooky Chesshire, "I was literally as sick as a dog. Wasn't I, Rodney? I'm still feeling horribly queasy."

"She threw up all over the bathroom floor," Rodney informed MacGregor earnestly. "And if I hadn't got the innards of a camel, I'd probably have done the jolly old same. *De mortuis* and all that rot, but old Peter did serve up some amazingly nasty plonk. Pity he wasn't poisoned, eh? Otherwise we could have told you exactly where to look."

One might have expected Dover to take an intelligent interest in a clinical discussion of this nature as he was something of an expert when it came to the malfunctioning of the human digestive system, but he didn't. He merely sat there, wrapped in gloom, while MacGregor plodded patiently through his list of routine questions. Nothing of interest was elicited, and since no invitation to tea was forthcoming, Dover prepared to cut his losses.

He didn't want the Chesshires to think, though, that they'd been let off the hook entirely. "You understand that these are only preliminary inquiries," he said when he was already out on the doorstep and his hosts thought they had seen the last of him. "We shall be pursuing our investigations in more detail when the results of various tests are to hand."

"Ah!" said Rodney Chesshire brightly. "You mean the ballistics report and the jolly old postmortem and what-have-you?"

Dover scowled. This blooming case was littered with clever devils trying to teach him how to suck eggs. "You just see you hold yourself in readiness, mate!" he advised as unpleasantly as he could. "No trying to skip the country!"

"Shouldn't you confiscate our passports?" asked Spooky Chesshire helpfully. "Not that we're likely to be going anywhere. No cash! Besides, we've already had our trip abroad for this year."

Dover now seemed anxious to prolong the conversation. "Oh, yes?" he said. "Where did you go?"

"We had a fortnight in Amalfi," cooed Spooky, rolling her big blue eyes in ecstatic reminiscence. "*Simply* gorgeous!" She slipped her arms through her husband's. "Wasn't it, darling?"

Dover waited until he and MacGregor were back in the police car. "Where the hell's Amalfi?" he demanded.

"In Italy, sir." MacGregor was feeling very apprehensive. Surely a steaming idiot like Dover hadn't spotted something he'd missed? "South of Rome. Why, is it important, sir?"

Dover leaned forward and poked the police driver in the

back of the neck. "Any chance of getting some tea down at your nick, laddie?"

The startled police driver reckoned that there was and was instructed to proceed to the local police station with all possible speed.

"While I'm having a cuppa," Dover told MacGregor, "you can see about getting the warrant."

"Warrant, sir?" howled MacGregor, his worst fears realized. "Who for?"

"That snooty beggar in there. Who else?"

"Rodney Chesshire, sir? But what's he done?"

"Murdered Who's-your-father, of course! 'Strewth, what's the matter with you? A kid of two could have worked that out. Look," Dover said, generously willing to explain his methods to the less gifted, "that chap who was croaked used to decorate the walls of his downstairs toilet with the picture postcards his friends sent him."

"Really?" MacGregor said weakly.

"One of the guests at that blooming wine-and-cheese party on the day of the murder went to the lavatory and removed one of the postcards."

MacGregor licked his lips. "I'm afraid I don't quite follow you, sir."

"Thank God for small mercies!" sniggered Dover before returning to more serious matters. "Look, the dead man—"

"Peter Zandarowski, sir!"

"—was a notorious womanizer, right? Well, what would you do if you found your missus had sent him a postcard with a very suggestive message on the back of it?"

"Sir, I really—"

"Peter What's-his-name's auntie remembers the postcard because it was some sort of special one from Italy. She also remembers the message on the back. It was unsigned, of course, but Derbyshire would recognize his own wife's handwriting, same as he recognized that very distinctive type of postcard when he saw it on the wall."

To his eternal credit MacGregor really tried to straighten all this out. "Do you mean, sir, that you're proposing to arrest Mr. Chesshire on the strength of a picture postcard which, if I understand you, you've not actually seen?"

Dover didn't take such petty nit-picking well. "'Strewth, there's a gap on the wall where the postcard was nicked from. Somebody at the party took it. You're not going to argue about that, are you?"

"But that doesn't mean Chesshire took it, sir."

"The card came from Italy! His wife must have sent it."

MacGregor forced himself to be both generous and fair. "Even supposing you're right about the missing postcard, sir, somebody else other than Chesshire could have removed it from the wall."

"But nobody else other than Chesshire would have then gone on and shot Peter Thingummyjig, would they?" demanded Dover, the end of his tether now in sight.

"Several of Zandarowski's lady friends were at that party, sir. Any one of them might have read the postcard and killed him out of jealousy. Hell hath no fury like a—"

"Listen, laddie!" snarled Dover, resenting MacGregor's tone of superiority. "You're talking through the back of your head as usual. It's got to be a man who murdered What's-his-name because it's got to be a man who pulled that postcard off his downstairs lavatory wall. Savvy? Well, there were only three men at the party and we can scrub that old fool of a doctor and it can't be this sixteen-year-old boy either, can it? Apart from anything else, neither of 'em can drive a bloody car. So that leaves Yorkshire, doesn't it? Well, you just get up off your backside and get somebody round to check his car. If it's capable of causing television interference, we've got him bloody cold."

MacGregor was not far from tears. "You're accepting

Miss Grut's evidence about the car on Sunday night, sir?"

"She'll be rock-solid in the witness box," claimed Dover, sitting back and rubbing his hands. "You'll not get her to change her testimony, not in a month of Sundays. In fact"—he lowered his voice so that the police driver shouldn't hear more than was good for him—"she'll be such a good witness that it might be worthwhile making sure Shropshire's car is unsuppressed. Get the idea? It probably won't involve doing more than pulling an odd bit of wire loose."

MacGregor had long since passed the stage when he was going to get upset about being asked to fabricate evidence. "I still don't see, sir," he insisted with dogged determination, "how you can be so certain that the postcard—if there was a postcard—was removed by a man."

"'Strewth!" exploded Dover. "You're as thick as two bloody planks, you are. That postcard was stuck at eye level on the back wall of the loo, right over the cistern. Get it? Well, that's precisely where it would catch a man's eye as he was standing there, isn't it? But women don't stand, laddie! They sit, and they sit facing the other way. Now do you see? It's a million-to-one chance that a woman would notice that postcard because it would be well above her head and she'd have her back to it." Dover eyed his sergeant speculatively. "I should have thought even you knew that much about the facts of life, laddie!"

"But—"

"But nothing!" said Dover, who was getting bored with the whole thing. "Wiltshire recognizes the postcard, reads it, discovers his wife's been two-timing him with What's-his-name, knocks her out with a sleeping pill when they come home from the party, drives back, and shoots Who's-your-father, and—if it hadn't been for me—he'd have bloody well got away with it, wouldn't he?"

—1979

Sweating It Out with Dover

Every English summer, no matter how awful the weather is in general, is blessed with one gloriously hot, really sweltering day—and in drought years we sometimes have two. The savage murder of young Elvin Garlick took place on one of these exceptional days when the sky was blue and the sun blazed down. So, too, did Detective Chief Inspector Wilfred Dover's "investigation." Indeed, his conduct of the case and the highly unseasonable weather were not unconnected.

It was getting on for midday when Detective Chief Inspector Dover, chaperoned as always by MacGregor, his young and handsome sergeant, arrived at Skinners Farm. The temperature was already pushing up into the eighties and most people would have been delighted at getting out into the country on such a marvelous day. Chief Inspector Dover, however, wasn't most people and, in spite of appearances, Skinners Farm was only twenty-five miles from Charing Cross and so not really country anyhow.

Charitable people might have thought it was the heat which had addled Dover's brains, but in reality he was just as slow-witted on the most temperate day. On this occasion, he didn't seem able to get it into his head that Skin-

ners Farm wasn't actually a farm but an over-restored Geor-
gian house standing in its own grounds and separated from
the hurly-burly of the outside world by a couple of fields
full of gently ruminating black-and-white cows.

"I suppose they call it a farm, sir," said MacGregor, surreptitiously dabbing at the back of his neck with a lightly
starched white handkerchief, "because it was once the
farmhouse."

"Bloody fools," said Dover, the sweat standing out in
beads on his forehead. As a concession to the weather, he
had left off his overcoat—but the greasy bowler hat, the
blue-serge suit, and the down-at-heel boots were the same
as ever. "'Strewth," he panted, "but it's hot!"

"Perhaps we could have the window down a bit, sir,"
said MacGregor, who'd been wondering for some time if
the peculiar smell in the police car was Dover or merely
something agricultural they were spraying on the fields.

"I hope they've shifted that blooming body," said Dover
querulously as he plucked at his shirt. "It'll be ponging to
high heaven else."

MacGregor glanced at his watch. "They may not have
moved it yet, sir," he warned. "It's only about an hour and
a half since they found him, and since I understand he's
lying in some sort of copse and reasonably sheltered from
the sun—"

"You won't get me going to see it," declared Dover flat-
ly. "I'll bet it's all crawling with flies. Here"—he roused
himself as the car turned into a driveway—"are we there?"

The married couple who lived at Skinners Farm were, understandably, in a state of some distress and they greeted
the arrival of the two high-powered detectives from Scotland Yard as though it was a heaven-sent solution to all
the horrors of that terrible morning. Anxiously hospitable,

they conducted a profusely sweating Dover through the house and out onto a comparatively cool and shady veranda.

Here they installed him on a cane chaise longue, plied him with cigarettes, and asked him what he would like in the way of a long cool drink. Dover, having graciously accepted pretty little Mrs. Hewson's suggestion of an iced lager, hoisted his boots up onto the footrest and flopped back. 'Strewth, this was the life! And it was going to take more than a bloody murder case to dislodge him from it.

When, a few minutes later, Mr. Hewson came out with the drinks, Dover was more or less obliged to open his eyes. Having half a pint of ice-cold liquid sloshing around in his stomach had quite a bracing effect on him, however, and for a few minutes he was actually sitting up and taking some interest in his surroundings. The veranda, he discovered, overlooked a large and well-kept garden which fell gently away from the house. In the distance was what appeared to be a clump of trees where several figures in dark blue could dimly be seen moving about.

Dover had no wish to strain his eyesight by peering through the heat haze, so he treated himself to a good look at his host instead. Mr. Hewson, he ascertained without much interest, was a man of about fifty, but very fit and youthful-looking. He was wearing a pair of powder-blue shorts and matching T-shirt, but his manner was far from being carefree and relaxed. As he explained with an uneasy laugh, he wasn't accustomed to stumbling over dead bodies in the middle of a Saturday morning.

Dover relieved his own inner tensions with a good belch and wiped the back of his hand across his mouth. "*You* found him, did you?"

"No, not exactly," said Mr. Hewson. "Tansy, here"—he indicated his wife, who was happily engaged in refilling

Dover's glass—"actually found him, but naturally I went down to have a look before I phoned the police. I hoped," concluded Mr. Hewson with a bleak little smile, "that she'd got it wrong."

"Still hanging around, are they?" asked Dover through a yawn which gave everybody a fine view of his dentures.

"The local police? Yes. The Inspector's using the phone in the sitting room and the rest of them are still down there in the old orchard." Mr. Hewson pointed toward the clump of trees which Dover had already more or less noticed. "They're searching through the undergrowth. Do you want me to tell them you're here?"

The last thing Dover wanted was a mob of local flatfoots swarming all over him in that heat. He leered encouragingly at pretty little Mrs. Hewson. "So what happened, missus?" he asked and rattled his now-empty glass.

Pretty little Mrs. Hewson grew tearful. She'd told her story four times already and really didn't want to go through it all again.

Dover had little sympathy for a woman who seemed incapable of recognizing an empty glass when she saw one. "Oh, get on with it!" he advised impatiently.

Mrs. Hewson gulped, dried her eyes on a wisp of handkerchief, clutched her husband's hand, and complied. "It's all my fault, actually. If I hadn't decided to grub up the old orchard and turn it into a vegetable garden, none of this would have happened. Freddie wasn't a bit keen on the idea—were you, darling? He said he'd do it himself sometime but—well, I know how busy he is, so I got hold of this young man from the village to come and do it."

"What young man?" demanded Dover, sportingly moving his empty glass even nearer so as to give Mrs. Hewson every chance.

"The young man who's been murdered. Elvin Garlick.

He works for a firm of landscape gardeners, so, of course, he's able to borrow their equipment."

"You mean he was doing the job for you in his own time?" MacGregor, sipping straight lemonade because he didn't drink when he was on duty, was taking notes. Well, somebody in that partnership had to behave responsibly, didn't they?

"Oh, yes!" said Mrs. Hewson with some pride. "And for cash. That way you get it cheaper because nobody has to pay income tax or V.A.T. or anything. The only trouble was," she added with a disconsolate little moue, "he could only come on weekends and that meant I couldn't keep it a secret from Freddie. I'd wanted to present him with a fait accompli, you see."

"Ugh," grunted Dover, just to show he was still awake.

"Well, Elvin arrived about half past eight this morning." Mrs. Hewson raised her pretty little chin defensively. "He told me to call him Elvin. He said everybody always did, especially when he was obliging them. Well, I told him exactly what I wanted doing and left him to get on with it."

"And where were you all this time, sir?" MacGregor turned to Mr. Hewson.

"I was still getting up. Saturday's my day off, too, you know." Freddie Hewson felt that further explanation was required. "I'm a stockbroker, so I'm in the City all week."

"So you didn't see Mr. Garlick?"

"No. I knew somebody'd come to the house, of course, and then later you could hear his rotovator or whatever churning away down there in the orchard. That's when this naughty little girl here"—Mr. Hewson squeezed his wife's hand affectionately—"finally had to tell me what she was up to."

"He was ever so surprised!" simpered little Mrs. Hewson happily.

"And then what, sir?"

"Well, then nothing, Sergeant." Mr. Hewson said, "Tansy and I had breakfast out here on the veranda. Garlick was all right then, because we could hear him—couldn't we, darling? After breakfast I went round to the back of the house to work on my car. I'm rebuilding a 1934 Alvis and there were a few things I wanted to get done before it got too hot."

"And you, Mrs. Hewson?"

"I was in the kitchen, getting as much as I could ready for dinner tonight. Well, you don't want to spend a glorious day like this slaving over a hot stove, do you?"

"The kitchen's on the far side of the house, too, Sergeant," explained Mr. Hewson, "so neither of us could see anything going on in the old orchard. And, as I told the other policemen, we didn't hear anything, either. We were both pretty absorbed in what we were doing and, of course, Garlick was a good way off and he wasn't using his machinery the whole time. Well, at about eleven, I suppose it would be, Tansy brought me out a cup of coffee to the garage. She said she was going to take some down to Garlick, too. I would have gone myself, of course, but I'd just started stripping down the clutch and it was all a big fraught and I didn't want to leave it."

"Oh, I didn't mind, lovie!" cooed Mrs. Hewson. "Like I said, I was glad to get out of that kitchen for a few minutes and stretch my legs."

MacGregor nodded. "So you walked down to the old orchard with the coffee, Mrs. Hewson?"

"That's right. Well, when I got there, I couldn't see or hear Elvin anywhere, so I shouted his name. I wasn't keen to go tramping about down there because it's waist-high in weeds and nettles and things." Mrs. Hewson stretched out her shapely bare legs for the general delectation and to emphasize the point she was making.

MacGregor did, indeed, begin to sweat a bit more freely, but it was many moons since any part of the female anatomy had sent the blood racing through Dover's veins. He merely pushed his bowler hat a bit farther back on his head and inquired if anybody'd got a cigarette to spare.

The murder investigation ground to a halt as the Hewsons obligingly rushed off in all directions to fetch cigarettes, matches, and ashtrays. They finally redeemed themselves by refilling Dover's glass, and it was only when they'd got Dover happily swilling and sucking away that Mrs. Hewson was able to finish her story.

The end proved something of an anticlimax. Having received no answer to her shouts, Mrs. Hewson had gingerly ventured farther into the old orchard and found Garlick just lying there, face down, with his own pitchfork sticking out of his back. Pretty little Mrs. Hewson wasn't sure whether she'd screamed, but she was certain she hadn't touched the body.

"I didn't have to," she explained unhappily. "I just knew he was dead. I dropped everything and came running back up here to tell Freddie."

Mr. Hewson took up the tale. "I went tearing down to the old orchard," he said, "and there he was. I couldn't see any sign of breathing—Garlick was stripped to the waist, by the way—and with that pitchfork pinning him to the ground, well, I knew it couldn't be an accident or anything. I left everything just as it was and came back up here and phoned the police."

"We had a patrol car here in less than five minutes." A man who had been waiting just inside the sitting room for a suitably dramatic moment stepped forward. There was an unmistakable drop of the jaw when he got his first clear look at Dover, but he recovered well and introduced himself. "Detective Inspector Threlfall, sir. I arrived at eleven twenty-six in response to an urgent summons from the patrol car and I have been in charge of the preliminary investigation since my arrival."

Detective Inspector Threlfall paused in case the seventeen and a quarter stone of solid flesh stretched out on the chaise longue wished to make some response. It didn't. With the mercury climbing that high in the thermometers, Dover had no energy to spare for social niceties.

Inspector Threlfall cleared his throat and tried again. "You'll want to see the body, sir."

That stung Dover into life. "I bloody shan't!" he growled, the mere thought of venturing out into the hot bright world outside making him feel quite sick.

"The doctor thought that Garlick had been knocked unconscious with a blow across the back of the head, sir." Inspector Threlfall would never have believed that Dover didn't care a fig either way. "Then he was run through with the pitchfork while he was still out. Crude, but effective."

MacGregor took pity on the Inspector. "Are there any signs as to which way the murderer came, sir?"

Inspector Threlfall shook his head. "Not so far, Sergeant. Mind you, Buff had been churning things up for a couple of hours before he bought it, so it's a tricky job trying to sort things out. The murderer could have come from almost any direction. Crept down this way past the house or come across the fields or"—Inspector Threlfall waved his arms about in the appropriate directions—"got into the orchard from the other side. You can't see it from here, but there's a road running along there not fifty yards from where Buff was killed."

Dover's chair creaked pathetically as he tried to find a more comfortable position.

"Buff?" queried MacGregor with a frown.

Inspector Threlfall shrugged. "That was his nickname. I've known him since he was old enough to appear before a juvenile court, you know, and he's been a regular customer ever since. We're going to miss him. He's had a go at pretty well everything—pinching old ladies' pension books, drunk and disorderly, breaking and entering, nicking cars, shoplifting—"

"Good heavens!" gasped Mrs. Hewson faintly.

Inspector Threlfall glanced at her with just a touch of contempt. "That's how he got his job with Wythenshaw's, madam. His probation officer swung it for him. Well, they'd tried everything else. Seems they thought a spell of honest toil might sort him out. I don't know what old Wythenshaw's going to say when he finds out Buff's been 'borrowing' all that expensive gear."

"But he told me his boss was only too willing to lend him the stuff," protested Mrs. Hewson, carefully avoiding her husband's eye.

"Well, he would, wouldn't he, madam?" asked Inspector Threlfall easily. "Always had a very smooth tongue, young Buff, especially where the ladies were concerned." He turned back to MacGregor. "That's where I'd start looking, if I was you, Sergeant. Buff's got more girls into trouble than you and I've had hot dinners. There must be hundreds of fathers and husbands and boy friends thirsting for his blood—and that's not counting any members of the fair sex who might have had it in for him."

"It hardly sounds like a woman's crime," said MacGregor doubtfully. He was dying to get down to the old orchard and see things for himself.

"I don't see why not. You don't need much strength to knock somebody out with a chunk of wood or something, and that pitchfork had prongs as sharp as a razor. It would go through him like a hot knife through butter."

"Oh, dear!" moaned Mrs. Hewson, clamping both hands across her mouth and going as white as a sheet.

Her husband leaped across and, wrapping his arms protectively round her, helped her to her feet. He smiled apologetically at the three stolidly staring policemen. "She's a bit upset, I'm afraid. I'll get her to have a little lie-down. You don't want us anymore just now, do you? I think we've told you all we know."

Nobody seemed much concerned one way or the other, though Dover did bestir himself to remark that, if Mr. Hewson was thinking of making his wife some tea, he—Dover—wouldn't say no to a cup.

"These cold drinks are all right," said Dover confidingly to an astonished Inspector Threlfall, "but there's nothing to touch a good hot cup of tea, especially in this bloody weather. It brings you out in a good muck sweat."

"Oh—quite," said Inspector Threlfall. "Er—I was wondering what your plans were, sir."

"Plans?" Dover squinted suspiciously.

"I thought you might like to pop down to the village, sir, and have a word with the lad's mother. He lived with her and she might just know something. I've got some chaps out making general inquiries around the neighborhood, but I thought I'd best leave Mrs. Garlick for you."

There was an awkward pause. Not that Dover was hesitating. Wild horses weren't going to shift him off that veranda until the temperature outside dropped by at least twenty degrees, but there was the problem of conveying this message to Inspector What's-his-name without too much loss of face. "How many people knew he was going to be working here this morning?" asked Dover in an attempt to give himself time to think.

Inspector Threlfall rubbed his chin. "Not many, I should think. Not if he was borrowing the gear without permission. Besides, it's not the sort of thing you'd expect young Buff to be doing in his spare time. Normally, if he wanted extra money, he'd just nick it."

MacGregor wiped the perspiration off his upper lip. The veranda was only comparatively cool. "Maybe he'd turned over a new leaf?"

"More likely casing the joint," said Inspector Threlfall. "The Hewsons must have been mad to let him come within a mile of this place."

MacGregor fanned himself gently with his notebook. "It was more Mrs. Hewson, wasn't it? I don't think her husband knew anything about it until Garlick turned up this morning."

"Seems he wanted that old orchard left just as it was," said Inspector Threlfall. "Claims it's a nature reserve or something. I reckon he'll pin her ears back for her when this is over."

Most untypically at this stage in the proceedings, Dover was wide-awake and listening intently. It wasn't, however, the lethargic conversation about the Hewsons' private life that was claiming his anxious attention, but the more interesting rumbles that were coming from his stomach.

MacGregor laughed a cool, sophisticated, man-of-the-world laugh. "Hewson'll just have to teach her who's boss, otherwise he won't be able to call his soul his own."

"Hark who's talking!" jeered Dover, for whom it was never too hot and sticky to be unpleasant. He left his guts to take care of themselves for a moment. "You could write all you know about married life on a threepenny bit, laddie, and still have room for the Lord's Prayer. Any moron can see that she's got him by the short and curly. What do you expect when a man goes and marries a flighty young thing half his age?"

"I don't think he's quite as—"

"Near as damn it!" snarled Dover, who didn't care to be contradicted, especially when he wasn't feeling too frisky in the first place. "There's no fool like an old fool."

"Speaking of marriage," said Inspector Threlfall—but nobody was listening to him.

Dover had tuned into those ominous visceral splutterings again and MacGregor was frantically trying to work out if Dover had spotted something he'd missed. "Do you think it might be a case of jealousy, sir?" he asked, eyeing Dover doubtfully.

Dover blinked. "Eh?"

MacGregor grew even more worried. "The elderly husband, sir, and the attractive young wife? Plus the sexy young man from the village? Do you think there could have been anything between Mrs. Hewson and Garlick?" MacGregor appealed to Inspector Threlfall. "You did say Garlick was attractive to women, didn't you, sir?"

"Like a honeypot to flies," agreed Inspector Threlfall.

"Or, maybe"—MacGregor was more interested in his own brilliant deductions—"it was *Mrs. Hewson!* She takes the coffee down to the old orchard, say, and Garlick makes improper advances towards her. She repulses him. He persists. She picks up the nearest fallen branch or what-have-you and—"

"Bunkum!" said Dover, coming out in a hot flush at the mere thought of such an expenditure of energy in that heat. "She'd not have the strength. She's only knee-high to a grasshopper."

"Garlick wasn't all that big a chap, sir," said Inspector Threlfall as he remembered that these two Scotland Yard experts hadn't yet even seen the body. "A woman might have done it. But what I wanted to mention, sir, was about the Hewsons."

"Well, why don't you spit it out, then? I haven't got all bloody day to sit around waiting for you to come to the point."

The training that Inspector Threlfall had received at the police school all those years ago stood him in good stead now. Otherwise Skinners Farm might have witnessed another and even bloodier murder. "They're not actually husband and wife, sir. Not legally, that is."

Dover shrugged his ample shoulders and folded his hands over his ample paunch. "So what? It's no skin off my nose." He closed his eyes against the glare coming in from the garden, only to snap them open again as the desire to score off a brother police officer proved stronger than the longing for a quiet forty winks. "She wears a wedding ring," he pointed out, much to MacGregor's amazement, because one didn't really expect Dover to notice such things. "And she calls herself 'Mrs.'"

"That's as may be, sir," said Inspector Threlfall, nobly swallowing the rejoinder he would have liked to have made. "But they are definitely not married—well, not to each other. Hewson's already got a wife. Or as far as anybody *knows,* he has."

"And what the hell's that supposed to mean?"

"It's just that I happened to be involved when she did a bunk, sir. The first Mrs. Hewson, that is. I was on duty when Hewson came in to report that she was missing. It must be six years ago now. He wanted us to find her."

"But you didn't?"

"There's nothing we can do about a runaway wife, sir. You know that. I carried out a routine investigation, but there was nothing suspicious about her disappearance. All I could do was suggest to Mr. Hewson that he try the Salvation Army. Not that it was her sort of thing, really."

Working on the principle that "talk, talk on the veranda" was a damned sight better than "walk, walk across that dirty great garden," Dover demanded more details about the first Mrs. Hewson and her mysterious disappearance. Inspector Threlfall was obliged to search his memory. As far as he was concerned, the whole incident had been totally unremarkable. It was true that the first Mrs. Hewson had cleared out without a word and nobody had heard from her since, but this could be attributed to pure spite.

"Spite?" queried Dover, almost as though he was interested.

"It makes it difficult for Hewson to divorce her, sir. As things stand now, he's got to wait all of seven years and then apply to the courts for permission to presume that she's dead. Meantime, his hands are tied. You can't serve divorce papers on a woman you can't find. Hewson himself reckoned she'd stay out of sight until the seven years was nearly up and then put in an appearance again, just to be bloody-minded. The marriage was pretty well on the rocks when she left home, but she seems to have made up her mind not to let him go without a struggle."

"You're sure there were no signs of foul play?"

"Quite sure, sir. She'd taken all her clothes and jewelry and her passport. There were a couple of suitcases missing and she'd cleared out their joint banking account. Her car turned up a few weeks later. It had been abandoned in the long-stay car park at Gatwick Airport, but there were no clues in it as to where she'd gone."

Dover ran a stubby finger round inside his shirt collar. 'Strewth, it was hot! He hoped What's-his-name wasn't going to be all bloody day with that cup of tea. "Was there another man?"

"Hewson thought there might be, sir, but he didn't know. She was on her own here quite a bit while he was off working in the City."

"What about her friends?" Dover might not have been the world's most brilliant detective, but in his long years in the police even he'd managed to pick up a few bits of technique. "Did she mention to any of them she was thinking of running away?"

Inspector Threlfall shook his head. "As far as I can remember, sir, she didn't have any friends. At least, not round here."

"Relations?" Dover had begun thrashing about in his chair like a stranded porpoise.

Inspector Threlfall watched these antics nervously. Was Fatty having some kind of heat stroke or was he merely trying to hoist himself to his feet? "Only a sister in Ireland, sir, and they hadn't spoken for years."

With a final wheeze, Dover managed to stand up. Too hot to move it may have been, but when Nature calls even the least fastidious of us is obliged to go. Especially if we have bladders as weak as Dover's. "Bloody foreign muck!" he grumbled. "It goes straight through you. I don't know why people can't give you proper English beer." He turned to MacGregor, who was trying to pretend that none of this had anything to do with him. "Where is it, laddie?"

Long association with Dover had taught MacGregor to give a high priority on every possible occasion to locating where "it" was. "I believe there's a small cloakroom at the foot of the stairs, sir."

Dover departed at an urgent trot, leaving a thoughtful silence behind him on the veranda.

Inspector Threlfall loosened his tie. "He's a bit of a lad, eh?" he said at last.

MacGregor responded with a thin humorless smile and changed the subject. "Have you any ideas about who killed Garlick, sir?"

"Some," said Inspector Threlfall, seeing no particular

reason to be helpful. Left alone, he reckoned he could have solved this case in a couple of hours flat.

"One of his fellow yobboes, sir?"

"Could be."

"Friday is usually payday," observed MacGregor carefully. "Garlick was a bit of a drinker, I think you said?"

"He liked his pint."

MacGregor closed his notebook to show that this was an off-the-record conversation. "You often get drunken rows blowing up on Friday night. Maybe this one didn't get settled until Saturday morning. I mean, who else—except his mates—would have known he'd be working out here this morning? Apart from Mrs. Hewson, that is. He'd have hardly spread the news around, would he? And it would only be a local chap who'd know there was easy access to the old orchard from the road."

Inspector Threlfall contented himself with raising his eyebrows in an enigmatic sort of way. If that was how the clever dicks from the Yard saw it, good luck to 'em! Inspector Threlfall wasn't going to stick his neck out just to show them where they'd gone wrong.

It seemed a very long time before Dover came waddling back. MacGregor tried to get him to continue on down to the scene of the crime while he was still on his feet, but Dover brushed his sergeant's efforts to one side and flopped back into his chair.

"I've just been out round the back," he announced.

MacGregor's heart sank. Oh, it was all so mortifying! "But, sir," he wailed, "I told you exactly where the cloakroom was!"

Dover flapped an impatient hand. "Not that, you fool!" he growled. "I went there first. It was after, when I went round the back of the house to have a look. Bloody good thing I did, too. Do you know what? You can't see the kitchen from the garage and you can't see the garage from the kitchen."

"Sir?"

"That means he did it, laddie!" explained Dover helpfully. He nodded cheerfully at Inspector Threlfall. "All we need now is a bulldozer and a warrant."

"I beg your pardon, sir?"

Dover's good humor began to evaporate. If there was one thing that really got to him, it was stupidity, especially on a blooming hot day like this. "You got cloth ears or something?" he asked Inspector Threlfall savagely. "I've solved your murder for you. 'Strewth, some people want it with bloody jam on!"

Inspector Threlfall very sensibly clung onto the one bit of this he could understand. "You've solved the case, sir?"

"It came to me out there," said Dover, not without a touch of pride. "I wasn't just twiddling my thumbs, you know. Then I went round the back and Bob's your uncle. It all fits. All you've got to do is dig up the evidence and charge him with murder."

"But charge—er—who, sir?"

"Well, What's-his-name, you bloody fool!" roared Dover. "Who else, for God's sake? Look, this morning he waits until his wife—or whatever she is—is safely shut up in the kitchen, right? Then he nips out of the garage, round the *other* side of the house—get it?—and down across the bloody garden."

The gesticulations which accompanied this vivid account were a little uncertain, as Dover had not actually seen the terrain he was describing. "He sneaks into this orchard place, finds young Who's-your-father, picks up the nearest blunt instrument, and knocks him out. Okay? After that, all he has to do is finish the job off with the pitchfork. Easy as shelling peas."

Rightly deducing that nothing useful was going to emerge from Inspector Threlfall's feebly gaping mouth, MacGregor himself tried to introduce a note of sanity into the proceedings.

"Are you saying that Mr. Hewson murdered Garlick, sir? But why should he? He didn't even know Garlick. In fact"—MacGregor riffled officiously through his note-book—"he claims that he'd never even seen Garlick until after he was dead. That's a very definite statement, sir, and easy enough to check."

Dover scowled. Trust MacGregor to start nit-picking! "He didn't have to know Garlick," he said sullenly, "he'd have croaked anybody."

"You mean Mr. Hewson is some sort of homicidal maniac, sir?"

Dover's scowl blackened. If it hadn't been for the excessively hot weather and MacGregor being such a big strapping chap, Dover might have been sorely tempted to go across and belt him one. Insolent young pup! "*Hewson,*" he snarled through gritted dentures, "would have killed *anybody* who started digging that old orchard up."

The penny dropped and MacGregor could have kicked himself. "You mean—"

"I mean that's where he buried his first blooming wife!" snapped Dover, making sure that MacGregor didn't steal his thunder this time. "She didn't run away. He killed her and then buried her with all her clothes and jewelry and stuff out there in that orchard."

Inspector Threlfall recovered his powers of speech. "But I investigated the first Mrs. Hewson's disappearance, sir, and there were no suspicious circumstances."

"'Strewth," sneered Dover happily, "you wouldn't know a suspicious circumstance if it jumped up and bit you! Hewson was just too clever for you, that's all."

"Well, it's true the marriage wasn't a very happy one," said Inspector Threlfall, meekly accepting the slur on his professional competence, "but we took that as a motive for her leaving him." He glanced across at MacGregor for support. "I suppose we could have Hewson in again and ask him a few questions."

Dover reacted to this suggestion with unusual passion. "Not yet, you bloody don't!" he spluttered indignantly. "I'm still waiting for that cup of tea he promised me!" This must have sounded a bit thin even to Dover's ears. "Besides," he added in an attempt to place his policy of inaction beyond all question, "I've been invited to lunch.

"Look, why don't you two just push off and get that orchard dug up? It'll probably take you two or three hours. Soon as you find the wife's dead body, you can come and tell me. But not before two o'clock at the earliest, mind! Then we can confront What's-his-name with the facts and get a confession out of him. There's nothing to worry about. He's not the stuff heroes are made of. He'll soon cooperate if we shove him around a bit. And now"—the Dover eyelids drooped slowly over the Dover eyes—"why don't you just bug off and leave me to have a quiet think?"

—1980

Dover Sees the Trees

Whoever murdered Randall Wainwright, the young man from Australia, must have jumped for joy on finding that Detective Chief Inspector Dover had been assigned to the case. Not that the general public knew much about Dover—considerable efforts were made to keep him out of the limelight—but anybody smart enough to commit murder which warranted the intervention of Scotland Yard would have no difficulty in spotting a real old dud like Dover a mile off.

It was three o'clock on a fine Saturday afternoon when he arrived at The Greensward Motel and he was already whining on all six cylinders. Why was it, he demanded of Detective Sergeant MacGregor, his long-suffering assistant, that everybody else could be out enjoying themselves while he, Dover, was condemned to spend the whole bloody day poring over a smelly corpse.

"I mean," he said, and had been saying every thirty seconds for some considerable time, "who cares? They're all descended from bloody convicts."

Sergeant MacGregor was an uncomfortably scrupulous policeman and would never have dreamt of sweeping any crime under the carpet just because it was less trouble that way. "Randall Wainwright was a rather unusual Australian, sir."

"Aren't they all, laddie? I tell you, I've seen some that'd look better up a bloody tree in a safari park."

"This one happens to have been the sole heir to the Wainwright millions, sir."

Dover was unimpressed. "The Wainwright millions?"

"The big chain of furniture shops, sir, that Sir Sydney Wainwright built up from nothing. When he dies, this lad who's been killed was down to cop the lot."

Dover perked up. "Piece of cake then," he declared confidently. "Collar whoever comes in for the lolly now, and Bob's your uncle. 'Strewth, you'd have thought the local wallies could have worked that out for themselves."

The management of The Greensward Motel, their booking arrangements already shot to hell by *someone's* lack of consideration, had begrudgingly allocated a large double room to the police for use as headquarters. By the time Dover and MacGregor put in an appearance, the transformation was almost complete. Beds and color-television sets had been moved out and typewriters and filing cabinets moved in. There were telephones everywhere, all ringing, and the room buzzed with keen young coppers, all intent on exploiting what might be the chance of a lifetime.

Dover came over quite faint, but his instinct for finding havens of peace and quiet in the most unfavorable circumstances stood him in good stead. Shoving MacGregor ahead of him, he withdrew nimbly into the private bathroom and locked the door.

The trouble with even the most well appointed bathrooms is that there isn't really anywhere very comfortable to sit. Dover subsided morosely on the best that was available and MacGregor balanced himself gingerly on a tiny three-legged stool.

"'Strewth," groaned Dover. "What a bloody life, eh?"

"Perhaps I could go on with telling you what the local police have found out so far, sir," said MacGregor, meanly taking what advantage he could of the situation. "Randall Wainwright was killed early this morning. He was stabbed once through the chest with a World War Two German bayonet while lying in bed. The blade went straight through his heart and the police surgeon reckons death would have been instantaneous. The victim was stabbed through the bedclothes so it's unlikely that the murderer would have got any bloodstains on him. The German bayonet—that's the murder weapon, sir—was the property of the deceased. He'd apparently bought it as a souvenir in Norway, of all places. It's brand-new and was never issued for use."

Dover blew most unpleasantly down his nose. "Fingerprints?"

"The bayonet had been wiped clean, sir, and there's nothing very promising in the rest of the room."

"You never see a decent fingerprint these days," grumbled Dover. "It's all those bloody detective stories." He tipped his bowler hat even lower over his eyes and sank a couple of inches deeper into the greasy collar of his overcoat. "How old was he?"

MacGregor consulted his notebook. "Nineteen, sir. He only arrived in England yesterday morning. He'd been doing a sort of world tour by motorbike. Hence, I suppose, the bayonet from Norway."

There were two small wrapped bars of soap on the washbasin. Dover put them away in his pocket and looked speculatively at the piles of towels on the towel rail. "Where does a half-baked young punk on a motorbike get the money for a place like this?"

MacGregor made a silent vow to defend those towels to

the death. Dover's contention that everything not actually nailed down was fair game had led to enough embarrassment on previous occasions. "The young man was
staying here as a guest of his grandfather, sir. That's the
one who was going to leave him all his money."

Dover had found some strips of paper specially impreg-
nated for cleaning shoes. They went into his pocket too.
MacGregor wondered why. To the best of his knowledge,
the Dover boots hadn't had so much as a duster near them
since the day Dover had "liberated" them from the Yard's
Lost Property Department.

Dover let his butterfly mind flit back to the case in
hand. "Any sign of a break-in?"

"Not according to the local police, sir, but I think we
ought perhaps to go along and have a look for ourselves."

"Wait till they've moved the body," grunted Dover.
"Some of those stiffs'd put you off your grub for a week."

"We can't sit here all day, sir."

The lavatory seat must have been harder than it looked
because Dover didn't usually plump for the work alterna-
tive. "We'll go and interview somebody."

MacGregor was on his feet in a flash. "Who did you
have in mind, sir?"

"The popsie. Or the boy friend. Whichever."

"Sir?"

"Use your brains, laddie," exhorted Dover irritably. "If
there's no break-in, that means What's-his-name must
have opened the door to the murderer himself. Would you
open your bedroom door to a total stranger in the middle
of the bloody night?"

"But, sir"—MacGregor was well aware of the hazards of
letting dubious hypotheses like this take root in Dover's
well-manured brain—"the position of the body indicates
that Wainwright was most likely fast—"

"Stuff the position of the body!" snarled Dover. "You just get your skates on, laddie, and fix something up. I'll be with you in a minute."

But when, after a good bit longer than a minute, Dover emerged from the bathroom amidst a hammering of pipes and the roaring of waters, he found that things had been taken out of his hands. Sydney Wainwright—furniture maker, millionaire, grandfather of the deceased, and fellow clubman of the Metropolitan Commissioner of Police—had expressed a desire to meet the two Scotland Yard detectives before they began their investigations.

Dover went like a lamb.

"Oh, that's too bad!" protested old Mr. Wainwright, raising himself bravely up from his pillows. "I could perfectly well have got up and come to you." Since his room was only just across the corridor, his concern for the inconvenience he was causing seemed a little excessive.

"Now, Father," warned the middle-aged woman who had ushered Dover and MacGregor in, "you know what the doctor said."

"He was as big a fussy old woman as you!"

The woman smiled apologetically at Dover. "I'm Miss Wainwright, by the way. I'm afraid Father's a little on the fractious side this morning. He's not used to being kept in bed. He's usually so active. Of course, it's been a big shock for him. For all of us, really."

"All of you?" echoed Dover as he settled himself down in the most comfortable armchair. His eagle eye had already caught sight of an impressive array of bottles of drink on the windowsill and he was prepared to be cooperative.

Mr. Wainwright was used to doing the talking. "My birthday party," he explained. "I've been celebrating it here at The Greensward ever since my wife died. Trying to cater at home for a large family get-together is simply too diffi-cult these days. Especially as Cora"—he flapped a hand in his daughter's direction—"is a somewhat indifferent house-keeper. So I bring everybody here. This year," he added with a sigh, "was to have been rather special."

"It's Father's seventieth birthday," said Miss Wainwright.

"Mind your own business, Cora, and give these gentle-men an aperitif! It's not too early for you, is it, Chief In-spector?"

The hour had not yet struck when it was too early for Dover to accept free liquid refreshment, from whatever source, and he smilingly indicated that a large whiskey might just hit the spot. MacGregor, on the other hand, refused, muttering something shame-faced about not drinking while on duty or in the middle of the afternoon.

"Actually," Mr. Wainwright went on, sipping a medici-nal cognac, "when I said that this year was to have been rather special, I was really meaning it was to be my first meeting with my grandson, Randy. Poor boy! I can still hardly believe it." He bowed his head. "What a waste!"

"Father, don't upset yourself." Miss Wainwright's admo-nition was little more than a reflex action.

Mr. Wainwright scowled at her. "Randy was my heir, Chief Inspector. You'll find that information of vital importance in your investigation. Mine is a one-man busi-ness, you see—always has been and always will be. I don't believe in this 'control by committee' nonsense. Whoever takes over when I'm gone is going to get the lot. The whole damned works. The rest of my family have nothing to complain about. They've got their allowances, they won't starve. In any case, Randy was the only son of my eldest son. It's not unnatural for me to nominate him as my suc-cessor. I didn't do it without considerable thought. Now all my plans and hopes have been wiped out by one savage, jealous blow."

Miss Wainwright had perched herself on the edge of the spare bed and taken up her knitting. "You'll have to choose a new heir now, Father."

"Don't you tell me what I've got to do!" came the response viciously. "Just you tell me what's the point in choosing somebody else if you and the rest of the family are going to kill him too."

Dover blinked. "You mean somebody in your family knocked this lad off?"

"Any fool can see that! The boy only arrived at Dover yesterday afternoon and he came straight here on his motorbike. The only people he had time to meet were the family. Who else could have killed him? It isn't as though there's any lack of motive. I've got a son and two daughters and three grandchildren—all bright green with envy and all nagging at me night and day to change my will and leave everything to them. They make my life a misery with their bloody sniveling."

Miss Wainwright looked up from her knitting and addressed herself to Dover. "You can hardly blame us for thinking it was unfair. My father had never seen this boy. None of us had. He was a complete stranger. My brother Jack—he was Randy's father—ran away from home when he was sixteen because he was so miserable. He hated Father. And Father hated him."

"I *didn't* hate Jack! He was the only one of the lot of you with an ounce of spirit or drive. All right, we didn't always see eye to eye, but the lad had backbone and I respected him for it. And Randy was the same." Mr. Wainwright broke off as the empty glass Dover was waving hopefully in the air finally caught his eye. "And why don't you give the Chief Inspector another drink?"

"Just to help settle my stomach," leered Dover as he watched the amber liquid gurgle into his glass. "It's been playing me up something cruel all day. You'd think the medical profession could pinpoint what's wrong, but it's got them baffled. It starts off with this sort of stabbing pain and—"

Mr. Wainwright cut callously through his tale of visceral woe. "I want my grandson's murderer found, Chief Inspector. And punished. You can rely on my full cooperation and on that of my family, even though one of them undoubtedly killed the poor boy." He straightened out his top sheet with a firm hand. "I don't anticipate much difficulty. Not with your professional expertise and my unrivaled knowledge of the characters of those under suspicion."

"My pleasure," said Dover with the smirk of a practiced bootlicker. He generally tended to take violent exception when outsiders tried to muscle in on the act, but Mr. Wainwright was clearly something different. His generous attitude toward alcohol, if nothing else, entitled him to special consideration. "Mind if I smoke?" asked Dover, snapping his fingers flabbily at MacGregor, who reckoned that keeping Dover in cigarettes was what was keeping him poor.

Mr. Wainwright, however, was a pearl among men. "Have a cigar," he said.

With a glass of whiskey in his hand and a fat Havana in his mouth, Dover was like a pig in muck. He sat back to enjoy the good life while it lasted and let MacGregor get on with the business of assembling a few basic facts.

These, it soon transpired, weren't either very complicated or very interesting.

Randy had been the last of the birthday guests to arrive at the motel, roaring up on his motorbike only a short time before everybody was due to forgather in Mr. Wainwright's room for a predinner drink.

"Cheaper than going to the bar," said Mr. Wainwright.

Randy had appeared at the party still wearing his leather gear and big boots. He was full of his travels across Europe and very proud of the souvenirs he'd collected.

"He insisted on showing us everything," said Miss Wainwright disdainfully. "You've never seen such rubbish."

Including the German bayonet?

Miss Wainwright shuddered. "He kept trying to spear the cocktail onions with it. Quite the life and soul of the party!"

"The boy felt uncomfortable," protested Mr. Wainwright. "Hardly surprising with you lot looking him up and down as though he'd come from Mars."

"And this was the first time any of you had seen him?" asked MacGregor, pencil poised importantly over his notebook.

"The very first time," agreed Miss Wainwright with an enigmatic little sigh. "It was not the most enjoyable of occasions. And when we moved into the dining room it got worse."

"Only because you were all determined to dislike the boy and find fault with him!"

"He was an ill-mannered, vicious young savage, Father, who couldn't hold his drink. You just don't want to admit that you made a mistake. Fancy that greedy little brute taking over Wainwright's!"

"Pour the Chief Inspector another drink!" yelped Mr. Wainwright. "And if you can't speak well of the dead hold your damned tongue!"

Miss Wainwright relieved Dover of his empty glass and fired a parting shot before heading for the whiskey bottle. "I'm only surprised it wasn't you we found murdered in your bed this morning, Father."

"Cow!" snarled Mr. Wainwright.

Dover, who was beginning to view the passing scene through an amber-colored haze, never did quite fathom why they then proceeded to interview the entire Wainwright clan in old Mr. Wainwright's bedroom. MacGregor knew how it had happened and had protested about it, but he'd got nowhere in the face of Mr. Wainwright's grim determination and Dover's flaccid inertia. With breaks only for more whiskey, afternoon tea, and several trips to Mr. Wainwright's bathroom on Dover's part—during which he acquired a box of tissues and a whole clutch of paper squares for blotting lipstick and wiping razors—the interrogations went on for hours. Mr. Wainwright determined the order in which the members of his family appeared, and even sent his daughter, Cora, to summon them. First, though, she had to complete her own evidence.

Knitting indefatigably away, she described the family dinner party at which young Randy, growing more objectionable by the minute, had chewed with his mouth open, talked with his mouth full, and swilled down the vintage claret as though it was so much Coca-Cola. She had been delighted when, about half past nine, her father announced that he was going to bed and the party broke up.

"He was as disgusted and fed up as the rest of us," said Miss Wainwright, "though he pretended not to be. I came back here with him and got him settled for the night. Then I went to my own room—I'm sharing with my niece, Priscilla. I got undressed and watched some rubbish on the television until she came in about midnight. Then I made a cup of tea for both of us and we went to bed. I'm a very light sleeper—I have to be with Father to look after—and I would certainly have heard if Priscilla had got up during the night. She didn't, and we both slept through till eight o'clock this morning."

"Which," Mr. Wainwright pointed out maliciously in

case the men from Scotland Yard had missed it, "doesn't prove that Cora herself didn't wield the fatal bayonet, because young Priscilla is capable of sleeping through the Last Trump. And don't let Cora's fragile appearance deceive you—there are some pretty powerful muscles under that mohair jumper."

"Mostly developed in your service, Father," commented Miss Wainwright sourly. "But why on earth should I kill Randall? You're hardly likely to leave the Wainwright empire to me, are you?"

"Not unless and until complete senility sets in," agreed her father. "Still, where there's life, there's hope. Any questions, gentlemen?"

"Who actually found the body?" asked MacGregor.

"The chambermaid. She wanted to clean the room." Mr. Wainwright nodded at his daughter. "All right, Cora, fetch Rose and Malcolm in!"

Rose Turner was Mr. Wainwright's younger daughter, and though it might seem slightly irregular to interview her and her husband at the same time Mr. Wainwright didn't seem unduly worried about it. Indeed he was soon demonstrating that he could cope with Turners at platoon strength should the need arise.

He kicked off by filling in the background. "In case Rose's pathetic attempts to look seventeen have confused you, Chief Inspector, she's thirty-six. Her husband has reached his peak as the deputy personnel manager in a small engineering works—which doesn't stop him thinking he could run my business if he got the chance. Malcolm is a very simple-minded man and killing off the current heir to the throne would be just about his mark. Rose, on the other hand, would favor a more subtle approach to the problem. Her first instinct would be to marry off her daughter, the sound-sleeping Priscilla, to Randy and get their hands on the money that way. However, I doubt if Randy was fool enough to be seduced by young Priscilla's limited charms. Rose may have realized this even as early as last night and so resorted—reluctantly, I'm sure—to murder."

"Father!" wailed Rose Turner.

"There is, you see," continued Mr. Wainwright, his withers quite unwrung, "another Turner. Young Piers. A ridiculous name, but I refused to have that brat called after me. Rose has tried on many occasions to get me to make this undistinguished youth my heir. Now, with Randy dead, Piers has the distinction of being my sole remaining grandson. You must make what you will of that, Chief Inspector. As to alibis, no doubt Rose and Malcolm will both claim to vouch for each other."

They did, and were dismissed.

It was at this point that afternoon tea was served. Dover was the only one who appeared to have much of an appetite and he was so busy stuffing his face that most of the examination of Joan Wainwright—wife of Mr. Wainwright's younger son, Alex—and her daughter passed clean over his dandruff-flecked head. This was a pity because Mr. Wainwright managed to elicit a new motive for Randy's murder—sex.

"Oh, don't be so daft, Grandfather," Leonie Wainwright said.

"You can't deny he was making overtures to you."

"He'd asked me to go to bed with him before we'd finished the soup," said Leonie calmly and to her mother's visible dismay. "So what?"

Mr. Wainwright eyed her accusingly. "Randy wasn't the sort of lad to take no for an answer. By George, I wouldn't have at his age."

"I'll bet you wouldn't, you old lecher!" Leonie laughed

delightedly. "And you're quite right, of course. Actually, he got much more masterful afterwards when you'd all gone off to bed or whatever. We went down to the discotheque in the cellar."

"Who's we?" asked MacGregor, snatching eagerly at the chance to prove he was still there.

Leonie ran a speculative eye over the handsome young sergeant. "Piers, Priscilla, Randy, and me."

"And what happened?"

Leonie shrugged indifferently. "Randy got a bit much. Talk about king stags in the rut! I thought one time he was really going to have me right out there in the middle of the floor."

"Oh, Leonie!" moaned her mother.

With the crass insouciance of youth, Leonie leaned across and helped herself to one of Dover's sandwiches. She was lucky not to be charged with murder there and then.

It was all crystal-clear to Mr. Wainwright. "So later on he lured you into his room and you were obliged to defend your honor. Well, you've nothing to worry about, Leonie. The courts are always pretty lenient with such cases. The most you'll get is probation."

Leonie swallowed her sandwich and giggled. "You're *sweet*, Grandpop."

Mr. Wainwright turned to his daughter-in-law. "What did you think about it, Joan?"

"Me? Think about what?"

"About Randy raping your daughter, of course."

"Oh, *Father!*"

"Don't tell me you didn't notice he was trying to get his leg over."

Joan Wainwright tried not to wince at the expression. "I knew Leonie could handle him."

"Well, she's certainly experienced enough, from what I

hear." Mr. Wainwright managed to catch Dover's rolling eye. "They could both have been in it together, mother and daughter."

"Ah," said Dover wisely, and belched.

"They were sharing a room, you know. Easy enough to wait till everything's quiet and then slip out and down the corridor. The whole thing wouldn't take more than a minute or two. They knew he'd got that damned bayonet, and who better than Leonie to get him to open his door in the middle of the night?"

"Just what I was thinking," agreed Dover thickly.

The worm, however, suddenly turned. Joan Wainwright rose to her feet and glared down at her father-in-law. "You're nothing but an evil-minded old troublemaker!" she sobbed. "Everybody knows you wouldn't leave us your rotten money if we were the last people on earth. You've never forgiven Alex for turning his back on your precious furniture business. So, since you can't accuse us of killing your precious grandson for money, you've dreamed up this absurd story. You know your trouble, Father? You're sick! Just because Alex couldn't come to your lousy birthday party this year! I knew you'd try and take it out on Leonie and me!" She turned to her daughter. "Come on, Leonie! Don't just sit there! We're going!"

When Dover returned from yet another sortie to the bathroom, he found to his dismay that there was now another member of the Wainwright clan sitting awaiting his ordeal. 'Strewth, how many more of 'em? He hoped that this beardless youth with the supercilious sneer and the SOD 'EM ALL! T-shirt was the bloody last.

Piers Turner was the son of Rose and Malcolm and, since about three o'clock that morning, Mr. Wainwright's sole remaining grandson. Not that the honor was humbling him in any way.

"Who cares?" he inquired scornfully of the room at large. "All property is theft and what difference does one cruddy Australian tick more or less make to the real problems of the world? Instead of sitting around here contemplating our navels we ought to be out doing something about whales and rain forests and mineral fuels."

Neither Dover nor Mr. Wainwright cared much for being lectured on their social responsibilities by a spotty fifteen-year-old.

Dover fell back on his usual tactics. "You hated him, didn't you?" he demanded fiercely.

Piers Turner smiled. "I save my hatred for more worthy targets, Chief Inspector. Where Randy was concerned, my main feeling was one of profound relief that I didn't have to share a bedroom with the loudmouth punk." He transferred his smile to Mr. Wainwright. "You must be slipping, Grandpa. You generally insist on double rooms all around, unless it involves a really unholy coupling. I'll say that for you—you do observe the bourgeois decencies most meticulously."

Piers Turner was in the process of making a formal declaration to the effect that he had not murdered Randy Wainwright during the course of the previous night when the telephone rang. Mr. Wainwright was nearer but MacGregor was quicker and grimly determined not to have any more of his prerogatives usurped.

It was the local police who had been trying to track down their colleagues from the Yard for some time. MacGregor was in no mood for explanations. "Well, you've found us now," he barked, "what do you want?"

The telephone squawked excitedly and Dover eased himself back in his chair in order to give his paunch the maximum possible lebensraum.

"Of course we want you to follow it up!" snapped Mac-
Gregor, who had been quite patient and understanding
before he got teamed up with Dover. "Need you ask? This
is a bloody murder case!" He dropped the receiver back
with a bang.

"Has something happened?"

The eager question had come from Mr. Wainwright, but
MacGregor did his best to preserve good order and discipline by directing his answer to Dover. "That was one of
the local inspectors, sir. They've been checking through
the list of guests staying in the motel last night. They've
found a couple of Australians—youngish men. They had a
room on this corridor and they left very early this morning. The girl on Reception remembers them. Tough-look-
ing types, and they turned up asking for a room *after*
Randy Wainwright had booked in."

"Sounds promising," grunted Dover.

There was a little flurry of activity. MacGregor bustled
off importantly to teach the local police how to do their
job, young Piers Turner was dismissed with his principles
still untarnished, and even Cora Wainwright was let off
the leash for a few minutes in the fresh air before resum-
ing her thankless task of ministering to her father.

Dover and Mr. Wainwright were left alone together.

"Do you think it could have been these Australians?"
Wainwright asked.

Reluctantly Dover roused himself. He sort of felt he
owed old Wainwright something. "Gangsters," he grunted. "Followed the lad all the way from Australia, I should-
n't wonder. God only knows what he might have been up
to out there—Mafia, drugs, diamond smuggling."

"Would they know about the bayonet?"

Dover puffed out his cheeks. "They might have seen it
when you were having dinner. Or they might have just
improvised. I dunno."

Mr. Wainwright frowned. "So you don't think one of the family killed him?"

Dover shook his head and a few flakes of dandruff floated gently onto the shoulders of his overcoat. "It was all so bloody quick," he grumbled. "The lad had hardly got here before he was knocked off. Besides, where's the motive?"

"The motive," said Mr. Wainwright with excusable exasperation, "is my money! I told you—Randy was due to get the lot—sole control of my entire business! The rest of them will just go on getting the allowances I pay them now, and that's all!"

Strangely enough, Dover had taken in more of the afternoon's proceedings than one might have imagined. The slack mouth, the closed eyes, even the occasional snore apparently didn't imply total oblivion. "There'd be a motive," he agreed, "if you were going to make one of them your new heir. But you're not, are you? I reckon you'd sooner leave it all to a bloody cats' home."

Mr. Wainwright grinned. Old Fatso wasn't quite as thick as he looked. "What are you going to do now?"

Not a lot, actually. However, seeing that Mr. Wainwright had lost a grandson, even Dover expressed it more diplomatically. "Oh, we'll keep soldiering on," he promised stoutly. "Never close the file on an unsolved murder, you know. Still, I doubt if we'll get very far. There aren't any clues, you see. Now if we could find somebody who saw somebody going into What's-his-name's room at the relevant time, that'd be different."

"Could you not follow up this business of the key?"

Dover sagged. "What key?"

"Randy's room wasn't broken into, so the killer must have had a key."

"The lad most likely opened the door himself."

Mr. Wainwright hadn't become a millionaire through bearing fools gladly. "Randy was stabbed through the bedclothes," he pointed out sharply. "Surely that indicates he was asleep when it happened?"

Dover clutched groggily at what straws were left to him. "We'll have to wait for the postmortem."

"But you could start making inquiries about the possible whereabouts of a duplicate key, couldn't you?"

Was there any wonder Dover's stomach kept playing up? "Waste of time," he said desperately. "This murderer's too cunning to leave a trail like that."

Mr. Wainwright drew in a deep breath and restrained his natural desire to leap out of bed and shake some sense into this idiot. Still, it was getting unbearably frustrating. "I told you," he said, trying to keep it casual, "that I've been holding my birthday party at this motel since my wife died. In the early days I used to invite the odd friend as well as the family. A lady friend. I might have found a master key rather useful."

Dover gazed longingly at the bottles which still lined the windowsill and wondered if it was worth the effort to jolly old Wainwright along. "I expect you would. Might be easier said than done, though, to get hold of one."

"I could have bribed a chambermaid," Mr. Wainwright snarled. "Borrowed her master key for half an hour and got it copied at the shop around the corner. And I might have hung onto the duplicate as a souvenir."

"Ah," said Dover.

"Have you ever thought, Chief Inspector, what it would be like to be a rich man, surrounded by a mob of greedy offspring who don't give a damn for you personally but just want your money?"

No, Dover hadn't.

"Well, I can tell you, it can be bloody frightening. You're a sitting duck either way. If you don't make a will, then it's equal shares all round. If you do make one, you can feel the chief beneficiary's finger itching on the trigger every minute of every live-long day."

"Nasty," said Dover, trying to sound sympathetic and look thirsty.

"You never feel safe. Not unless you've left your money to somebody thousands of miles away. As long as your heir is safely on the other side of the world, you can rest easy. And everybody else is intent on keeping you alive. It's their only chance of getting a will made in their favor."

Dover was rapidly coming to the conclusion that mental telepathy was a load of old codswallop.

"But supposing," Mr. Wainwright went mercilessly on, "you learn that your heir is about to turn up on your doorstep? A sensible man would start taking a few precautions, wouldn't he? Fix things up so that there was no shortage of suspects. Think about a weapon. Make sure there's going to be a suitable opportunity. Stop behaving as though you're as fit as a fiddle and twice as active as men half your age. Make plans, but stay flexible. Of course"—Mr. Wainwright treated himself to a death's-head grin—"all this may turn out to be a wholly decent young man who wouldn't hurt a fly, much less his benefactor. On the other hand, he might turn out to be a right ruthless little bastard, merciless and very quick."

Dover's stomach was rumbling most alarmingly. "You could always change your will," he said. "Cut the beggar off with a shilling if you didn't like the look of him."

Mr. Wainwright denied himself the luxury of pointing out that it wasn't easy to get hold of your solicitor over the weekend. He'd already said enough. It was one thing to want somebody to appreciate your cleverness but quite another to face spending your declining years behind bars. He let his voice assume an old man's quaver. "But I'm boring you, Chief Inspector. How about you and me having another little drink, just to cheer ourselves up, eh?" He waved his hand feebly. "I'm afraid I shall have to ask you to pour it out."

Dover's face broke into a sunny beam. "My pleasure!" he said.

—1981

Dover Weighs the Evidence

"Wadderyemean, there's no bloody body?"

The young policeman who'd been left holding the fort looked close to tears. It was his first encounter with Scotland Yard's most notorious detective, and nothing in his training had prepared him for the shock. That appallingly scruffy overcoat, that greasy bowler hat, those mean little button-black eyes, that sullen pasty face . . . "The gentleman died in the ambulance on the way to hospital, sir. Didn't they tell you?"

Having gazed his fill at the fatal staircase, Detective Chief Inspector Wilfred Dover shoved his way back through the narrow doorway into the main hall and sat down weightily on the nearest chair. He merged well into his surroundings which were comparably decrepit, unlovely, and none too clean. "Nobody," he whined in a bid for cheap sympathy, "ever bloody well tells me anything."

The young policeman glanced curiously at the third member of their little group who was standing as far away as he dared in an attempt to disassociate himself from the proceedings. Detective Sergeant MacGregor, Dover's long-suffering assistant and whipping boy, was dying to point out that he had regaled his chief inspector with every known fact about the case in the police car which had brought them racing out to one of London's grottier suburbs, but—police discipline being what it is—he didn't say a word. Besides, he blamed himself really. Who knew better than he did that, when Dover sat there with his eyes closed, it wasn't because the fat old fool could concentrate better that way.

"Cat got your tongue?" Dover muttered.

The young policeman pulled himself together and decided to keep it short and simple. "The deceased is a Mr. Humbert Mew, sir, aged about fifty-five. He was a faith healer, sir."

"'Strewth!" said Chief Inspector Dover in tones of the utmost disgust.

"He was due to hold one of his faith healing sessions here in the Quine Street Social and Recreation Rooms at two o'clock this afternoon. It's a regular booking, sir. Well, Mr. Mew arrived at about half-past one, sir, with his wife and a Mr. Glossop, his business manager."

"Business manager!" scoffed Dover.

The young policeman struggled on. "While the other two were getting the hall ready for the meeting, sir, Mr. Mew retired as was his custom to the room at the top of the stairs for a period of quiet preparation. As you will see, sir, the stairs are shut off from the main hall by this door here.

"It was Mr. Mew's habit, sir, to remain alone in that upstairs room until two o'clock. Meantime, the people who'd come to attend the meeting and consult him were gathering here."

Dover looked round with little enthusiasm. Several rows of uncomfortable chairs, on one of which he was sitting, had been set out facing a small raised platform at the far end. And that was it, apart from some grimy windows set up high near the ceiling and a badminton court laid

out on the floor. "One born every minute," he commented sourly.

"Yes, sir."

"Mind you, laddie," added Dover with more than a
touch of self-pity, "when you've got a stomach like mine,
faith healing's about all there is left."

MacGregor knew what could happen if Dover's stomach
was allowed to intrude into the conversation. He smiled at
the young policeman in an effort to show the human face
of Scotland Yard. "You collected names and addresses?"

"I've got a list for you, Sarge."

"How many are there, by the way?"

"About thirty, Sarge."

"Damn!" snarled Dover, for whom work was a four-
letter word. "We'll be at it till Christmas!"

It was not the young policeman's place to speculate on
the accuracy of this prediction so, after a moment's understandable hesitation, he went on with his story. "At two
o'clock, sir, Mr. Mew came out of his room and began to
descend the stairs. That's when it happened. People out
here in the hall said they heard a sort of shout followed by
several bangs and thuds. Mr. Mew was quite a heavy gentleman, sir, and those stairs are pretty steep.

"Well, Mr. Glossop was sitting just here by the door and
he got to the foot of the stairs first. He realized Mr. Mew
was in a bad way and an ambulance was phoned for. P.C.
Roberts and I were on patrol in the vicinity and we also
responded to the call. Mr. Mew was removed in the ambulance, sir, accompanied by his wife, and P.C. Roberts began
questioning the people in the hall in an endeavor to pro-
cure an accurate picture of the incident.

"I proceeded to examine the staircase, sir. I ascertained
that, although uncarpeted and none too well lit, it could-
n't be classified as dangerous. I was about to attribute Mr.
Mew's fall to an unfortunate trip or him coming over faint

or something, when my eye was caught by an object on the wall at the top of the staircase. It was a small hook, sir. Painted black and screwed into the wall about a foot up from the second tread down, if you follow me, sir."

Dover was glowering balefully. So this was the interfering little upstart he had to thank for a ruined weekend!

"Perhaps I could show you, sir? It would be easier than trying to explain."

The suggestion that Dover should rise to his feet fell very flat.

"Well, sir, I investigated further and found another similar hook, in the baluster, opposite the first one. Hanging down from this second hook, on the outside of the staircase, was a length of thin twine, also painted black. There is a coat rack on the side of the staircase, sir, and the length of twine was partly concealed behind the coats hanging there.

"I checked the length of the twine, sir, and noted that it had been snapped in two. I had no doubt that it had originally been stretched across the staircase between the two hooks, and that Mr. Mew had broken it in his fall. With the release of tension it had then flipped away to hang down the side of the staircase."

Dover's eyes weren't closed this time, but they were glazed.

The young policeman hurried to get it over. "At this moment, sir, news came through that Mr. Mew was in fact dead and I had no hesitation in concluding that we had a case of murder. P.C. Roberts concurred, sir."

"Good work, constable!" said MacGregor, because somebody had to. "So you think somebody fixed up this booby trap after Mr. Mew had retired to the room upstairs so that when, at two o'clock, he emerged to conduct his healing session, he'd trip over it, fall, and kill himself?"

"That's about it, Sarge. Except I think the screws could have been put in much earlier. It's unlikely anybody would spot them and it would save time. All the murderer would have to do then is thread the twine through and tie it tight. Presumably he was counting on being able to remove all the evidence in the confusion after Mr. Mew's fall. If he'd managed that, of course, we'd have just put it down as an accident."

At this point, and somewhat belatedly, a police photographer and a fingerprint expert arrived and the young policeman broke off to conduct them to the scene of the crime.

Dover crooked a finger at MacGregor. "Come on, this place gives me the creeps!"

"But hadn't we better wait to see if they find anything, sir? There may be prints or—"

"The day I rely on bloody scientific experts to solve my cases for me'll be the day I hang my bloody boots up!" declared Dover who favored what one might call, for want of a better word, the psychological approach.

"Where were you thinking of going, sir?" MacGregor was quite prepared to learn that the old fool fancied a cinema or even a stroll along the Embankment in the pouring rain.

"We'll go and see the wife," said Dover. "The odds are she croaked him and we might get a confession if we get to her quick."

With a sinking heart MacGregor realized that they were probably in for another dose of the Dover Method. This was a simple technique which consisted of harassing the spouse of the deceased until he or she pleaded guilty to murder. It was surprising how often it worked.

Mrs. Mew, however, got Dover's measure very quickly. Good-looking and in her late thirties, she spotted that he

was unlikely to be lured from the path of duty by woman-
ly wiles, so she gave him a chair by the fire, a stiff drink and
a cigarette—and got herself crossed off the list of suspects
before you could say Adelaide Bartlett. She forestalled any
doubts as to the depths of her grief with the same skill.

"I was never one to wear my heart on my sleeve, even
as a girl," she confided. "Not that Humbert and me was
exactly setting the world on fire. It wasn't so bad before he
went on this faith healing kick, mind you. He'd got a good
job and things were ticking over quite nicely. Then, a couple of years ago, he discovers he's got this strange power
and he chucks everything else clean out of the window.
Not that you can't make a bomb out of faith healing," she
admitted ruefully, "but Humbert wasn't interested. Said he
couldn't prostrate his gifts for sordid gain."

"Was it a con?" asked Dover.

"You tell me, dearie! All I can say is sometimes he really did do extraordinary things. Not always, mind you.
There was some he couldn't do anything for, but—well,
take my knee."

Dover and MacGregor stared solemnly as Mrs. Mew
stretched out one black-stockinged leg.

"You wouldn't believe the trouble I've had with it for
donkey's years, and the pain. Humbert cured it in a matter
of seconds. Honest! And he was wonderful with migraines.
Or take old Mrs. Pretty—the doctor had given her a fortnight at the most when she called Humbert in and look at
her now! She won't ever run a four-minute mile, but she
gets around. Comes to our Saturday meetings at Quine
Street as regular as clockwork. She was there this afternoon—and it's over a year since they reckoned the next
stop was the crematorium."

"Ah, yes," said MacGregor quickly, "this afternoon!" He
knew that, once Dover got comfortable, he tended to lose

what sense of urgency he ever had. "Perhaps you could tell us about that. Now, I understand that your husband always retired to that room at the top of the stairs before the meeting began."

"He sort of had to psyche himself up," agreed Mrs. Mew, solicitously refilling Dover's glass. "Fanatic about that, he was. Half an hour's complete peace and quiet. Me or Glossy used to stay by the door to see nobody got through to disturb him."

"Glossy?" grunted Dover, just to show he had the interview well under control.

"Glossy Glossop, our business manager, dear. You've got to have somebody to see to all the arrangements. Glossy's like me—he wanted Humbert to break into the big time."

"Who was on guard today?" asked MacGregor.

"Glossy. He wouldn't let anybody through."

"Nobody at all?"

Mrs. Mew gave Dover another cigarette. "Only the ushers, dear. We let them hang their coats up at the foot of the staircase. It's one of their little perks. There is a sort of cloakroom by the entrance, but it gets a bit of a scrum there and we have had the odd thing pinched. Oh, lord!" Mrs. Mew's face crumpled. "I've just thought! What's going to happen about my bad knee now?"

MacGregor, while not unsympathetic, had more serious problems on his mind. "What are the names of these ushers?"

"There's only two, dear." Mrs. Mew tucked her handkerchief away down her cleavage. "Cyril Watterson and Douglas Pretty."

"Does Mr. Glossop hang his coat at the bottom of the stairs?"

"Of course he does, dear."

"And how about you, madam?"

Mrs. Mew was nobody's fool. She grinned. "Oh, I kept mine on, dear. That hall can strike very chill. You can ask anybody. I was wearing my mutation Chinese mink, you see, so they're sure to have noticed."

There is no doubt the questioning would have proceeded even more penetratingly if there hadn't been an interruption. The door burst open and a sporting-looking gentleman came breezily into the room.

He was only momentarily disconcerted at finding the place full of policemen. "Ah," he said, deftly slipping his bunch of keys back into his pocket, "you left the front door ajar, Iris." He indicated the bottle of champagne and the large heart-shaped box of chocolates with which he was burdened. "Just thought I'd pop round and see if I could cheer things up a bit. I'm Glossy Glossop, by the way."

MacGregor turned a little ostentatiously to a clean page in his notebook while Mr. Glossop made himself at home, pouring out a drink and sitting on the sofa next to Mrs. Mew. "You were the late Mr. Mew's business manager, I understand."

"Business manager, publicity agent, counselor—what's in a nomenclature, squire?" Mr. Glossop dropped his voice to a sincere baritone. "I was Humbert's *friend*." He got his cigar case out and offered Dover one.

"How long had you been with him?"

"Eighteen months. Long enough to fully appreciate the man's amazing gifts but not long enough, unfortunately, to persuade him to share them with the waiting world. Still, we were working on him, weren't we, Iris, my love?"

Dover took his free cigar out of his mouth and examined it with considerable alarm. The back of his throat felt as though somebody'd been at work with a blowtorch. He put the next question himself, just to make sure his vocal cords hadn't been damaged beyond recall. "What did you do before you became a con man?"

It was difficult to offend Mr. Glossop. He explained good-naturedly that he'd been a commercial traveler of sorts.

He was much more precise when it came to describing how Mr. Mew had fallen to his death that afternoon. When Mr. Mew had withdrawn for his normal bout of spiritual preparation, Mr. Glossop had, as per usual, taken up his station out in the main hall. It was a chore to have to sit there guarding the door for the best part of half an hour but bitter experience had shown how disastrous it was to allow the faith healer to be disturbed.

"Remember what a shambles we had at Brighton, Iris? When that stupid Welsh female broke in on him? God, the state he worked himself into he couldn't have cured a side of bacon. No, I learned my lesson at Brighton, squire. Since then, nobody—but *nobody*—has got past me."

MacGregor looked up. "But you did let some people go through the door from the hall, didn't you?"

"Only Pretty and Watterson. I don't count them. They know what the score is."

"Did they arrive together?"

"No, Pretty came first. Young Watterson didn't show up till ten to two. I remember wondering if the spotty little git was going to let us down again."

"How long did they take, hanging up their coats?"

"Not long enough to fix that trip wire up, if that's what you're after, squire. A few seconds."

"But the door from the hall was closed, wasn't it? You couldn't actually see them?"

Glossy Glossop handed his empty glass to Mrs. Mew and she got up to replenish it. Dover gulped the dregs of his down at top speed so as to save his hostess' legs.

"Out of sight is out of mind, squire! We had a number of newcomers at this afternoon's session and I wanted our two acolytes out there mingling. That's what they're appointed for—to mingle."

MacGregor watched Mr. Glossop carefully. "And how long were you hanging your coat up, sir?"

"Look, squire"—Glossy Glossop leaned forward to make sure MacGregor got the message—"I had a damned good look at those screws your young bobby found, and do you want my considered opinion? Five minutes! At least. That's if you'd got everything ready to hand like tools and things. Now, in those meetings in the Quine Street Rooms I'm a public figure, squire. If I'm not visible during the pre-liminaries, folk are going to notice, believe me. Five min-utes? If I'm not back in that hall in ten seconds flat I've got a queue forming to speak to me."

"Collusion," said Dover.

He and MacGregor were back in the police car again, driving through wet and deserted streets.

"Do you think so, sir?"

"'Strewth, even you must have spotted what was going on there."

MacGregor clenched his fists in the darkness of the back seat. Dover's habit of regarding his unmarried sergeant as a sexual ignoramus had ceased to be even mildly funny several years ago. "Extramarital liaisons are hardly grounds for murder these days, sir," he said coldly. "Not when divorce is so easy. Besides, I doubt if either Glossop or Mrs. Mew would be so foolish as to kill the goose that lays the golden egg."

"What golden egg?" demanded Dover. "That's what they kept sniveling about—that What's-his-name wouldn't turn himself into a money spinner."

"I fancy they were both better off financially with him, sir, than they are likely to be without him."

Dover switched tactics and plumped for blinding Mac-Gregor with higher mathematics. "So, what about the time element, eh?" he inquired. "If it takes five minutes for one person to fix those screws and things, two people could do it in half the time. It's like I said—collusion."

"Well, actually, sir," said MacGregor, "I've been thinking about the length of time it must have taken."

But he had left it too late. They had arrived at their destination and Dover was already legging it up the garden path with all the urgency of a man with a notoriously weak bladder.

What Mr. Pretty thought when he answered the impassioned hammering on his front door to find a large fat man—red of face and askew of bowler—charging over the threshold and demanding to be told where the karzi was, is not known. Suffice it to say that he kept his head, and with Dover closeted in the downstairs powder room, it fell to MacGregor to make the necessary introductions, explanations, and apologies.

"'Strewth," puffed Dover when he joined MacGregor and Mr. Pretty in the front room, "that was a near thing! I reckon that booze must have been off or something. If they weren't trying to poison me." He smacked his lips. "Left a hell of a funny taste in my mouth."

Mr. Pretty rose to the bait. "Would you like a cup of tea?"

Dover's sense of outrage was almost tangible. "Is that all you've got?"

"There's cocoa," said Mr. Pretty. "And I wonder if I could ask you to keep your voice down. Mother's in the next room. Mr. Mew's death has been a terrible shock to her and I've had to give her a sedative." He ran a trembling hand over his bald head. "I shudder to think what's going to happen now. Humbert Mew was all that's been keeping Mother alive. She was literally at death's door before we met him. And now . . . with him gone . . ."

He dabbed feebly at his lips with his handkerchief. "Mother is all I have, gentlemen. There's just the two of us. We've always been together and looked after each other." He swallowed hard. "I just don't know what I'll do if anything happens to her."

MacGregor began the routine questioning and it soon emerged that not only was Mr. Pretty unmarried but he didn't have a job either. Well, Mother had needed constant attention for many years and luckily there was enough money to keep them both in modest comfort.

Dover stared enviously at Douglas Pretty. Some people have all the luck! Not, mind you, that he—Dover—would have whiled away his leisure hours making crummy model airplanes, if he'd been blessed with a private income. Kid's stuff! He sneered comprehensively at the table which was littered with all the paraphernalia of Mr. Pretty's hobby— bits of cardboard and plastic, little tins of paint, glue.

Meantime, Mr. Pretty was wending his uninspired way through that afternoon's events at the Quine Street Rooms. He had little new to offer, even when Dover informed him, in a laudable attempt to liven things up, that he was the Number One murder suspect.

Mr. Pretty, it turned out, had arrived at the hall well before the meeting was due to start. "I have to get Mother settled, you see, and she doesn't like to be rushed. And then I have this usher's job to do, too."

"Ah, yes! You and Mr. Watterson." Dover liked to demonstrate that, unlike some, he kept all the facts at his fingertips.

"He was late," grumbled Mr. Pretty halfheartedly. "Last week he didn't show at all. It makes it very difficult for me, you know. They're nearly all on crutches or in wheelchairs or old or something."

Mr. Pretty had not, of course, noticed if there'd been a piece of string stretched across the top of the stairs. He'd never thought to look. He'd just hung up his coat and gone straight back into the hall to get on with his duties.

Dover bestirred himself to ask a question. "Was Who's-your-father already in that room upstairs when you hung your coat up?"

"Oh, yes. Mr. Mew was always the first to arrive. He had to be, didn't he? Because of the key."

"What key, for God's sake?"

Mr. Pretty couldn't understand what his two visitors were getting so excited about. It was only the key to the Quine Street Rooms. "The caretaker lives a couple of doors away and he's a proper little dictator. He won't hand the key over to anybody except the person who made the booking. He won't even let Mr. Glossop have it just because it's Mr. Mew's name on his list." Mr. Pretty managed a sketchy smile. "Whatever else you can say about the Quine Street Rooms, their security was good."

Detectives like concrete things like keys, so MacGregor make a careful note of this one before pressing on with his interrogation.

No, Mr. Pretty couldn't imagine who would want to kill Mr. Mew—a man universally loved and respected and who had, after all, devoted his life to the service of others.

A disgruntled patient?

Mr. Pretty shook his head. "He never promised to cure anybody. He just said he'd do his best. And he was so obviously sincere that I can't see anybody bearing a grudge against him."

Could money be a motive?

Mr. Pretty looked shocked. "Mr. Mew wasn't making

any money out of this! I know there was a small charge to attend the healing sessions, but that was only to cover the cost of the hall. People did make donations, of course. Mother did. But they were only small sums that people could afford."

MacGregor sighed. He could see that Dover was getting restless. No doubt hunger was gnawing at the fat slob's vitals yet again. Or thirst. "One last question, Mr. Pretty. Where were you when Mr. Mew fell?"

"Oh, out in the hall. I was talking to that lady with the rheumatism in her knees. I rushed over as soon as I heard the sound of Mr. Mew falling. I found Mr. Glossop already on the scene. He was just standing there, looking. Well, I could see that Mr. Mew was still alive and I was just about to kneel down and see how bad he was when Mr. Glossop sort of pushed me out of the way. Quite roughly, actually. He told me to go and phone for an ambulance.

"Well, that seemed awfully silly to me because I'm really quite experienced when it comes to handling sick people, whereas Mr. Glossop isn't. I suggested it would be far better if he did the telephoning while I tried to do what I could for Mr. Mew." Douglas Pretty's eyes glinted almost spitefully behind his thick glasses. "Mr. Glossop seemed to lose his head completely. He shouted at me to do as I was told and stop arguing, and to shut the door leading out to the hall behind me because, by now, people were crowding round and staring in."

"Stingy creep!" said Dover as they waited for Mr. Watterson's landlady to tear herself away from the television set and answer the door. "Him and his damn cocoa!"

MacGregor rang the bell again. "I don't suppose there's anything much stronger in that household, sir."

"Which proves how bloody little you know about it,

laddie!" retorted Dover, giving the door a kick. "If there's one thing folk keep handy for sick old ladies, it's brandy. 'Strewth, I could just do with a drop of Three Star to keep the chill out."

To Dover's fury, Cyril Watterson's hospitality didn't even extend to cocoa. His landlady provided two cooked meals a day (three at weekends) and it would have been a foolhardy lodger who asked for anything more. She didn't hold with smoking, either.

"Your problem, laddie!" said Dover, taking a deep drag on the cigarette he'd cadged from MacGregor.

Cyril Watterson, a gangly youth, scrabbled around frantically for something that would do as an ashtray. The best he could find was a tin of zinc ointment and it took him several attempts to get the lid off.

"Nervous, are you, laddie?" asked Dover with a leer. "Got a bit of a guilty conscience, eh?"

Cyril Watterson shoved his hands deep out of sight in his pockets. "I hardly knew Mr. Mew," he protested, backing into a small table and almost knocking it over. "I only started going to him four or five weeks ago, and for all the good it's done me I might as well not have bothered. Bloomin' acne!" he moaned. "Girls think it's catching, you know." He remembered to whom he was speaking. "Not that I blamed Mr. Mew," he declared hurriedly. "I'm sure he did his best. And he's been no worse than the bloomin' doctors, has he?"

"You were acting as an usher this afternoon?" asked MacGregor.

"They're a bit short on people who've got their health and strength." Cyril Watterson was giving most of his attention to Dover. Dear God, the old beggar wasn't really flicking his ash all over the floor, was he? "Not that I minded helping out. Not when I thought Mr. Mew was going to cure my spots. But lately, well . . . It's not as though you ever meet any birds there, is it? I skipped it last week," he added proudly. "I went to that Rock Festival in Dorset. Smashing! No shortage of crumpet there, eh?"

As a would-be, latter-day Don Juan, young Mr. Watterson was singularly unconvincing with his prominent Adam's apple and his acne bouncing back the light from the naked, overhead bulb.

MacGregor averted his eyes. "Have you any thoughts about who might have killed Mr. Mew?"

"Glossy Glossop," said Cyril Watterson, flattered to have his views canvassed by experts from Scotland Yard. "I suspected him the minute it happened. I never bought that accident theory, you know."

If there was one thing Dover could do without it was this young punk's half-baked ideas. "You could have fixed that bit of string across as easy as him, laddie."

"Ah, but I haven't got a motive, have I?"

"Has Glossop?"

"Hasn't he just!" In his eagerness to assist the police in their inquiries Cyril Watterson sent a pile of girlie magazines slithering to the floor. He ignored them, and so did Dover. It was many a long day since the real thing had sent the blood coursing through the chief inspector's veins, never mind a few crummy photographs. "Money!" said Mr. Watterson. "Mind you, he's been fooling around with the fair Iris, but I don't reckon that as a reason for bumping Mr. Mew off. I mean, why buy a garage when you can hire a car?"

Dover eyed Cyril Watterson with intense dislike. "What car?"

Cyril Watterson decided, very sensibly, to come straight to the point. There had been instances when various clever devils had attempted to take Dover with them on their flights of fancy, and had ended up in the dock facing very serious charges. "I work in an accountant's office," he explained, "and I get a bit of commission if I introduce new business. So, I put it to Mr. Mew that it might be a good idea to have his books done properly, by experts."

"And?"

"He was very taken with the idea. Said Glossy Glossop was forever going on about them being short of money and Mr. Mew couldn't understand it because he was doing such good work and the people he helped always seemed to be grateful and generous. He said I'd given him a whole new slant on things. It wasn't that God or whoever wasn't providing enough of the ready, it was just that old Glossy couldn't cope with the bookkeeping."

MacGregor, at any rate, was interested. "When was this?"

"Two or three weeks ago. Well, that's it, isn't it? Mr. Mew tells Glossy he's going to have the books audited by my firm, and Glossy sees the game's up. I reckon he's been fiddling things for years. That's why Mr. Mew wasn't killed last week."

"What do you mean?"

Cyril Watterson sighed. If this was Scotland Yard! "Because I wasn't there, was I? Glossy maybe hoped I'd gone for good and all this business about proper accounts would die the death. But this afternoon there I was again. So Glossy had to knock Mr. Mew off quicker than that before he could contact me and give me the go-ahead. Get it?"

There is no doubt that MacGregor would have pursued the matter further if it hadn't been for the ominous rumbles coming from Dover's stomach. Dover feeling peckish could be pure murder, so MacGregor lost no time in rushing him off to the nearest pub which sold bar snacks.

A pork pie, two cheese and pickle sandwiches, a piece of

apple tart, and three pints of best bitter later found Dover
in more amenable mood. Indeed, he would have been well
nigh comatose if the pangs of hunger hadn't been replaced
by those of indigestion.

Dover belched loudly before summing up his investigation thus far. "You can't win 'em all."

MacGregor was taken aback. Dover usually gave a murder case at least forty-eight hours before writing it off as
insoluble. "But, sir—"

"Waste of the taxpayer's money," said Dover, as if he
cared. He leaned back and undid the top button of his
trousers. "It'll be one of that lot we've seen," he added
with a grunt, "but we'll probably never know which one."

"But don't you think we ought to follow up this business of Glossop and the money, sir?"

Dover's determination to throw in the towel overcame
his natural instinct to speak ill of people. "Glossop doesn't
look like a murderer to me, laddie."

Desperate times call for desperate measures. MacGregor
got his wallet out. "Can I get you another drink, sir?"

"I'll have a large rum and peppermint. This flatulence is
giving me hell."

Having thus purchased five minutes of Dover's butterfly
attention, MacGregor couldn't afford to waste it. "I think
we've been going slightly off course, sir," he began cautiously because Dover didn't take kindly to criticism.
"We've been assuming the murderer set the booby trap
after Mr. Mew retired to that upstairs room."

"Have we?"

"The screws could have been put in at any time, sir.
Then, today, the twine could have been fixed across in a
matter of seconds."

"That just makes everything even more bloody complicated."

"Not quite, sir. We'll need to check, of course, but because of the caretaker it doesn't look easy to gain unauthorized access to that hall. The murderer would therefore probably have put the screws in when he was there in the normal course of events. Say a week ago, at the last faith healing session."

Dover, who seemed to be having some difficulty in focusing his eyes, refrained from comment.

"And our murderer would need to be pretty good with his hands, sir. Getting those screws in would be quite tricky."

"That eliminates acne-face, then!" said Dover as the mists cleared for a moment. "Fingers like a bunch of bananas!"

MacGregor began to feel quite hopeful. "We may be able to eliminate Mr. Watterson on another count, sir," he said encouragingly. "He wasn't there last week."

"It's all bloody theory," grumbled Dover. He removed his bowler hat and wiped the sweat from his brow. "And it still leaves three of 'em—What's-his-name, Who's-your-father, and the woman."

"Only Glossop and Pretty, actually, sir. Mrs. Mew kept her coat on, you remember, and didn't go near the staircase. She wouldn't have had the opportunity of making even the final adjustments to the booby trap."

"So she says," mumbled Dover, feeling vaguely uneasy as the rum started fighting it out with the other contents of his stomach.

"She's not likely to have lied about something so easy to check, sir. Which leaves Glossop and Pretty."

Some people would have tossed a coin. Dover simply recalled that heart-shaped box of chocolates that had never been handed round. "It's Glossop!" He amplified this theory. "Cooking the books and adultery."

"I rather fancy Mr. Pretty, sir."

"You would!" sniggered Dover. He loved a good joke at the expense of his somewhat fastidious sergeant. "Just your type! Couldn't say boo to a goose. Besides, what's his motive? According to him, What-do-you-call-him was all that was keeping his mother alive."

Family affection was not one of Dover's weaknesses, so even he got the point. "'Strewth, that's clever! Murder your rich old mother and the finger of suspicion's pointing straight at you. But knock off the one person who's keeping the old bird alive—"

"With his mother dead, sir, Pretty gets his freedom and the money while he's still young enough to enjoy it."

Dover thought hard. If it was MacGregor's theory, there must be something wrong with it. "It won't hold water, laddie!"

MacGregor frowned. "Sir?"

"When the Cat man—"

"The Cat man, sir?"

Dover's entire body wobbled with mirth. "Mew-cat!" he guffawed. "Get it laddie?"

One day, MacGregor promised himself grimly, he was going to cast prudence to the winds and stick a straight right on Dover's chins. "Very amusing, sir."

"You know your trouble, laddie," snarled Dover. "No bloody sense of humor. Well, like I was saying, when he fell downstairs, they all came running—right? And there was a bit of an argey-bargey about who should phone for the ambulance and who should stay alone with the body—right? Well, you nit, it was *Glossop* who insisted on staying and on having the bloody door shut! He wouldn't have done that if he hadn't been the murderer."

MacGregor could never keep that stuff about grandmothers and eggs at the forefront of his mind. "On the contrary, sir, that's the clincher! Don't you see? If Glossop was the murderer and he'd been left alone for even a couple of minutes back there by the staircase, he'd have removed those screws and the twine—the only evidence we have that it was murder at all. The fact that no attempt was made to get rid of such incriminating evidence proves that the real killer was never given the opportunity."

There was a long pause after Dover chewed this over. "Pity," he said at last.

"Sir?"

"You should have mentioned it earlier, laddie." Dover began gathering his overcoat round him and generally preparing to get to his feet. "We might have jostled What's-his-name round a bit and got a confession."

"We could still confront him with the evidence, sir."

Dover shook his head. "It's all theory, laddie. Even the grounds for calling it murder are pretty shaky."

MacGregor didn't approve of intimidating suspects but, damn it all, they couldn't just fold their tents and steal away. "If we persuaded Pretty to confess, sir—"

"Easy as pie," agreed Dover. "One hard push and he'd spill the lot. Trouble is, it would never stand up in court. He'd get himself one of these shyster lawyers, shout 'police brutality,' and then where'd we be? No"—Dover made a supreme effort and achieved the vertical—"I reckon we're just going to have to forget about this one. Chalk it up to experience." He looked round. "You spotted the privy in your travels?"

"It's out at the back, sir. But, sir"—MacGregor so far forgot the most elementary rules of hygiene as to catch hold of Dover's sleeve with his bare hands—"we can't just let Pretty get away with murder."

"He won't get away with it, laddie," said Dover reassuringly. "What's the first thing the silly beggar'll do now that he's not tied to his old mother and he's got a nice bit of cash? He'll get married, won't he? That's punishment enough for any man. Now, you've just got time to get another round in, laddie, before they put the towel over the pumps. I'll be back in a minute."

—1982

A Souvenir for Dover

"Ongar."

The two other men in the police car realized that Detective Chief Inspector Dover had woken up and was taking notice.

"Ongar," he said again, savoring the word.

The police driver stared woodenly ahead but Dover's assistant, the young and dashing Detective Sergeant MacGregor, couldn't avoid the burdens of social intercourse so easily.

"Sir?"

Dover bestirred himself and his fourteen and a half stone of unlovely fat oozed even farther across the back seat of the car. "'Buy Ongar, it's longer and stronger,'" he quoted.

Sergeant MacGregor, already squeezed as far as he could go into his corner, noted this unwonted display of animation with alarm. It was a swelteringly hot day but Dover refused to have a window open on the grounds that fresh air went straight to his stomach. The atmosphere in the police car had to be breathed to be believed, and the last thing anybody wanted was Dover getting excited and making things worse.

"Indeed, sir."

"It's the best damned lavatory paper there is!" snapped Dover, who didn't care for subordinates arguing with him. "We've used it for years."

"Really, sir?"

"I've tried to get 'em to buy it at the Yard. Like I told 'em—it's educational, really."

Recalling the considerable portion of the working day that Chief Inspector Dover already spent closeted in the gentlemen's toilet, MacGregor was not surprised that the Scotland Yard authorities were reluctant to make their facilities even more attractive. Though how anybody could find the motley collection of humorous anecdotes, household hints, medical advice, conundrums, advertisements, and inspirational Thoughts for the Day which were printed on every sheet of Ongar toilet paper in any way educational was beyond MacGregor's somewhat limited imagination.

"It's the ink that does it," observed Dover.

"Does what, sir?"

"Doesn't come off, you fool! It was old Mrs. Ongar herself who invented it."

"I didn't know that, sir."

"You would have if you read Ongar's toilet rolls, laddie. 'Strewth, she must have made a bloody fortune." Dover devoted a few moments' silence to pea-green envy before his enthusiasm reasserted itself. "Did you see the one with the cartoons? Bloody funny, that was. Oh, well"—he sighed deeply—"it's the end of an era, I suppose."

"What is, sir?"

"Old Mrs. Ongar getting wiped out."

MacGregor clenched his teeth. Dear God, you would have thought the stupid bastard . . . "It's not Mrs. Ongar who's been murdered, sir. It's her great-nephew. A young man called Michael Montgomery."

Dover's interest waned. He eased his greasy bowler hat back on his head and cautiously undid the top button of his overcoat. "'Strewth, it's hot in here." He dragged out a handkerchief that few people could have cared to touch without surgical gloves and mopped his brow. "Got a fag, laddie?"

"I think we're just arriving, sir."

Dover glanced out of the window as the car turned into a driveway and approached a large, rambling house standing in its own grounds. He perked up a bit. Not exactly Buckingham Palace, but not bad. Not bad at all. There should be good pickings here.

The local constabulary had been on the scene for some time and were still milling busily around. Most of the available space in front of the house was occupied by their vehicles, lights flashing and radios chattering. Alerted by an underling, a uniformed inspector appeared in the doorway, but Dover, incensed at having had to walk all of fifty yards from his car, was in no mood to bandy compliments with power-mad bumpkins.

"Where's the stiff?" he demanded, pausing, as he waddled painfully across the threshold, only long enough to deliver one of his better full-frontal scowls.

It was the uniformed inspector's first experience of the Dover Method of detection but he was a highly disciplined man who fully appreciated the consequences of ramming a superior officer's false teeth down his throat. Prudently unclenching his fists, he led the way to the back of the house.

The scene of the crime was a poky, apparently disused pantry which had been perfunctorily converted into a bedroom. Tight-lipped, the uniformed inspector indicated the salient features. Pride of place was occupied by the late Michael Montgomery, pinned to the mattress of a camp bed by a World War II German army bayonet, the hilt of which was still sticking up out the middle of his chest. There were no signs of a struggle and only a modest path of brown blood stained the top sheet, through which the blade had passed.

"The murder weapon was the property of the deceased, sir," said the uniformed inspector, "and there are no fingerprints on the handle. It has been wiped clean."

Dover tipped what might have been a pile of vital evidence off the only available chair and sat down with a grunt of relief. "Access?"

"Sir?"

"How did the bloody murderer get in, numbskull?"

"Well, through the door you came in by, sir. There's no other way."

Dover raised a meaty and none-too-clean forefinger. "What about that then, eh?" He pointed at a second door across which the camp bed had been somewhat awkwardly jammed.

"We checked that, sir. It leads into the back yard, but it's not been used for years. It's locked and bolted on this side."

"In any case, you can't open it," said MacGregor, "because the camp bed's in the way."

Dover ignored him. "Windows?"

"Just the one, sir." By now the uniformed inspector was realizing that he'd drawn Scotland Yard's only purblind detective. He carefully picked his way through the obstacle course of discarded clothing, canvas grips, dog-eared girlie magazines, and plastic bags from the Duty Free Shop which littered the floor, and triumphantly indicated the window. "It's heavily barred, sir. Nobody could gain entry that way."

MacGregor went to look for himself. "Was it open last night?"

"No."

"It was very hot."

"Not hot enough to melt the layers of paint on that window, sergeant. You'd need a chisel to get it open."

Dover's chair creaked impatiently. "Time of death?"

"The doctor reckons in the small hours of this morning, sir. He'll have a better idea when—"

"Instantaneous?"

"Virtually, sir."

"Need any expert knowledge or strength?"

"The doctor thought not, sir. A heavy, fairly sharp blade plunged into the chest of a man lying on his back and most likely asleep—well, you'd have a job not to kill him."

"And no bloody fingerprints," complained Dover. "Just my bloody luck!"

"None that can't be accounted for, sir. No clues at all, really."

"Never are these days," said Dover. "It's all this detective stuff on the telly. Talk about an Open University course in bloody crime!"

The ambulance men came for the body. They got no resistance from Dover. Bloodstained corpses put him right off his food, and he didn't care who knew it.

On the pretext of trying to arrange for a cup of coffee, MacGregor slipped away and managed to achieve a slightly more professional debriefing of the uniformed inspector, though he wondered why he bothered. This case already bore the hallmarks of one of those typical Dover cock-ups in which the last person likely to be inconvenienced was the murderer.

When MacGregor returned, he found Dover still sitting on his chair, halfheartedly leafing through one of the victim's girlie magazines. Instantly abandoning the soft porn, Dover struck straight for the jugular vein of the situation.

"Where's my bloody coffee?"

"Just coming, sir," lied MacGregor. "I thought you might care to see Mrs. Wilkins first."

"Mrs. Who? 'Strewth"—Dover's butterfly flitted off on one of its many tangents—"what a tip!" He swept a lethargic arm round the room. "Catch me spending the night in a crummy dump like this."

"It is a bit basic, sir," agreed MacGregor, "but that's no reason for this Montgomery chap to have dumped all his belongings on the floor."

"No wardrobe."

"There are some hooks behind the door, sir."

"No dressing-table. No bedside lamp. And it pongs."

MacGregor wondered if the pong had been quite so pronounced before Dover had arrived.

"Suppose you got taken short in the night?" demanded Dover with all the caring concern of one who frequently did. "Have you seen where the blooming light switch is?"

MacGregor, a trained detective, had. It was on the wall next to the locked and bolted door across which the camp bed had been pushed. "I thought it was quite handy, really, sir. Well, when you're in bed, that is. A bit awkward, perhaps, when you come into the room by the other door."

"You could break your bloody neck," insisted Dover indignantly, "groping around for that in the bloody dark. In an emergency. Speaking of which, laddie"—he rose ponderously to his feet—"have you spotted a lavatory in your travels?"

By the time Dover got round to questioning Mrs. Wilkins—he'd found the roll of biblical quotations in the downstairs loo almost totally absorbing—the good lady herself had had ample time to sort out precisely what she intended to tell him. Seated on the camp bed—it was either that or stand—she delivered her statement with a succinctness that left Dover floundering.

Mrs. Wilkins was housekeeper-companion to old Mrs. Ongar and the only living-in servant. The others came in daily but on that particular morning they had, of course, been turned back by the police. How Mrs. Wilkins was supposed to cope with a prostrate Mrs. Ongar, a houseful of guests, and all these blessed repetitions about how she found the body she simply didn't—

Dover clutched at the one straw he could see. Mrs. What's-her-name had found the body, had she?

At seven-thirty that morning. She'd gone in to waken this Montgomery boy—

"With a cup of tea?"

If that was a hint, Mrs. Wilkins ignored it. She'd gone in to waken this Montgomery boy because he was the sort of idle ne'er-do-well who'd spend all day lolling in bed given half the chance. Mrs. Ongar liked her guests to be up with the sun. Mind you, Mrs. Ongar didn't have to try rousing people who were as dead as mutton with nasty great knives stuck in their chests. Not that Mrs. Wilkins had lost her head. She had broken the news to Mrs. Ongar and then phoned the police. She hadn't touched anything and neither had anybody else because she'd kept the door locked until the police came, and if that was all she'd be going because she'd only got one pair of hands and they'd all be screaming for their lunch before she'd had time to turn round.

For all Dover cared, she could have dropped down dead, but MacGregor took the fight against crime more seriously. To the accompaniment of baleful looks from both Dover and Mrs. Wilkins, he insisted on asking a few questions.

When Mrs. Wilkins went to waken Mr. Montgomery—
Well?

—was the door closed?

Yes. Mrs. Wilkins had given a perfunctory tap and come straight in, having no intention of standing on ceremony with the likes of him.

Was the light on?

It had better not have been. Mrs. Ongar had a thing about wasting electricity.

So the room was in darkness?

Bright as day. Which was just as well, seeing the state his room was in. Why youngsters like him couldn't hang things up in a civilized manner was beyond her. Mind you, she blamed the parents.

MacGregor frowned. So the curtains were open?

The curtains were closed. They were also paper-thin. Mrs. Wilkins was surprised that MacGregor hadn't spotted that for himself. They let in more light than they kept out. And with the sun blazing down out of a clear blue sky—

MacGregor tried again. "I understand that Mr. Montgomery was only a guest. He didn't live here."

He lived in Australia and it was a pity he hadn't stayed there. Of course he was only a guest—and an uninvited one to boot. That's why he'd been put in the old pantry. It was the best they could do at short notice with the house being full. Waltzed in the day before yesterday, he had, large as life and as handsome if you didn't count those shifty eyes and the pimples. Straight from Heathrow without so much as a phonecall first to see if it was convenient. As if Mrs. Wilkins hadn't enough on her plate without hordes of foreigners descending without so much as a by-your-leave.

MacGregor had looked up from his notebook some time ago, but Mrs. Wilkins was not one to yield the floor until she was good and ready. "You say the house was full?"

Of course it was full. Still was. Full of Mrs. Ongar's sponging relations, any one of whom would walk barefoot over a bed of nails for a free meal.

But they had been invited.

Mrs. Wilkins tossed MacGregor a final crumb before she brought the interview to a close. Of course they'd been invited. They'd come to celebrate Mrs. Ongar's seventy-fifth birthday yesterday. There'd been a posh dinner party and Mrs. Wilkins still hadn't got straight after it—a situation she proposed to rectify forthwith. Meantime, she would like to remind everybody that it was nearly a quarter past and Mrs. Ongar didn't like to be kept waiting.

"Mrs. Ongar?" echoed MacGregor.

"Across the entrance hall," said Mrs. Wilkins crisply. "Turn left. First on the right. Knock before you go in."

Mrs. Ongar was in bed. Propped up amongst her pillows, she gave an impression of frailty and vulnerability, belied only by a formidable jaw line of which the late Benito Mussolini would not have been ashamed.

Two chairs had been placed in readiness and Dover sank gratefully into the nearest. This hot weather played hell with his feet. When a few moments later Mrs. Wilkins marched in with coffee and biscuits, the chief inspector was almost happy. Munching rhythmically, he stared with some curiosity at the woman who single-handedly put toilet rolls on the map. Mrs. Ongar handed a sheet of paper to MacGregor. "The name of the murderer is on that list."

MacGregor tried to look grateful.

"It contains the names of the five people who were staying in the house as my guests last night."

"For your birthday party, eh?" asked Dover, wondering if there'd been a cake.

Mrs. Ongar had got Dover's measure as soon as he entered the room. She continued to address herself to MacGregor. "They are the sole surviving members of the family, on my side and on my late husband's. Three of them—Christine Finch, Daniel Ongar, and young Toby Stockdale—would like to think of themselves as potential heirs to the Ongar empire. I don't believe in rule by committee and it has always been my aim to leave the entire concern to one person. Since I own ninety-eight percent of the shares, whoever I appoint as my heir will get the lot."

"It sounds more like a motive for your murder than for your great-nephew's," said MacGregor diffidently.

Mrs. Ongar's nostrils flared. "If I might continue without interruption . . . Some years ago I made a will leaving everything to my great-nephew, Michael Montgomery, in Australia. I have had ample time to study my other relations and none of them is fit to run a multi-million-pound business. Daniel Ongar, Toby Stockdale, and Christine's husband, Major Finch, have all been given jobs in the firm and their achievements have been no more than average. If they hadn't been members of the family, I should have dispensed with their services long ago."

Dover shifted unhappily in his chair. Having drunk his coffee and eaten all the biscuits, he was beginning to find time hanging heavy on his hands. His gaze wandered idly about in search of diversion. Mrs. Ongar's bedroom was on the ground floor and had a bathroom en suite. Dover envied her that convenience. Not that it stopped the old biddy keeping an old-fashioned chamber pot under her bed. In fact, Mrs. Ongar seemed to be a real belt-and-braces character. Everything had a back-up system. On the bedside table there was not only an electric bell-push but a large handbell as well, to say nothing of a police whistle dangling on a ribbon from the headboard of the bed. And she'd got two wheelchairs, one manual and one battery-driven.

Mrs. Ongar was still telling MacGregor about her family. "Toby Stockdale is a junior sales representative—in other words, a commercial traveler. David Ongar, my late husband's younger brother, is Chief Personnel Officer, when he can tear himself away from the golf course."

"And Major Finch, madam?"

"He is in charge of security. After an undistinguished career in the Army, he seemed well suited for the position. There is," observed Mrs. Ongar drily, "comparatively little crime in the toilet-paper industry and, as far as industrial espionage is concerned, I myself safeguard the formula for our ink."

Dover was losing interest in the desultory inventory he'd been making of Mrs. Ongar's possessions—an electric torch *and* a candle, wires denoting an electric blanket on the bed *and* a rubber hot-water bottle on one of the chairs, a pair of stout walking-sticks *and* one of those Zimmer frame things. His eye slipped indifferently over a single red rose drooping terminally in a vase. Security officer at Ongar's? That didn't sound a bad job. The sort of thing an experienced ex-copper should be able to do with his eyes closed.

"What's the screw?"

Mrs. Ongar blenched, but she hadn't got where she was by letting trifles like Dover throw her. Quite calmly and dispassionately she studied the crumpled suit, the dandruff epaulettes on that disgusting overcoat, the unspeakable bowler hat, the pale podgy face with the mean little eyes, the moth-eaten mustache. Then she took a deep breath and put the whole sordid spectacle right out of her mind.

"You must realize," she said, addressing herself exclusively to MacGregor, "that while Christine Finch is actually my niece, her husband—the major—and her daughter have just as good reasons for killing poor Michael. They would both benefit if I were to leave Ongar's to Christine."

"Oh, quite," said MacGregor.

"One of the reasons, you know, that I made poor Michael my heir was that I thought he would be safe, far away in Australia, from the murderous machinations of the rest of the family, safe from their greed and jealousy. You can imagine my feelings"—Mrs. Ongar raised a lightly starched handkerchief momentarily to her eyes—"when the poor boy just walked in. It was a terrible shock. And when I saw the hatred on *their* faces—I blame myself. I should have known they would kill him the moment they had the chance."

MacGregor tried to lower the emotional tension by asking a few routine questions. Predictably, Mrs. Ongar was of little help.

"Last night was my birthday party," she reminded Mac-Gregor. "A happy day, but a tiring one. I didn't get to bed until after eleven and then I slept like a log. All the noise and the excitement and the rich food . . ." She relaxed back deeper into her pillows. "Oh, well, it's not every day that one reaches the age of seventy-five, is it?"

There seemed little point in prolonging the interview. Mrs. Ongar seemed tired and so, if the sagging jowls and the drooping eyelids were anything to go by, did Dover.

MacGregor smiled sympathetically at Mrs. Ongar. "Well, we'll leave you to get some rest," he murmured.

"Rest?" Mrs. Ongar's head jerked up. "There's no rest for me, young man."

"No?"

"I have to draw up a new will. I've already sent for my solicitor."

"A new will?"

Mrs. Ongar looked cross. "Haven't you realized that it's *my* life that's in danger. Michael was killed for my money."

"But if you leave your money to one of the others—"

"Precisely! And if I don't make a will, my niece, Christine, will inherit everything. Suppose it was one of the Finch family that murdered Michael? Do you think they would hesitate to kill me in my turn?"

MacGregor tried to suppress the thought that a second murder in the Ongar household might make it a good deal easier to solve the first. "What are you going to do, then?"

"That's my secret!" snapped Mrs. Ongar. "But you can rest assured that I shall take every precaution. In the meantime I want Michael's murderer found without delay. And I also want all the remaining members of my family out of this house as soon as possible. My safety must be your prime concern."

Dover and MacGregor retired to the dining room, which had been set aside for their use. Dover propped his elbows on the highly polished mahogany table and glowered disconsolately at Mrs. Ongar's list of potential murderers. "We're never going to solve this one."

MacGregor tried to take a more positive attitude. "Oh, I expect we'll get to the bottom of it, sir."

Dover pushed the list away and reached for the packet of cigarettes MacGregor had laid out on the table as a sweetener. "Not a single bloody clue for a start," he grumbled as he accepted a light from MacGregor's elegant gold lighter. "This joker creeps downstairs in the middle of the night, stabs What's-his-name with his own bloody bayonet, and creeps back to bed again. No fingerprints, no footprints, no bloodstains, didn't drop anything, and a motive that's shared with half a dozen other people. We're on a hiding to nothing."

MacGregor opened his notebook and laid his pencil ready. "Careful questioning of the suspects, sir—"

"Why don't you grow up, laddie?" demanded Dover. "Careful bloody questioning? Look"—he dropped his voice to a tempting murmur—"why don't we rough 'em up a bit?"

"We can't do that, sir."

"Why not? As long as we're careful not to thump 'em where it shows, it'll be their word against ours. And, if we stick together—"

MacGregor was reluctant to waste time discussing the extent to which Dover's fist could be considered a legitimate instrument of justice. "Why don't we just see how far we get playing it by the book first, sir?"

Dover's thirst for violence was a good deal less passionate than his desire for a quiet life. "Oh, suit yourself!" he grunted as a lump of cigarette ash joined the rest of the debris on his waistcoat. "Let's have this security fellow to start with. Major What's-his-name. I rather fancy him."

Major Finch knew the value of reinforcements and arrived accompanied by his lady-wife and his less than ladylike teenage daughter. "We're all three in exactly the same boat," he explained, "and I thought it would save time."

Dover shrugged his shoulders to indicate that it was no skin off his nose.

The Finches had heard nothing, seen nothing, and knew nothing.

"We were all dog-tired," drawled Mrs. Finch, who tried to distance herself from her lavatory-paper connections by affecting an air of languid sophistication. "That ghastly dinner party! I had a splitting head. I had to take a sleeping pill, so the whole house could have gone up in flames for all I cared."

"Pretty grim," agreed her husband. "And the way Auntie fawned over that disgusting young punk didn't help. Talk about killing the fatted calf!"

"You'd have thought the rest of us simply didn't exist," complained Mrs. Finch. "I'd like to know what she'd have said if we'd turned up without a birthday present. That damned paisley shawl cost over fifty quid and for all the thanks we got you'd think we'd bought it in a sale at Woolworth's."

Samantha-Ivette, the teenage daughter with four earrings in one ear and pink hair, found contradicting her elders more natural than breathing and twice as much fun. "Mick didn't know it was her birthday."

"Then it was an amazing coincidence, darling, that he arrived all the way from Australia just in time for it."

"And he got her that red rose."

"A single red rose!" snorted Major Finch. "Very romantic! Especially when he'd had the damned cheek to touch me for a fiver to buy the old girl something, and then comes back with that damned bayonet for himself. Well, much good it did him!"

MacGregor tried to muscle in. "Who knew about the bayonet?"

"Everybody knew about the bayonet," said Major Finch impatiently. "He was fooling about with it all through dinner, the damned idiot. I suppose we ought to be grateful he didn't buy himself a submachine gun and a couple of live hand-grenades while he was about it."

"He didn't buy the bayonet," Samantha-Ivette chipped in proudly. "He nicked it. From that shop by the post office. I helped him. I had to keep the old man talking while Mick pinched the bayonet. It was terrific fun."

"Samantha-Ivette!" wailed Mrs. Finch.

"He pinched the red rose, too. From the cemetery."

"My God!" exploded Major Finch. "Well, I just hope all this has taught Auntie Beryl a lesson."

"You mean you hope she'll leave Ongar's to Mummy now, don't you?" inquired Samantha-Ivette pertly. "Why should she? I think she liked Mick, really."

"She was appalled by him! And with good reason."

"Well, at least he wasn't a fuddy-duddy old stick-in-the-mud."

"He was a vicious young lout!"

"You think everybody who smokes a bit of pot is a moral degenerate."

"Smokes pot?" Mrs. Finch clutched her heart. "I didn't know he smoked pot. Why didn't somebody say? Auntie would have thrown him out of the house."

"Oh, Mummy, don't be so prehistoric!"

Dover got enough of this sort of thing at home without having to put up with it at work as well. He fixed Major Finch with a beady eye. "Hear you're a security officer," he grunted. "Thought that was a job for an ex-copper."

Major Finch took a second or two to catch up, but eventually he agreed that many security officers were indeed former policemen. "Not that background is all that important, you know. Any conscientious, reasonably intelligent man with good organizing ability can cope."

Dover was less interested in the qualifications than the rewards. "How much do you get paid?"

Major Finch was shocked. "I'm afraid my salary is a confidential matter," he said coldly. "Strictly between myself and Ongar's."

And five minutes of intensive browbeating failed to make the major unseal his lips, in spite of Dover's repeated warnings that such an uncooperative attitude did a murder suspect little good. In the end it was Dover who got fed up first and the Finch family, more than a little confused about what was going on, were allowed to take their leave.

Daniel Ongar, when he was shown into the dining room, got a smoother ride as Dover harbored no pipe dreams about becoming a personnel officer. However, his suggestion that the murderer had been some passing maniac tramp was received without enthusiasm.

"But why should any of us want to kill the little blackguard?" he asked, adjusting his cuffs and running a hand over his thinning hair.

Dover told him.

Daniel Ongar waved the explanation aside. "Nobody knows which one of us will get Ongar's now," he pointed out. "Beryl's quite potty on the subject or she'd never have made that nasty Montgomery boy her sole heir in the first place. Dear God, she'd never even seen him. Now, I don't pretend to be any more moral than the next chap, but you don't really see me committing murder, do you, just to see the whole kit and caboodle go to Toby Stockdale or one of Dickie Bird's lot?"

Dickie Bird?

"Richard Finch. That's what they used to call him in the Army. And what about *him* as a prime suspect? He was in the infantry and if you want somebody who knows how to use a bayonet—"

"Have you no idea who the next heir will be, sir?"

Daniel Ongar stared imperturbably at MacGregor. "None, except that it's unlikely to be me. I'm sixty and, in dear Beryl's book, that's geriatric. She talks about keeping it in the family but it could be the cats' home or the Chancellor of the Exchequeur or something equally daft. I mean, where was the logic in leaving it all to young Montgomery, apart from the fact that he was tucked away safe on the other side of the world and unlikely to come bothering her? Poor Beryl, she thinks everybody's after her money. I'll bet she's told you one of us is going to murder her next."

"Don't you think she's every reason to be anxious, sir?"

"No, I damned well don't! Can't you see that Beryl is more valuable to us alive than dead? Dickie Bird, Toby, and I have got pretty well-paid jobs. Mrs. Wilkins, too, if it comes to that. What guarantee have we got that Beryl's successor, whoever it is, won't give the whole bang shoot of us the sack?"

"Speaking of well-paid jobs," said Dover, "how much will your chief security officer be getting?"

Daniel Ongar frowned. "Dickie Finch? A damned sight more than we'd pay an outsider, that's for sure. About twenty thousand, I should think."

"'Strewth!" said Dover.

While MacGregor went off to fetch the last suspect for questioning, Dover busied himself with some simple arithmetic on the margins of the girlie magazine he had absent-mindedly removed from the scene of the crime. After much head-scratching and a heavy precipitation of dandruff he achieved a result which took his breath away. With his pension, even allowing for early retirement, and twenty thousand plus perks—well, there was bound to be a bit of a fiddle somewhere—he'd be bloody rolling in it!

Even when Toby Stockdale, an uninspiring young man in his middle twenties, was sitting opposite him across the dining-room table, Dover seemed unable to drag his popping eyes away from the girlie magazine, an apparent preoccupation which did little to enhance his public image.

Toby Stockdale claimed to have slept the sweet sleep of the deeply inebriated. "Still feeling a mite fragile," he admitted with a sheepish grin. "Took me by surprise, really, the old girl pushing the boat out like that. Usually it's one small dry sherry and a glass of grocer's plonk."

MacGregor looked up from his notebook. "Did Michael Montgomery drink a lot?"

"Swilling it down like there was no tomorrow. Well, you know what Australians are like when it comes to booze. Paralytic. Funny, really."

"What is?"

"Auntie Beryl letting her hair down like that. I mean, when he first turned up, right out of the blue, I thought she looked pretty sick. Cheered me up because I reckoned she'd have second thoughts about leaving Ongar's to a yobbo like him. Talk about your wild colonial boy! And when he came in at tea-time with that stupid bayonet thing, I thought he'd really cooked his goose. Well, it was a bit much. Pretending to stab people with it and everything. Childish. Still, that single red rose must have done the trick because she was all over him at the birthday dinner. Egging him on, laughing, joking, dancing with everybody."

"Dancing?"

"Hopping around like a two-year-old. We had the radio on. Bit obscene, I thought, at her age. Not that I said anything, of course."

A loud rumble from Dover's stomach warned everybody that it was lunchtime, and Toby Stockdale, although somewhat bemused, didn't wait to be told twice that he could go.

Dover, usually such a rapacious trencherman, didn't however move.

MacGregor eyed him anxiously. Was the old fool sickening for something? If so, dear Lord, please let it be lingering, painful, and fatal.

Dover sighed and, folding up his girlie magazine, stuffed it into his pocket. "We could pin it on one of 'em, I suppose," he said without much enthusiasm. "Fiddle the evidence a bit. Just for the look of things."

MacGregor's heart sank.

"Wouldn't stand up in court, of course. Still, I wouldn't mind putting that Major What's-his-name out of circulation for a bit."

"Major Finch, sir?"

"On remand six months at least before the case came to trial," mused Dover, demonstrating that even his sluggish brain cells could be galvanized into life with the right motivation. "And no bail on a murder charge. You couldn't expect Ongar's to do without a chief security officer all that time, could you?"

MacGregor flattered himself that he could see the light at the end of this particularly murky tunnel. "You're not thinking of applying for the job yourself, are you, sir?"

Dover grinned with nauseating complacency. "Mrs. Ongar took quite a fancy to me."

MacGregor resisted the temptation to debate the point. "She might like you a great deal more, sir, if you found out who really murdered her great-nephew."

"Use your head, laddie! All that old biddy wants is the whole thing to just fade away."

"Surely not, sir?"

"She hardly knew the joker," insisted Dover. "And, I ask you, who cares about some blooming foreigner getting knocked off?" He dropped his cigarette in the general direction of the ashtray and hauled himself up. "Think I'll go and have a word with her. See how she'd like to play it."

"You mean whether she'd sooner have Major Finch framed for the crime or just let the whole investigation fizzle out?"

Cheap sarcasm was wasted on Dover. "You wait here, laddie. I shan't be a tick."

In the event, Dover was away for ten minutes—a period of time which left MacGregor perplexed. It was too long for Mrs. Ongar just to have sent Dover off with a flea in his ear but too short, surely, for any meaningful discussion to have taken place.

Luncheon was taken, on the recommendation of the uniformed inspector who finally got a bit of his own back, in a low-class pub full of hot and sweaty customers swilling pints of beer and carefully avoiding the bar snacks. Dover, having opted for the shepherd's pie with a double helping of chips and half a bottle of tomato sauce, gobbled his way to apoplexy in as much silence as his distressing table manners would allow. Steamed ginger pudding and custard followed. Dover thought about cheese and biscuits but decided it was just too hot and went for a large brandy instead, just to settle his stomach. In the meantime, a quick trip to the Gents wouldn't come amiss.

Dover stood up and made the supreme sacrifice to a temperature now soaring up into the nineties. He dragged his overcoat off and dropped it, with an audible clunk, on his chair.

MacGregor watched Dover waddle clumsily out of the bar. Although the sergeant's mind was mostly occupied with the probable cost of a double brandy, his keen ears had caught that clunk—and it set the alarm bells ringing.

The Ongar house had contained many valuable knick-knacks and trinkets which would fit quite nicely into the overcoat pocket of any light-fingered detective chief inspector who happened to be passing. MacGregor lived in dread not of Dover actually nicking something—he'd got used to that long ago—but of Dover being caught red-handed actually nicking something. The situation called for drastic action, and MacGregor was not found wanting. Hesitating only for a second, he plunged his bare hand into the pocket of Dover's overcoat and found, together with several other articles too disgusting to bear close examination, an electric torch.

MacGregor put the torch on the table in front of him. Why in God's name had Dover purloined an electric torch? It was neither valuable nor especially attractive. Of course, Dover's standards, even of dishonesty, were not high but—

Fifteen minutes of considerable discomfort spent in the pub's outside convenience had done nothing to sweeten Dover's mood. For one thing, there had been no Ongar's toilet paper with which to while away the time.

"Just lousy little squares of newspaper threaded on a string," he complained, and would no doubt have developed the theme further if he hadn't spotted the electric torch on the table. "What the hell. . . ?"

"Sir—"

"I didn't steal it," said Dover quickly. "Old Mrs. What's-her-name gave it me."

"Mrs. Ongar gave it you, sir?"

Dover scowled. "As a souvenir."

"And she'll confirm that, sir, will she? If asked."

"Don't be so bloody wet, laddie! She'll deny she's ever set eyes on it." Dover dropped his overcoat onto the floor and sat down. "Where's my bloody brandy?"

MacGregor's brain was in turmoil. It was humiliating enough when Dover failed to solve a crime, but it was a thousand times worse when, by pure fluke of course, the disgusting old fool spotted the solution first. MacGregor nodded at the torch. "That's a vital clue, isn't it, sir?"

"You want your brains examining!"

"It's the only electric torch in that house, isn't it, sir?"

Dover's bottom lip stuck out. "How do I know? I haven't looked and neither have you. Could be hundreds of 'em. I just suggested to Mrs. Ongar that she'd be better off without this one."

"My God," breathed MacGregor, "the murderer must have had a torch! He couldn't have put the main light on if he'd wanted to because the switch was right on the other side of the room beyond the camp bed. And with all Montgomery's possessions strewn over the floor . . . And then he had to locate the bayonet . . . He had to have a torch. And there was no moon last night, either."

"You're so sharp it's a wonder you don't cut yourself," muttered Dover.

"But, sir—"

"Go and get my brandy and stop sticking your nose into what's none of your business! And give us a fag while you're at it."

MacGregor got his cigarette case out. "But this *is* my business, sir! And yours. We're supposed to be investigating a murder."

"Ah," said Dover, delighted to have his entire argument handed to him on a plate, "investigating's the word, laddie! I'm with you there. It's solving the bloody thing that's going to drop us right in it. Look at it this way—there's millions of unsolved crimes every year. This is just another one."

MacGregor could be very uncooperative. "Sir, it's our duty—"

"We'd be crucified in court!" Dover was twitching with exasperation. "Accusing somebody as rich and famous as Mrs. Ongar—a frail, bedridden old duck of seventy-five—

of killing her teenage heir from Australia the day after she'd met him for the first time. Bloody hell"—he shuddered dramatically—"it doesn't bear thinking about!"

"But she isn't frail and bedridden, is she, sir?"

"Of course she is!" Dover's voice rose to a near scream. "You saw her!"

"That was mostly for our benefit, sir." MacGregor had ceased grasping at straws and was now beginning to make good, durable bricks. "She wasn't bedridden on the night of her birthday party. She was even dancing. Stockdale said so. She sounds perfectly capable of getting up in the middle of the night and walking as far as Montgomery's room. She wouldn't even have to go upstairs afterward."

Dover scowled. "She's still an old lady."

"A babe in arms could have stuck that bayonet in Montgomery, sir, especially if he was drunk. And who was it who'd—most untypically—been plying him with drink all evening?"

"You want your head examining!"

But MacGregor wasn't going to be put off by vulgar abuse. "Mrs. Ongar had Montgomery put in that downstairs room, sir, well away from everybody else. She ensured he'd be sleeping soundly, and she had a torch. She also knew how awkwardly placed the main light switch was."

"Anybody could have known that!" squealed Dover. And had a torch. And what about motive? Montgomery was her blue-eyed boy. She was going to leave him all her money."

"We don't have to prove motive, sir."

"Sometimes it bloody well helps!" snapped Dover. "'Strewth, she'd barely clapped eyes on the little bastard. You going to claim she suddenly ran amuck or something?"

"Didn't she give you a hint?"

Dover squinted suspiciously at MacGregor. "Who?"

"Mrs. Ongar, sir."

"When?"

"When you went to see her, sir, just before we left the house. When you—er—acquired the torch, sir."

Dover had had time to work out his answer. "We didn't discuss the matter," he said firmly.

"You must have talked about something, sir."

Dover shrugged his meaty shoulders. "I was asking her about getting a job at Ongar's, if I took early retirement. You know, something in the security line." He grinned to himself. "She was very helpful. Thought she might be able to shift that major joker to another department. Said it'd be simpler than trying to pin the murder on him. Give her her due," said Dover generously, "she's got a good head on her shoulders, that woman."

"You don't think she was perhaps trying to bribe you, sir?"

Less convincing displays of indignation have won Oscars, and Dover brought his performance to a sizzling conclusion by advising his sergeant to go and boil his head and reminding him that there was still a double brandy outstanding.

MacGregor reached reluctantly for his wallet. "If it had been Montgomery who'd killed Mrs. Ongar, I could have understood it. That would have been normal."

"I used to think I had an ulcer," said Dover, "the pain was so bad."

But MacGregor's thoughts were soaring far above Dover's stomach. "I wonder if that's what Mrs. Ongar thought—that Montgomery was going to kill her? She was terrified of being murdered for her money—Daniel Ongar or somebody said that. With Montgomery in Australia, she felt safe. But, when he turned up here—"

"The doctor's quite definite, though. It's just the wind."

"He was a right young tearaway by all accounts," Mac-Gregor went on, "and when Mrs. Ongar found she had him under the same roof with her, she must have panicked. And when he started fooling around with that army bayonet, it must have confirmed all her fears. He intended killing her."

"Chronic gastritis," said Dover. "There's only one treatment. Lots of rest."

"Sir"—MacGregor was so pleased with himself that he burst straight through Dover's favorite daydream, in which the chief inspector was a semi-invalid for life—"I've got the motive! It was a preemptive strike. Mrs. Ongar killed her great-nephew because she thought he was planning to kill her."

Dover was getting very bored with all this Ongar business. "You'd be laughed out of court," he grunted. "Not that you'd ever get into court. Like I said, no bloody evidence."

"There's that torch, sir."

Quite slowly and deliberately, Dover picked the torch up off the table and put it back in his pocket. "What torch, laddie?"

MacGregor nodded slightly to acknowledge defeat. The torch didn't really make a ha'porth of difference. Dover was right. They'd never be able to make a case out against Mrs. Ongar. "I'll get your brandy, sir."

MacGregor stood up and walked over to the bar. He arrived just in time to see mine host drape the last towel over the beer pumps.

"We're closed, mate. I called last orders ten minutes ago."

MacGregor appealed to the landlord's sense of decency, fair play, and compassion.

"We've all got sick friends, mate, and if I was you I'd get

mine out into the fresh air before I give the pair of you something to take to casualty with you."

MacGregor swore under his breath. Damn Michael Montgomery and damn old Mrs. Ongar. If he hadn't been so preoccupied with their blooming troubles, he wouldn't be faced with the problem of telling Dover that he couldn't take his medicine for at least two and a half hours.

—1985

Afterword

My sister, Joyce Porter, was born in a place called Marple in the county of Cheshire, which lies in the northern part of England. In those days, Marple was a large village that ran down a long hill, not far from the industrial towns of South Lancashire but also bordering on a large area of unspoilt hilly moorland. It was quite a mixed community: There were a couple of cotton mills, some small farms, various professional people but also a few somewhat decayed gentry. This is where Joyce lived for the first eighteen years or so of her life.

I mention all this because I think it is Joyce's early background that contributes a good deal to the distinctive flavour of her work. The early Dover novels in particular are set in the north, for which the complaining Chief Inspector sets off from London, and the little towns and villages where the crimes take place are just what one would have found there. Behind many of the brilliant caricatures I can recognize the lineaments of people we knew in our youth. And the clearly marked and so very English class structure, which contributes so much to the action, was something we were very conscious of. Even the generally atrocious weather in the stories reflects that part of northern England, which has an unenviable reputation for the amount of rain it gets.

Joyce attended, as did I, the local church elementary school, and then gained a scholarship to the High School for Girls in the neighbouring town of Macclesfield. From there she proceeded to King's College, London, where she took a degree in English. I do not think that there was anything particularly special about her education: It gave her that solid basic grounding and the ability to work hard that the British system of those days provided. Her university period coincided with the Second World War, towards the end of which she had a brief spell in the ATS, the women's section of the army. She then drifted through some secretarial jobs before, in 1949, she decided to join the Women's Royal Air Force and was launched on her first career.

Immediately Joyce was sent on a two-year course to learn Russian, including six months with an émigré family in Paris, after which she became a cog in the Cold War machine, engaged in confidential intelligence work. Naturally, she never spoke about this—though one gathered that training others was an important part of her work— but it was clear that she greatly enjoyed what she did. After a successful service of some twelve years, the air force, in its inscrutable wisdom, switched her to a recruiting job, for which she went round schools trying to persuade not overly enthusiastic girls to join up. For this, she felt she had neither the capacity nor the interest, and in 1963 she finally left the air force.

I well remember a conversation when our mother and I asked her what she proposed to do next. "I'm going to become a writer" was her reply. It might be going too far to say that we flung up our hands in horror, but we certainly expressed our doubts as to whether she would be able to make a living at it. "Well," she then said, "I've written three novels and they've been accepted by a publisher."

These, of course, were the first three Inspector Dover stories, which established her reputation in her new career. Dover has always remained Joyce's most popular character, but just how she came to create him always remained something of a mystery to her. She never envisaged herself at the outset as a comic author. She used to say that she wished she wasn't. As she once wrote, "Personally, I wouldn't read a funny detective story if you paid me." She was inspired to write by Georges Simenon, for whom she always had an immense admiration and all of whose books she possessed in the original French. Dover was originally intended as a sort of English Maigret, but Joyce soon realized such a character could not be made to fit the English scene: In her words, "My detective wasn't a bit like any of the coppers I actually knew. So, I just turned him inside out. It was as simple as that."

Perhaps not quite so simple. In a short article published in 1977 (in the form of a letter to a would-be detective-story writer), Joyce wrote of the problem of creating a really original detective figure who would so capture the interest of readers that they would go on buying books just to read about him. With Dover, she seems to have succeeded triumphantly. Dover was certainly meant as a contrast to the favourite sort of detectives in much English crime fiction: good-looking, well-connected, scrupulously well-behaved, and so highly cultured that it sometimes looks as though they had swallowed the entire *Oxford Dictionary of Quotations*. Contrast that with the revealing little passage from *Dover Three*. When Dover uses a popular phrase, with a slightly naughty innuendo, MacGregor responds with a line from Gilbert and Sullivan, and then we read: "Dover scowled crossly. He couldn't stand people who always had to cap one Shakespearean quotation with another." And, of course, the great detective is virtually omniscient; he can see things that nobody else does and eventually produce a solution that explains everything and leaves no loose ends. Dover is really a takeoff of such a figure: He has one bright idea after another, most of which turn out to be red-herrings, and at the end of the novel, loose ends are as plentiful as leaves in Vallombrosa (which one suspects is true of the outcome of most real-life investigations).

Dover is a policeman, but he is very different from another type of fictional detective: tough, "realistic," tangling with professional criminals and the sleazy underworld. Dover's world is basically that of the middle, or more often the lower-middle, class. Again, I think this is very much a reflection of Joyce's own early background. We were a lower-middle-class family and most of the people we came across were the same. The Dover novels of course present this world as a riot of satire and farce, but satire and farce only hit their mark if they are commenting on something real, and this was a reality that Joyce knew, understood, and conveyed. She described her method of working as starting "with notes listing the names and ages of the characters, their family relationships and plans of rooms or streets." What sticks in the mind after reading the novels is not an elaborately contrived plot, but the succession of hilarious individual episodes and personalities. One is reminded of the tradition of the English picaresque novel, as with Sterne and Smollett: essentially a string of scenes. The action is largely carried on by means of dialogue, and Joyce had a wonderful ear for the kind of earthy language she could have heard both in a northern village and in the air force. That, it seems to me, is very much where her genius lay, and she knew it. The "beauties of literature" was not her forte. As she once wrote: "The only thing that I can think of that I do deliberately is to reduce description to the bare minimum. This is simply because, whenever in my reading I come to two-page word pictures of the view from the study window or three hundred lines on the beauty of the heroine, I skip. In big jumps."

The first Dover novel received great acclaim, and Joyce always thought that the ending—the tantalizing suggestion that we might be dealing with a disgusting case of cannibalism—was the cleverest thing she ever wrote, and probably most readers would agree. That acclaim continued with the two following books, and encouraged her to continue with her literary career. She soon moved to a small thatched cottage in a little village in the southern county of Wiltshire, in a setting of beautiful countryside, where she would sit at her desk for four hours a day, seven days a week. She was always very clear that this was how she earned her living, that writing was a job. As she herself wrote: "I have one virtue as a writer. Once I've started a book, I finish it. Always." But she never pretended that she did not find the mechanics of composition a hard slog during which boredom often set in. In her view, the aim of successful detective authors had to be "to keep on writing the same story—for a lifetime if necessary—and publish it under different titles." With the popularity of Dover she no doubt could have achieved this. But I think she sometimes felt she was in danger of becoming something of a Frankenstein, and she confessed that each Dover book was a little bit harder to write than the one before.

So, in and between producing fresh Dover stories, she turned to inventing two other central characters to give her, as she put it, "a bit of a busman's holiday." The first was Eddie Brown, the subject of a series of spy stories. Just as Dover is the antithesis of the great detective, the Eddie Brown novels are a comic takeoff of espionage as portrayed in the very popular books of such authors as Len Deighton and John le Carré. Like Dover, Eddie is an antihero, bungling and incompetent, and the butt of outrageous adventures. In one novel Eddie, disguised as a female, has to fend off the advances of a lesbian Soviet officer. But again, behind the farce and satire there is sound knowledge and acute observation. From her own air force experience, Joyce would have known—as we now increasingly know—that the antics of the Cold War were marked as much by incompetence and idiocy as by dramatic successes. Also, the Eddie Brown stories—perhaps the best of which, *Neither a Candle nor a Pitchfork,* is titled after a Russian proverb—gave Joyce the opportunity to use Russian backgrounds and her knowledge of the workings of the Soviet Union as she could not do when writing about Dover.

The second figure she created was an aristocratic amateur female detective, the Honourable Constance Ethel Morrison-Burke, known as the "Hon Con." Not unlike Dover, she was a grotesque character, an exaggeration of those female battle-axes (such as Lady Bracknell) in books, plays, and films who have always appealed to English tastes. But woman sleuths are not very common, and I suspect that, with the Hon Con, Joyce may also be having a sly dig at Agatha Christie's wholly different Miss Marple.

These other endeavours did not lead Joyce to abandon Dover. In 1969, she contributed a short story, "Dover Pulls a Rabbit," to *Ellery Queen's Mystery Magazine.* Thereafter, others of her short stories regularly appeared, and these are now collected in the present volume. At first, Joyce found writing short stories something of a challenge: They did not give her the elbow room that a full-length novel did. But she soon acquired a true facility in the genre. It enabled her to tighten up the control of her plots and she found herself able to convey the essence of Dover remarkably well in a brief compass.

Joyce continued to publish one or two novels, as well as these stories, every year until 1980, when her last Dover book, *Dover Beats the Band,* appeared. Thereafter, she gave up detective fiction. Following Dr. Johnson, she used to say that she only wrote for money, and when she had made enough from her novels she simply stopped. But I suspect there may have been more to her decision than that. I think she felt that she had made her distinctive and permanent contribution to literature, and that writing the "same detective story for a lifetime" was not so inviting a prospect after all. Instead, she devoted her last years to researching and planning for a biography of the Grand Duchess Elizabeth, an aunt of the last Tsar. Joyce had long developed a great interest in Imperial Russia, building up a valuable library on the subject, and the project enabled her to make full use of her knowledge of the language. One can see the appeal to Joyce of the Grand Duchess, a somewhat exotic figure who, after the assassination of her husband, became a nun and had her habits made by a Parisian dressmaker. She was later murdered by Bolsheviks, buried in the convent she had founded at Jerusalem, and finally canonized by the Orthodox Church. Joyce collected a mass of material on the Grand Duchess, mostly from original sources, but had barely began to write at the time of her death. I think she was in no great hurry, enjoying the research for its own sake and feeling, as Stevenson has it, that "it is better to travel hopefully than to arrive." But her archive has been preserved and it is hoped that others will draw on it to complete her work.

Joyce's life in her Wiltshire home was happy and uneventful. She settled into village life and took a real interest in its activities, while viewing the inhabitants with a sardonic, yet invariably kindly eye. Among the things she most enjoyed in connection with her research on the Grand Duchess were the foreign trips to discover new material. In the course of her travels, Joyce visited Russia, Israel, and Darmstadt, the Grand Duchess's family home, where she was entertained by the Princess of Hesse. Indeed, travel was always one of her delights. Her books were translated into many languages, and it has never ceased to somewhat intrigue me that so quintessentially English a writer, with such a distinctive regional background, should enjoy such an international success. Her visits to the States and Japan, in both of which countries her books have become notably popular, were particularly memorable for her.

It was perhaps appropriate, then, that Joyce should meet her end on a holiday abroad. In December 1990, she and I, along with a friend (curiously enough by the name of MacGregor), went on a short tour of China. The weather was extremely cold and Joyce contracted some sort of virus. She grew steadily weaker but, typically, she was determined to carry on and not go into hospital. A doctor in our party, as well as a Chinese physician, did what they could for her and thought she would be able to make it back to England, but she died quietly on the plane home. We were put off at the Gulf State of Sharjah, from where, after oceans of paperwork, her body was flown home and buried in the country churchyard of her village. It may seem a suitably dramatic end for a writer of detective stories, but the local Sharjah English language newspaper's headline simply read, "Elderly Woman Dies on Plane." I can imagine Joyce giving this a wry smile and a resigned and satisfied nod.

—*The Reverend Canon J.R. Porter*